EVA CHASE

FOUL CONJURING

ROYALS OF VILLAIN ACADEMY #6

Foul Conjuring

Book 6 in the Royals of Villain Academy series

First Digital Edition, 2019

Copyright © 2019 Eva Chase

Cover design: Fay Lane Cover Design

Ebook ISBN: 978-1-989096-52-9

Paperback ISBN: 978-1-989096-53-6

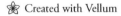 Created with Vellum

CHAPTER ONE

Rory

My first step onto the university green held the promise of a perfect day—or near-perfect, anyway. The midday sun beamed down from the clear sky with more warmth than you could usually expect in upstate New York at the beginning of fall. A fresh leafy scent carried on the light breeze. The students ambling across the lawn between Bloodstone University's three primary buildings chatted with each other in upbeat voices.

I drank in all that and the presence of the guys around me: three of my fellow scions, who'd stood by me through an awful lot here at the school more accurately known as Villain Academy. Who'd become much more than colleagues or even friends. I hadn't exactly gotten an easy time of it since I'd discovered my heritage as heir to one of dark magic society's ruling families and been whisked away from my former home, but this day with them could be a brief respite.

My birth mother, Baron Bloodstone, long-lost and until recently presumed dead, wouldn't be woken from her medical treatment until tomorrow at the earliest. Then, the four of us—and the fifth scion we were heading over to the garage to meet—would find out what her return meant for our alliance against most of the current barons. Right now, I wanted to enjoy the momentary peace while we had it.

"Do you really think Connar's parents could have talked him into joining a tournament?" I asked. That was the official story the Stormhurst scion had offered for his absence from campus, but the other guys had seemed puzzled by it. Connar might look the part of a fighter, all chiseled features and brawn—and if anyone threatened his friends, he could act the part too—but I'd discovered how much gentleness lay beneath that front.

A grimace crossed Malcolm's divinely handsome face. I'd clashed with the heir of Nightwood and self-appointed king of the scions in pretty extreme ways when I'd first gotten to campus, but over the last couple months we'd moved from tentative understanding to what was becoming a deeper affection.

"If I'd been here, I probably could have pulled some strings to get him out of it," he said, running his hand over his cropped golden-brown curls. "That's what I've usually done in the past. Easier than him trying to explain to everyone why he doesn't want to jump into a bunch of competitive magical brawls."

Declan, the Ashgrave scion and the only one of us currently close to full baron, tipped his head in acknowledgment. The breeze ruffled his smooth black hair. "Especially with the tensions still lingering after your hearing, Rory, he might have figured he was better off going along with their demands this once rather than rocking the boat even more."

Just a few weeks ago, I'd been framed for murder and forced to pull out all the stops to prove my innocence. The other scions had spoken on my behalf at the hearing, to most of their parents' dismay, considering the Barons Nightwood, Stormhurst, and Killbrook had been behind the plot in the first place. Connar had convinced his mother that he was playing a long game so he could get inside information from me and manipulate me, but who knew how long he could deceive the Stormhurst baron?

"He might not have enjoyed himself, but I'll bet any mages he went up against had a much worse time than he did," Jude said with a cheeky grin. The supposed Killbrook scion tended to treat most things as a joke, but his careless demeanor covered up an awful family secret—one he hadn't yet dared to reveal to anyone but me. When he caught me studying his expression, he shot a softer smile my way and clasped his slender hand around mine.

I squeezed his fingers in return. Jude and Connar were the only two in our... unusual arrangement that I was openly dating. If Connar was feeling low after whatever he'd been drawn into, I could hope that seeing I'd made it back from my own trip across the country would lighten his spirits. I could kiss him hello right here on the green without needing to worry about who saw.

Inspiration sparked in the back of my head. "What plans do you all have for the rest of the day? After the month I've been through, I can probably get away with skipping my afternoon seminar. We could get away, just the five of us, for a little bit—cheer Connar up, regroup…"

"As always, I like the way you think," Jude said with a glint in his dark green eyes. "I'm sure I can finagle my way out of any supposed responsibilities for the next few hours at least."

"Saying there's scion business we need to attend to can excuse a lot," Malcolm put in. "I wouldn't mind a day off that's actually *off.*" He'd joined me and the squad of blacksuits that had gone down to California to rescue my mother from her captors. Despite the fancy hotel we'd stayed in, the trip had been far from a vacation for any of us.

"My classes are finished for the day, and anything else on my plate I can postpone." Declan aimed his bright hazel gaze at me. "Did you have anywhere in particular in mind?"

I paused to consider that question just before we reached Killbrook Hall, the main building at the front of the campus. I hadn't had the opportunity to do much exploring beyond the university and the small town just down the road. My family's nearby country property offered a certain amount of privacy, at least until my mother was up and about again, but two hours' drive was still a bit of a hike.

The guys had all attended the university for years longer than I had. I was about to ask what they'd suggest when the school headmistress, Ms. Grimsworth, came out of Killbrook Hall leading a group of at least a dozen students. From their wide-eyed glances at the buildings around them, these were newcomers. That would have been strange on its own, considering that the mages who attended the college usually arrived individually at random times during their fifteenth year, as soon as their magical powers first appeared. What was really odd, though, was the gold leaf-shaped pins gleaming by all of the newcomers' shirt collars.

They weren't just new students—they were Nary students. Short for "ordinary," or as my adoptive mother had liked to say, "Nary a bit of magic," the Naries were an expected presence at Blood U, but only in small numbers. The university invited them as scholarship students to a few special programs, partly to help the rest of us practice keeping our magic concealed in the company of non-mages and partly to give us easy targets for stirring up the emotion that powered that magic: fear.

Because of the second factor, the Nary students didn't tend to be treated all that well by my fellow students. I'd stepped in to protect my friend and dormmate Shelby from various sorts of bullying more than once. Seeing a whole bunch more unknowing innocents brought in for the fearmancer students' use made my skin crawl.

Ms. Grimsworth didn't look all that happy about the

situation either. Her thin lips were tight and her posture stiff inside her fitted dress suit as she gestured to Nightwood Tower in what I guessed was a campus tour.

"What's going on?" I asked the guys, keeping my voice low. "Why are they bringing in so many new Nary students all of a sudden?" The usual number had arrived at the beginning of September when the regular school term began.

Declan frowned. "I don't know. No one mentioned it to me—but then, I'm not on staff anymore, so I wouldn't necessarily have expected them to." He'd stepped down from his position as teacher's aide a couple weeks ago.

Malcolm shot Jude a questioning look, having been out of the loop for the last couple days just as much as I'd been. The other guy held up his hand in a gesture of bewilderment. "Beats me. I haven't heard anyone talking about a change in policy." His grin had faltered. "They've got no idea what they're in for, do they?"

We were distracted from any further speculation by a well-built figure coming into view around the side of the hall. Connar walked toward the green with his usual muscular stride. A smile sprang to my lips. We all moved to meet him, my eager anticipation of the reunion carrying me to the front of the pack.

As I slipped past Malcolm and started to form a greeting, the Stormhurst scion's gaze settled on me. He halted in his tracks, his light blue eyes so icy cold that my mouth snapped shut and my legs locked.

The other guys stopped around me, glancing from him

to me and back again, clearly picking up on the unexpected tension.

"Conn," Malcolm said in his usual confident tone. "What—"

Connar cut him off. "You're still letting her string you along."

His voice was even chillier than his expression. The bottom of my stomach dropped out. My lips parted, but I couldn't summon any words that seemed adequate.

Who else could he mean by "her" but me? But... why the hell would he talk about me like that? It jarred against everything we'd been through together, all the tenderness he'd shown me. Even the one time months ago when he'd torn into me to prove his loyalty to Malcolm, he hadn't looked at me like *that*.

Declan stepped forward, his forehead furrowing. "Connar, what's going on? Where have you been?"

Connar drew back a step. His whole body had gone rigid. "There's no point in talking to you while she's here. Can't you see how she's taking over everything?"

Jude cocked his head. "I don't know, buddy. If anyone has been taken over around here, I'm starting to think it's you." His usual teasing tone had taken on a nervous edge.

Connar scoffed. "Of course you'd say that."

None of this made any sense. None of this was *right*. I forced myself to move toward him, my hands open and empty at my sides. "Connar, this isn't you. You *know* me."

"*You* don't know a fucking thing about me," he snapped, recoiling even farther. "Stay the hell away."

He swerved around us to march toward the senior

dorms, leaving those last words ringing in the air. They'd punched a hole straight through my heart. For a few seconds as I watched him stalk away, I couldn't catch my breath.

"Fuck," Malcolm muttered, his expression dark. He looked as if he was about to say more, but then his gaze skimmed the green around us, and his jaw tensed.

We had an audience. The gaggle of Naries hadn't paid us much mind, not knowing we were anyone all that important anyway, but the fearmancer students who'd been out on the green had turned our way with expressions both wary and curious.

A public dispute between scions didn't happen very often. And after the supposed murder not everyone was convinced I'd deserved to be cleared of, any hostility toward me was going to draw extra interest.

Declan glanced toward Ashgrave Hall, which held our private scion lounge in the basement, but considering that was the building Connar had just disappeared into, he must have decided it wasn't the best venue for a conversation. He motioned for us to follow him between the buildings onto the wilder field between them and the forest that ringed the campus on three sides.

We stopped in the middle of an open grassy area where we could easily see all around, not close enough to any buildings to have to worry about eavesdroppers there. Without any prompting, Malcolm intoned a casting word with a flick of his hand. A quiver of magic touched my skin. He'd cast some kind of privacy bubble around us for extra protection against being overheard.

"He's obviously not in his right mind," he said the second he'd finished the spell. "I've never seen Conn act like that, even when he's angry. And what the hell could he have to be angry with Rory about when she hasn't even been here in days?"

Jude folded his arms over his lean chest. "I suppose we're assuming at this point that whatever his mom roped him into, it wasn't any tournament."

Declan shook his head. "It can't have been that. She's got him in the grips of some kind of spell—persuasive, probably—and sent him back to mess with Rory. Maybe she figured out he was lying about being on his parents' side and decided to force him into loyalty."

"Or she threatened him with something that made him feel he has to pretend he hates me," I said hesitantly. There hadn't been any magic involved when he'd turned on me before for Malcolm's sake.

Declan looked at me. "Do you really think he could bring himself to talk that way to you, no matter what she said? I didn't get the sense he was conflicted about it."

My head drooped. The perfect day around me had dulled. It was hard to focus on anything except the ache in my chest, twice as searing as it'd been before. I'd lost my familiar during our attempts to free my mother. That had been painful enough. If I'd lost Connar too…

I'd known I'd lose him eventually. Of all the scions, he had the least choice when it came to his future life partner. He was the only remaining heir of Stormhurst, so there was no way he could leave that role behind to become a Bloodstone, which would be required of any man I married since I was a sole heir too. But I hadn't expected the separation to happen like this.

"I'm not sure," I said. "I wouldn't have thought so, but... You've all known him a lot longer than I have."

"Connar's capable of a lot, but he's no master of deception," Malcolm said. "And I've seen how the guy feels about you. There's no way that was him. It's got to be magically induced."

The Nightwood scion hadn't been all that keen on the idea of sharing my affection with the other guys in the first place, so the vehemence with which he'd defended Connar reassured me. "What do we do about it, then? Can we counteract the spell?" A spell cast by a baron was going to be pretty potent, even if the Stormhursts' primary strength wasn't persuasion.

Declan rubbed his mouth. "We'd need to determine exactly what the spell is and have at least some cooperation from him while we worked at unraveling it, which might not be a quick process. I'm not sure how likely he is to cooperate with anything we suggest at the moment."

"It can't last forever." Jude clapped Malcolm on the arm. "Even Mr. Persuasion here can't make a command stick for days on end. His parents got their little revenge and shook us up, embarrassed Rory in front of the other students, but once it's worn off, he should be his regular self again."

"Unless they've implemented one of the various methods for extending a spell's impact," Declan said. "But for now, it might be best if we give him his space and see if he comes out of it on his own. Pushing some kind of immediate intervention on him could make things even worse."

I definitely had no desire to face Connar and his sudden frostiness all over again if I could help it. But if he needed more help than that, I wasn't going to abandon him either. "We'll check on him in the morning, then?"

Malcolm's mouth twisted as if he disliked the idea of letting Connar's parents get away with their gambit even that long, but he nodded. "That's a fair plan." His tone turned softer as his gaze caught mine. "Looks like we'll have to wait on that group getaway."

"Well, maybe tomorrow," I said with as much optimism as I could dredge up, which to be honest wasn't a lot. Worry sat heavy in my gut, and there was nothing I could do except wait to find out how much more worried I needed to be.

CHAPTER TWO

Rory

In the parking lot, I got out of my Lexus and hesitated with my hand on the door. After Lillian Ravenguard, a senior officer in the fearmancer law enforcement ranks and one of my mother's closest friends, had called this morning, I'd driven to the blacksuits' main building of operations as fast as I could. But something about the shape of it looming over me made the situation so much more real.

My mother was awake. The woman who'd given birth to me and raised me the first two years of my life. The woman everyone had thought was killed by the opposing faction of mages, the joymancers, two of whom had been the only parents I'd ever really known. I had no memories of Baron Bloodstone, no real sense of who she was other than scraps of impressions from recordings and photographs and bits of hearsay picked up from my fellow scions.

Fearmancer parents weren't known for warmth and compassion, and the barons seemed to be worse than most. Malcolm's father subjected him to intense physical torment when he needed to make a point. Connar's parents had driven him to a near-deadly battle with his twin brother years ago. Baron Killbrook had arranged Jude's conception through what amounted to the magical rape of another man and then shunned the false heir he'd brought into this world. From what Declan had said, the Ashgraves were the exception to the rule, at least in recent times.

I didn't know what my mother would be like, but she'd been friends and allies with Baron Nightwood. He and the other barons had seen her supposed death as a grave loss. That was reason enough to approach what felt to me like our first meeting with extreme caution.

Gathering myself, I walked up to the main doors. There was a desk just inside the foyer where one of the blacksuits monitored comings and goings. He glanced at me and tipped his head—a very different welcome than I'd gotten the first time I'd come here, escorted in magic-suppressing cuffs under guard.

"She's waiting for you, Miss Bloodstone," he said. "I'll have someone bring you up."

Would they have insisted on an escort if it'd been any of the other scions visiting? I wasn't sure how much they trusted *me* after their failed attempt to prosecute me, but I wasn't going to argue about it.

Almost immediately, another blacksuit opened the locked inner door and beckoned for me to follow her. It was a short walk to the medical wing. At the door to my mother's room, I paused to peek through the small window. No one was in the room around the bed—Lillian must have had other business to attend to after her initial visit with my mother.

That was fine. I now knew that Lillian had not only carried out the murder of my dormmate and friend that I'd been framed for, but had done so as part of an ongoing conspiracy involving the three older barons and some of the blacksuits. I'd rather experience this first encounter with my mother without Lillian's alert eyes looking on.

My mother was sitting up in the bed, flipping through a book that she appeared to be skimming more than actually reading. Her hair, the same dark brown as mine mixed with a sprinkling of silver, hung sleek to her shoulders, and her face, though still narrow, had filled out a little from the gauntness I'd seen when we'd first rescued her from her imprisonment. There wouldn't have been any indication she'd ever needed medical attention if a sudden tremor hadn't come over her hand as I watched, the page she'd been holding slipping from her fingers.

I drew in my breath and pushed open the door. The blacksuit who'd led the way stayed in the hall outside.

My mother looked up the second I stepped in, her hands going still over the book. Her whole body froze as she took me in with her dark, considering gaze.

It occurred to me with a skip of my pulse that I didn't even know what her magical specialty was. I bolstered the shield around my mind instinctively, as if she might attempt to prod inside my head before so much as talking to me.

"Hi," I said awkwardly, my hands clasping together in front of me. A tart, faintly floral scent tickled my nose, though I didn't see any Get Well bouquets around. The click of the door shutting behind me sounded way too loud in the silence.

A smile crossed my mother's face, bright and pleased but somehow not entirely warm, although maybe it only seemed that way to me because of my nerves. "Persephone," she said. "Look at you. I—I've missed so much. They couldn't take the Bloodstone out of you, could they? As much as I'm sure they tried."

I guessed Lillian had filled her in on what had happened to me after the attack in which my mother had been captured. But not on the name I'd been going by— or maybe she had mentioned that, and my mother was choosing to ignore it. Faced with her, I didn't know how to say that I felt more connection to a name given to me by the people who'd stolen me from her and imprisoned her for seventeen years than the one she'd bestowed on me at my birth.

I stepped closer to the bed, and she motioned to the chair next to it. "The couple that raised me suppressed my magic and didn't tell me anything about who I really was," I said as I sat, "but they didn't mistreat me other than that. I was okay."

"More than okay. I hear you've impressed all of Blood U right from the start. All four strengths." She shook her head with the same smile. "My father was the same, you know. I didn't quite manage it myself, although your father's specialty was the one area I wasn't quite impressive in, so you have him to thank too."

Lillian had filled her in on an awful lot. I opened my mouth, closed it, and opened it again, grappling for words. It didn't feel right to discuss my school victories with a woman who'd just been through so much. As far as I knew, my adoptive parents hadn't been aware that my birth mother was alive, but the joymancers who'd held her captive obviously hadn't treated *her* well. When the blacksuits had dragged her from confinement, she'd looked half dead.

"Are *you* okay?" I had to ask. "I had no idea—no one knew the joymancers had you. What did they want with you?"

The mages who fed their magical power by encouraging happiness had attacked me when I'd gone to them in California to try to negotiate, so I had no illusions about their hostility toward fearmancers. Still, my joymancer parents had not just avoided mistreating me but been actively loving. It was hard to wrap my head around the immense deception and cruelty their colleagues had pulled off.

"I feel much better now." My mother gave a low chuckle. "I'm embarrassed they perpetuated that scheme as well as they did. There were so many of them, and I think they must have intended from the start to take both of us, so they were prepared... They wore down my magic quickly and were careful not to give me any opportunities to spark more power. Otherwise I'd have been able to reach out to make my situation known sooner."

She rubbed a forehead with a slight wince. I leaned forward in the chair. "Do you need me to call one of the doc—"

"No, no." She waved me off. "Lingering effects of the magical depravation and… the rest. Better that we don't dwell on that. They wanted me as weak as possible so they could keep control, but we Bloodstones recover quickly."

"So, they just locked you away because they could?" I didn't want to say this either, but I didn't understand why the joymancers would have gone to all that effort rather than simply killing her like they had my father and Declan's mother, the previous Baron Ashgrave.

"They didn't include me in their discussions on the subject, as I'm sure you can imagine. But from the bits I was able to gather over time, I believe they were hoping to deal a severe blow to our pentacle of barons. As long as there was no Baron Bloodstone to weigh in, any major decision could only be delayed." Her mouth tightened. "Of course, they only needed *you* alive to ensure the heart of the family's power wouldn't pass on to someone else. But I suspect the joymancers didn't realize that, and held onto me as well out of caution. No doubt they meant to off me when you'd come of inheritance age."

At twenty-one. Less than two years, and if the blacksuits hadn't tracked down my location, the woman in front of me would have been dead after all. "But then I got away from them."

"Yes. That must have ruined their plans quite a bit."

Her smile came back, but it was definitely cool now. "I didn't know why at the time because I didn't know what had happened to you, but in the last few months, they'd become more tense around me. I sensed that they might be re-evaluating my usefulness. But that uncertainty also opened up a few minor opportunities for me to stir anxiety and fuel enough magic to make some attempt to send out a signal."

"I helped as much as I could as soon as Lillian told me," I said.

She shifted her hand on the bed toward me. "I know. I felt you there, once or twice, even if I wasn't sure I could trust my impressions or whether it was a hopeful hallucination. My mind… was not as clear as I'd prefer for much of that time." With a rustling of the sheets, she sat up straighter. "But that's in the past now. They will regret their attempt to crush me and mine. As soon as we're in a position to turn those tables—"

Her eyes had flashed so fiercely and her voice turned so sharp that I stiffened without realizing it. My mother cut herself off when her gaze came back to me.

I wavered, not knowing what to say. I'd insisted on coming to California and I'd approached the joymancers on my own specifically because I'd wanted to avoid as much bloodshed as possible. Several people had died in the fighting all the same. And my mother clearly wanted more.

Nearly every fearmancer I'd spoken to had scoffed at my pacifistic tendencies. It was already becoming clear that my mother wouldn't approve of them either.

But even though I kept quiet, she could clearly pick up on my discomfort. She let out a rough, rueful sigh. "There will be time enough for that in the future. We have so much to catch up on. I…" She touched her temple again. The color was starting to leach from her face. "I'm afraid my recovery isn't quite complete yet. I'm not sure I'll be the best company right now."

"Don't strain yourself," I said quickly, with a pang of concern. I *would* send a doctor over here when I left the room, whether she liked that idea or not. "It's all right."

She caught my eyes, hers filled with both longing and what felt like a command. "You'll come back to see me soon so we can talk more? I expect I'll be back at the Bloodstone manor before very long."

How could I say no to that? "Of course. As soon as you're ready."

I didn't need to ask for a doctor after all. As I got up, she made a surreptitious gesture that presumably triggered some sort of call system. She sank lower on the bed, and a blacksuit who must have had medical training appeared in the doorway before I'd taken more than a few steps. I left her to his administrations, my stomach balled tight.

My mother wasn't a terrifying figure at the moment, and she'd acted nothing but happy with me and what she knew of who I'd become. Who knew how much Lillian had told her about the frictions that had risen up around me, though, or the attitudes I hadn't kept totally quiet during my time at Blood U?

And the fury I'd sensed in her during the locating spells was still there too. I couldn't blame her for being angry with her captors, but that didn't mean I wanted to see her lead the charge into wholesale slaughter for revenge.

She was still getting a grip on herself, adjusting to being back. She might have spoken out of more emotion than she'd have allowed herself in her official capacity as baron. The fearmancers had steered clear of any unprovoked offensives against the joymancers for decades, from what Declan had said. To outright attack them now would be a huge change in approach.

That knowledge wasn't as comforting as I'd have liked, but it did make the uneasiness inside fade as I made the drive back to campus. The meeting could have gone a lot worse; that was for sure. Why not look on the bright side?

I made it back to the university with less than fifteen minutes to spare before my early afternoon seminar. Cursing myself for not having thought ahead, I jogged from the garage to my dorm to grab the reference book I'd need. As I was hustling back down the stairs past the third floor landing, Connar stepped into the stairwell.

He jerked to a stop when he saw me, and I caught myself against the railing before I could stumble in my surprise. His icy gaze cut straight through me. Before he even spoke, I knew whatever his parents had done to him, it hadn't worn off overnight.

"What are you standing around for?" he spat out. "If you think I'm giving you another chance to mess with my head, you can forget it."

My stomach knotted twice as tight as it had before. I couldn't keep my thoughts from slipping back from our last interlude together, out at the Shifting Grounds—the affection that had radiated off him as he'd admitted he loved me, the way he'd lit up even more when I'd told him I loved him too. That had been less than a week ago. How had Baron Stormhurst managed to bury that guy so far?

The love I still felt for that guy wouldn't allow me to just let go, even for a moment, without trying. "Connar," I started, "I swear to you—"

"I don't want to hear it," he snapped, and jabbed his hand toward the stairs. "Go on already."

I hugged the book to my chest and headed down, my throat squeezing tight. As soon as I'd turned around the bend, out of his view, I pulled out my phone to text the other scions.

Connar's still not himself. We need to talk—soon.

CHAPTER THREE

Declan

Looking at the four of us assembled in the scion lounge sent a twinge through my chest. It wasn't that many weeks ago when a different four of us had been making use of the space for similar reasons—all of us but Malcolm working out plans to deal with the murder accusation against Rory while we hadn't been sure whether the Nightwood scion would help or hinder that cause.

We'd only just found our footing in a new, cohesive status quo with all five of us united, and now we were having to leave out someone else who deserved to be here.

That was exactly why Baron Stormhurst would have taken this tactic with Connar, wasn't it? Punish him for being more loyal to Rory than to her and rattle the entire pentacle of scions at the same time. The older barons might not *know* that Malcolm or I were actively working on Rory's behalf now, but I wouldn't be surprised if they suspected it of one or both of us, and Jude had made his allegiance known ages ago.

Even if we'd been on the fence about Rory, having one of our number verbally attacking her at every opportunity put her in a much more precarious position.

I sipped the bitter espresso I'd made with the machine in the corner, although the shock of caffeine wasn't making my thoughts all that sharper than they'd already been. Ice cubes clinked as Jude fidgeted with the drink he was mixing at the bar cabinet. Jack and Coke in hand, he came over to the sofa where Rory and Malcolm were already sitting, but after he'd sunk down at Rory's other side, he simply cupped the glass between his hands rather than drinking.

I stayed standing by one of the armchairs, too restless to take a seat. "So," I said, because someone had to kick off the conversation, "we can be reasonably sure at this point that whatever's happened to Connar, it's not going to fade away without some kind of intervention."

"I'm sure it's a spell," Malcolm said, his expression dark. "I tried talking to him last night, and he didn't budge on the anti-Rory rhetoric. There's no way he'd be able to keep it up that consistently if he was forcing himself to act that way."

"A master thespian, Conn is not," Jude said, but he couldn't manage to put his usual wry spin on those words. None of us liked seeing one of our number under this kind of influence.

Rory maybe least of all. It'd only been a few hours since she'd called for this meeting, but her face was as drawn as if she'd been worrying about Connar nonstop for a week. I'd seen the way they were together, the softer side her presence brought out in him, how comfortable she'd become in turning to him for support.

She had the rest of us, absolutely, but hearing those accusing and disdainful words from his mouth had to cut deep. And if he had any normal awareness beneath the spell right now, I couldn't imagine how much agony *he* must be in, forced to lash out at her against his will.

"If it's a spell and it's not fading naturally, then it must be contained in something on him or at least that he's near a lot, right?" she said, tucking her dark hair back behind her ears. "That's what— When Professor Banefield was sick, whoever put that spell on him embedded it in a mole on his calf that worked like a conducting piece. I had to… break the structure before the spell would release him."

She hadn't talked about her attempts to save her mentor in that much detail before, at least not with me. I hadn't realized she'd needed to go through a process quite that complex. She'd only discovered her magic a matter of weeks before she'd been faced with that challenge—she'd barely begun her education here, and still she'd managed to foil the barons' first plot against her and those supporting her nearly on her own.

If she'd been prepared for the violent spell that had activated in the illness's aftermath, she might have foiled them completely, without Banefield needing to take his own life to save her.

I nodded. "That's what I'd expect. More likely it'll be on Connar than an outside object, since that would be a greater guarantee of continuing influence and harder for anyone to interrupt. He was gone for a day and a half—they had plenty of time to work a spell that thorough."

Malcolm leaned forward, his expression turning intent. The sooner we could switch from conversation to action, the happier I knew he'd be. "Then we figure out where they've planted the spell on him and unravel it, and problem solved. That shouldn't be so hard."

"I don't know." Rory frowned. "Professor Banefield was sick, so he wasn't really in a position to protest. I had to focus *really* carefully to destroy the enchantment on him. Connar's definitely not going to let me get close enough to him to check him over for unexpected physical marks. Do you think he'd go along with any of you examining him if I'm not there?"

Jude turned his still-full glass between his slim fingers. "The Stormhursts had to realize that we'll try to counteract the spell. They might be more on the blunt side than subtle, but they're not *stupid*. They'll have put this construct somewhere on him we're not likely to get a casual glimpse of, just to make it as hard for us as possible. I don't relish the idea of finding out how he'll react if we attempt to de-pants him."

"I could see if I can talk him into going for a swim in the pool and take a look in the change room," Malcolm said, but he sounded doubtful.

"He always complains about the chlorine," I pointed out, remembering.

"Yeah, even in ideal circumstances, it might be a tough

sell." He rubbed his hand over his face. "And he's definitely wary of me even without Rory there."

Rory glanced up at me with a flicker of inspiration in her indigo-blue eyes. "Maybe we can find out indirectly. If one of us can pull off an insight spell on him—with someone else distracting him to make it easier to get past whatever mental barriers he's got up, maybe?—asking specifically about what his parents did to him, we'd have a decent chance of sensing not just where they placed the spell but possibly more about what it involves too. That'd make picking it apart easier."

As the pentacle's original Insight expert, I should have been the one to think of that. Of course, Rory had been catching up in her skills in leaps and bounds. I shot her a small smile. "That's a good idea. Connar's mental defenses aren't the strongest ever—his focus has always been more on the external arts."

"The mood he's in, he'll have them up at the best of his ability, though." Malcolm cocked his head. "I can figure out a good way to put him off-balance—and for long enough to give one of you time to really delve in there. Give me a little while to think on it and work out the best timing. We'll only get one shot. Once he realizes we're trying to get into his head…"

He didn't need to finish that sentence. With the spell acting on Connar, we'd be lucky if he agreed to come within ten feet of any of us if he decided we were all the enemy.

Jude finally took a gulp of his drink. "It doesn't sound as if I'll be of much use in the current scheme, but keep me in the loop if you need any illusionary work. I do *not* want to see how much worse Connar's temper can get."

The comment about tempers reminded me of the irritable state Jude's father had been in during the last meeting of the barons. The others had needled Baron Killbrook about his heir having moved away from the family properties, but Jude still hadn't breathed a word about that development to any of us. Their relationship had always seemed chilly, but if things had gotten worse, if *he* needed someone to intervene on his behalf—

He might not appreciate me bringing up his familial dirty laundry in front of Rory, though. I'd never seen him care anywhere near as much about what anyone thought as he clearly did with her. It might be better to wait to broach the subject when it was just us guys, and if we needed her help, we could determine it then.

"If we can set it up so he won't notice me there and be triggered by that, I think I should do the insight spell," Rory had started saying when my phone buzzed in my pocket. "It was only a few months ago that I had to help Professor Banefield—I'd be able to recognize the signs faster."

I didn't know the number on the screen. I turned away from the others, raising the phone to my ear. "Hello?"

"Hey. Declan?" said an uncertain and rather young male voice, fractured by shaky reception. "There's been—I think Noah's had an accident. He might be hurt."

Might be? How could this guy not know what had happened one way or another if he'd been there for this "accident"? All my nerves jangled to high alert.

My younger brother had only just arrived at Blood U a few days ago, after spending the first two years of his education abroad—my attempt at keeping him out of the political fray. Now he'd been thrown straight into that fray, and apparently his peers were already challenging him every way I'd been worried about.

"Where are you?" I demanded. "What exactly happened?"

"It's… hard to explain," the guy said weakly. "We're out about an hour's hike east along the lake—I can make a magical signal so you can find the spot. I'll show you what I mean when you get here."

"Is he going to need more help than just me?"

"I… I don't know."

The back of my neck prickled with the instinctive awareness that this could just as easily be some kind of attempt to mess with *me*, although the other students wouldn't generally have dared to pull a major prank on a near-baron.

"I'll be there as fast as I can," I said. "Don't go anywhere, and keep that signal going."

As soon as I'd hung up, I tried texting and then calling Noah, just in case he was actually fine. The call didn't even ring, just went straight to voice mail as if his phone was off. Shit.

I debated going to the health center first to ask for backup, but the chances that anyone would have seriously injured my brother seemed slim. I'd only make him look weaker—and like a more appealing target—if I showed up with the full cavalry. If I couldn't handle the situation, I'd call for extra help then.

When I turned back to the others, they were watching me. My distress must have been obvious.

"What's going on?" Malcolm asked, tensed in his seat.

"I think my brother's facing a little more than the standard newbie razing," I said. "I can handle it—but it sounds like I'd better handle it quickly. When you come up with a definite plan for Connar, let me know."

Unfortunately, once I'd set off, there was no way to speed up the journey along the lake. Even if I'd had access to a motorboat, the shoreline east of campus rose up twenty to thirty feet of nearly sheer cliff over the waterline, leaving nowhere to dock. Even the path that meandered through the forest not far from the shore petered out after about twenty minutes' brisk walk.

After that, I had to pick my way as quickly as possible through the brush, twigs tugging at my clothes. Normally I'd have enjoyed the brightening autumn colors around me and the crisp fall scent in the air, but I was too distracted by thoughts of what Noah's new "friends" might have wrapped him up in. Every few minutes, I sent out a thread of magic seeking the signal the caller had said he'd conjure.

Even at the pace I was keeping, it took three quarters of an hour before I picked up the tingle of magic in the distance. I pushed myself even faster, wincing as a thin branch whipped against my cheek. As I followed my sense of the signal, the ground slanted up even higher.

I emerged into a rocky clearing between a stretch of

pines. A junior fearmancer I recognized from Noah's dorm was standing in the middle of it, his expression turning vaguely terrified at my arrival. He still had his phone clutched in his hand.

"All right," I said in the firmest tone I had in me. "What's going on? Be quick about it."

The guy shifted on his feet and jerked his head toward the ground several feet away from him. "A bunch of us came out here exploring. One of the guys dared Noah to go down into the caves. I don't know what happened down there, or whether it was on purpose—it sounded like some rocks fell. He wasn't answering us."

My skin turned cold. And of course the other perpetrators of this ploy had fled when they'd realized it'd gotten out of hand. I stalked closer to the spot he'd indicated, where I could now see the mossy rocks opened with a crevice large enough for a person to squeeze through. All I could make out below was darkness.

"Noah?" I hollered.

No answer. When I looked back around, all I caught was the last guy's back as he hightailed it into the woods. He didn't want to stick around to take the blame either. I guessed I should thank him for bothering to call me in the first place, even if I suspected he'd been more involved in this setup than he'd wanted to admit.

I conjured a small ball of light and sent it down into the crevice. It highlighted craggy walls and a rough floor several feet down. Well, there was nothing for it. I dragged in a breath and concentrated on forming a thin rope with my magic.

As I clambered down into the caves, a quiver of energy passed over my skin. The second I'd dropped below it, the cave's silence fell away. Water was dripping somewhere nearby, and a pebble rattled. Then a voice carried, hoarse but determined, from deeper in the darkness.

"Hello? Guys?"

Noah. Someone had cast a silencing spell beneath the cave entrance so no one could communicate with him from above. What the *hell* had these assholes been thinking?

My jaw clenched, I scrambled the last few feet down and waved my conjured light in the direction the voice had come from. I had to hunch to squeeze deeper into the caves. "I'm coming!" I called.

"Thank fucking God," Noah muttered, with enough spirit that my lips twitched with relief even as anger continued churning in my gut.

I had to take a couple of turns before I found him. My brother was sprawled on his ass in a particularly narrow section of cave, where several rocks ranging from skull size to whole person size had tumbled down to fill the gap—and pin his legs in place from the thighs down.

Noah's expression tensed when he saw me, as if he expected me to be angry with *him*. I knelt down next to him, setting a careful hand on his shoulder.

"Don't worry about it. We'll get you out. You tried moving the rocks?" His arms wouldn't have been much help in his current position, so he'd have needed to turn to magic.

He nodded, his mouth twisting. "It—it really hurts. I

managed to shift a few of them, but my control wasn't great because the pain messed with my concentration, and I accidentally knocked more down, so then it didn't seem like such a great idea to keep trying. The guys..." He gave me a questioning look.

"They took off on you," I said. "But one of them stuck around long enough to give me a heads up."

"I think they did it on purpose," he said grimly. "Some of them, anyway. I wasn't planning on going this far, but this force that must have been conjured started shoving me, and before I could get around that, all this crap crumbled down." He ducked his head. "You tried to warn me people would pull shit like this. I just didn't think—I didn't want them to think I was *scared* of them."

"It's okay." I squeezed his shoulder. "I wouldn't have thought anyone would go this far either. Just imagine their faces when you show up back on campus acting like nothing was ever wrong. That'll throw them off. Now let me get you free."

This once, I wished Physicality had been one of my strengths. I wasn't outright weak in it, but the magic to lift the stones out of the way came with noticeably more effort than my regular spells did. Even in the chilly air underground, sweat started to seep down my back and across my forehead. I had to be careful, or I could bring down more rubble on my brother instead.

When I'd finally cleared the rockslide, I winced at the sight of Noah's legs. One of them was twisted at an unnatural angle from the knee. Something was broken there. No wonder he'd been in too much pain to effectively cast his spells.

We weren't making that hour-long walk back with him like this. I could numb the pain and fix a splint on him to make sure the break didn't get any worse, but that was about it. I pulled out my phone to call back to campus and grimaced at the No Reception message. Of course there wouldn't be down here.

"Not that I wanted you to have to learn this lesson," I said, "but I don't think you're going to forget to be cautious around your classmates anytime soon. I'm going to steady your leg as well as I can and get you out of here, and then we're going to have a nice long talk about how to deal with assholes while we wait for the medical team to get here."

CHAPTER FOUR

Rory

It was pretty normal for me to emerge from my dorm bedroom and find Shelby, my friend and only Nary dormmate, making her breakfast in the kitchen area. What was a little strange was the fact that she didn't look up or say anything in greeting when I came over to make some toast for myself.

"Hey," I said, not particularly loudly, but she startled so badly that the spatula she'd been holding ready to scoop up her frying eggs flew from her hand. It clattered onto the floor.

Shelby blushed pink and ducked to grab the utensil with a swing of her mouse-brown ponytail. "Oh my God," she said, swiping the back of her hand across her forehead. "I'm sorry. Somehow I didn't even notice you there."

She was usually more alert than that. She'd needed to be, considering the fearmancer students made her as much a target of their pranks and bullying as they did all the other Nary students. And Shelby had become even more of a target since my friendship with her had become obvious. Victory Blighthaven, who'd been queen bee over the dorm before I'd arrived, had taken every chance she could get to undermine me and my friends until Malcolm had warned her off a month ago, and that had included tearing up Shelby's property.

Sometimes I had to worry about Shelby's own sense of self-preservation. During my first term here, she'd kept going to classes despite running a high fever for a week, scared of losing her spot in the music program if she didn't appear committed enough. The staff didn't cut the nonmagical students any breaks.

I studied her expression, noting with some relief that she was wearing the violin pendant I'd gifted her. The deflective spell on the silver charm should prevent most direct spells from affecting her, although if someone hit her with anything really powerful, I wasn't sure how well it would hold. I'd have to bolster the magic in the pendant as soon as I got the chance.

"Are you okay?" I asked. Maybe she was coming down with something again.

"Oh, yeah, same as usual." She flashed me a little smile, rinsed the spatula under the faucet, and turned off the water. A second later, she turned the water back on and rinsed the spatula again. Then she repeated the process a third time without any sign she'd realized she was redoing her efforts. My stomach sank as she finally wiped off the utensil with one of the dish towels.

"Are you sure everything's fine?" I pressed. "You slept okay? No one's been hassling you? No problems in class?"

"Everything's good. You don't need to worry about me." Her tone was bright, but her gaze jerked to me at the same instant, and I caught a sensation I didn't think I'd ever felt from her before. A small but clear shiver of fear shot from her to me, prickling through my chest to join the rest of my magical energy where it thrummed behind my collarbone.

She was scared of me? Of something I'd said? I didn't think I'd come on so strong with my concern that she'd take it as a threat. I eased back a step anyway, swallowing hard.

It might not really have anything to do with me. The other fearmancer students could have shaken her up so badly that she couldn't help remembering them when she looked at me, just because I was another regular student rather than a scholarship kid. She'd often downplayed the treatment she'd faced in the past.

I wouldn't have thought she'd completely brush off an incident that had rattled her this much, though.

The last thing I wanted was to make her more uncomfortable by harping on the subject. "Well, if you need any help or just want to talk to someone, you know where to find me."

"Thanks," she said, sounding genuinely appreciative, so maybe nothing was wrong after all. She dropped the eggs onto her plate and headed for her bedroom. "Gotta study the piece we're going to start performing today. I'll see you later!"

I forced down my worries and opened up the fridge to grab my raspberry jam. At the sight of my stash of cheese and grapes in the corner, my throat tightened for a totally different reason.

Those had been mainly for my familiar's benefit. Deborah might have kept most of her human mind after her fellow joymancers had transferred her consciousness into the mouse's body so she could watch over me as a supposed pet, but her tastes had definitely been influenced by her new state of being. Just a week ago, I'd have been adding a chunk of cheese, a few grapes, and some crackers to a plate so she could have her own breakfast.

I'd never be bringing her those little offerings again. I'd never have to lower my voice while we talked, me out loud and her inside my head through the familiar bond, to make sure my fearmancer dormmates didn't realize I'd brought an intruder into their midst. I'd never hear her dry but affectionate voice calling me "Lorelei" the way no one had since I'd lost the parents who'd raised me.

Other than the glass dragon charm hanging from its chain around my neck, Deborah had been the only connection I'd still had to my life with the joymancers I'd thought of as Mom and Dad. She'd been a contrasting voice when the fearmancers tried to convince me of their ideals. And in the end, it'd turned out she'd had too much faith in her own community.

The joymancers in California had refused to listen to her or me when we'd tried to convince them I wanted a peaceful negotiation to get my birth mother back without the bloodshed. When I'd escaped, they'd tried to kill me.

Deborah had thrown herself into a spell I hadn't been fast enough to deflect and taken that blow in my place.

Her loss had left not just an emotional ache but a physical discomfort from the severed familiar bond. Over the days since, it had dulled but not vanished. The pain still throbbed faintly in my chest. I didn't know how long it would take for it to fade completely, and maybe I didn't want it to. I should remember the sacrifice she'd made for me.

With those solemn thoughts hanging over me, I nibbled my way through my toast. I was just finishing my breakfast when Victory and her two besties, Sinclair and Cressida, sauntered out of their respective bedrooms to converge on the dining table. Sinclair appeared to have been assigned to grab their chef-made pre-prepared breakfasts out of the fridge.

Victory didn't look directly at me, but I felt her attention on me all the same. She flipped her light auburn waves over her shoulder with a huff. "Almost twice as many feebs wandering around campus now. It really is ridiculous. I guess we should just be glad they didn't stick one of the newbies in our dorm."

I suspected she'd brought up that subject specifically to needle me, even though in theory she was talking to her friends. She knew I hated the insulting slang so many of the fearmancers used for Naries and that I'd come to the defense of the school's Nary students more than once.

"I know," Cressida said in a bored tone, but she gave me a wary glance when I got up, her fingers fidgeting with the end of her ice-blond French braid. She and I hadn't exactly called a truce, but we'd made a magical deal where I owed her a favor in exchange for the testimony that had cleared me of the murder charge. I couldn't tell whether she was worried she might somehow lose my end of the agreement or if she'd gained a little respect for me somewhere along the way.

The "feeb" comment had rankled, but I held my temper as I rinsed my plate. The three girls were from major families among the fearmancers. It was possible they'd heard something about the new students that my fellow scions hadn't, especially since *their* parents had gotten particularly cagey about sharing information with their heirs.

"It's odd that Ms. Grimsworth brought them in partway through the term," I said casually, as if I'd been included in the other girls' conversation. "I wonder why she made that decision."

Victory pursed her lips as if she'd eaten something sour, but Sinclair piped up, apparently eager to show off her inside knowledge. "I heard they were off the waiting list," she said, flicking her black bob back from her face. "It was getting really long, and the feebs recommending people were starting to ask awkward questions."

Victory gave her friend a look both puzzled and pointed. "You heard that where?" Obviously she hadn't known even that much.

Sinclair's cheeks turned pink. She ducked her head with an awkward shrug. "It was just some teachers talking. I don't know the whole situation. It was something like that."

I wouldn't have thought Ms. Grimsworth would be intimidated by a few impatient Naries, but admittedly, I didn't know much about how she ran the school. Having more nonmagical students might not be such a bad thing anyway. It could mean the bullying would be spread out more, and who knew, there was even the slight chance a fearmancer student or two would get to know one well enough to realize they weren't so "feeble."

It didn't look like I was going to get anything else out of the trio, so I rinsed my dishes and headed out. I didn't have class for another hour, but being in my dorm bedroom reminded me too much of my familiar's absence. I went down to the library to catch up on the studies I'd missed while I was in California.

As I reached the library doorway, a young woman hurried over to me. "Miss Bloodstone?" she said in a hushed voice. "You're wanted in the maintenance building, as soon as you can stop by."

The maintenance building? I'd only been to the squat structure at the west side of campus once—with Imogen, when she'd still been alive, to ask for her father's help with a construction project I'd been encouraging the Naries in. Mr. Wakeburn was head of the department, though I'd heard he'd understandably taken leave since his daughter's murder. I didn't know anyone else who worked there at all.

"What about?" I asked.

The woman twisted her hands together in front of her, looking nervous but not malicious in any way I could decipher. "It's a personal matter. If you're busy, you don't have to come right away. I was just asked to deliver the message."

If I didn't find out what this was about right now, it'd distract me until I did. I turned away from the library. "I can come now. Is there someone specific who wanted to see me?"

She bobbed her head with a grateful smile. "Just go to Mr. Wakeburn's office."

I didn't actually expect to see Mr. Wakeburn and not a temporary replacement *in* his office until I knocked on the door in the maintenance building a few minutes later and a familiar voice called out, "Come in." Imogen's father sounded wearier than when I'd talked to him before, but his tone managed to hold some of the same warmth.

I eased open the office door tentatively. When I'd met the man, he'd struck me as a California surfer type: shaggy dark blond hair, eyes that crinkled with his smile. Today, his hair was brushed back in much more somber fashion, and he didn't smile at all, although relief crossed his face at the sight of me. He stood up as I closed the door behind me. All his clothes were mourning black.

"Miss Bloodstone," he said. "I'm glad you came—and so quickly."

His grief came through so clearly in everything from his demeanor to his outfit that my chest clenched up. "I should have come by sooner—I would have if I'd known you were back. I'm so sorry about Imogen. If I could have done anything to help her—"

He raised his hand to stop me. "I've read the reports. By the time you found her, it's clear there was no saving her. That's not— It never sounded right to me, the accusations— I can't place any responsibility for that on your shoulders."

I was responsible, though, on a deeper level than he'd have let himself consider. My enemies had arranged Imogen's murder specifically so they could frame me for it, knowing they'd be able to exert much more control over my actions if I were convicted. If Imogen and I hadn't been friendly, if she'd happened to be in another dorm, they wouldn't have picked her.

The knowledge added to the pressure in my chest, even though I couldn't admit any of it to the man in front of me.

"It shouldn't have happened," I said, not knowing what else to say.

"No. It shouldn't." Mr. Wakeburn dragged in a breath. "I know the two of you were friendly, even if you had your disagreements in the past. I was hoping you'd consider doing the one thing that might help her in some small way now. The blacksuits haven't made any progress—I'm not sure who else to ask. In your position as scion, you might be able to accomplish something."

A quiver of suspicion passed through me. I resisted the urge to tense up. "What are you asking?"

He looked me straight in the eyes then, his gaze steady and pleading. "No one can bring my daughter back, but that doesn't mean her murderer should get away unpunished. She deserves some kind of justice. Will you do what you can to see that happen?"

That's what I'd thought he was getting at. He wanted

me to help find and bring in her killer. How could he ever imagine that the woman responsible was high up in the exact organization he trusted to bring him that justice? I knew who'd murdered Imogen... and I wasn't sure I had any hope in hell of ever proving it, let alone making Lillian Ravenguard pay for that crime.

I couldn't admit to any of that either, but with Imogen's father looking at me like that, I couldn't rebuff him either. Imogen *did* deserve that justice, and so did Mr. Wakeburn. And if I couldn't make that happen, no one would.

"I want to see her get justice too," I said. "If I can make that happen, I promise you I will."

CHAPTER FIVE

Rory

Bloodstones recover quickly, my mother had said a couple days ago, and from the moment I arrived on the main family property, I had proof of that right in front of me.

She sat straight but not stiffly in the sitting room armchair kitty-corner to me, her eyes alert and her hand steady as she brought her cup of tea to her lips. I sipped from my own cup, the sweetly nutty flavor of the green tea she'd said was her favorite coating my tongue. The click of the grandfather clock's swinging pendulum carried through the room. My mother closed her eyes as she drank.

How long had she gone without this favorite tea? Without so many other things she must have enjoyed that the joymancers would never have supplied her with?

Despite my trepidations about her interest in vengeance and the fact that she still wasn't much more than a stranger to me, a flicker of my own anger shot through me at the thought.

The joymancers had stolen all that from her. And on top of it, they'd stolen from me the chance to know this woman as more than a stranger when she should have been the pinnacle of my world. Maybe I would discover that separation had been for the best, but it wasn't as if they'd done it for my benefit. They'd wanted to control and contain me as much as they had her. It'd just been easier with a child who couldn't remember where she'd come from.

"You picked Insight as your specialty and your league," my mother said, her gaze returning to me. "Tell me about that."

As I was often finding with her, I couldn't tell whether the request contained any judgment or only curiosity. Insight had turned out to be a valuable skill, but many fearmancers saw it as lesser than the other areas of magic simply because its effects were subtle rather than vividly impressive. It probably wasn't a coincidence that out of the other four baronies, the Ashgraves were the ones who tended toward that area. I wasn't sure whether the Bloodstones had a particular pattern.

I thought back to the moment when Ms. Grimsworth had asked me to choose after the assessment that had shown my strengths in all four areas of magic. "I was torn between that and Physicality. I used to make sculptures and things, before… I do like constructing with magic too. But when there were so many people around me who seemed to want a lot from me, not all of it good, I wanted every chance I could get of recognizing unkind intentions ahead of time."

I'd also picked it to honor the attitudes I'd inherited from my joymancer parents. Mom and Dad had always encouraged me to pay attention to people's expressions and actions to figure out what might be important to them, the way they did when deciding how to most easily stir up joy to power their magic. I didn't think my birth mother would react well to that part of the explanation, though.

She made a humming sound that sounded accepting if not outright approving.

"What's your specialty?" I had to ask. Almost as much, I'd have liked to know which area she wasn't quite powerful enough in to call it a strength, but that question might have raised eyebrows.

A slight smile curled my mother's lips. "I'm fond of a good conjuring myself. But I find it's most useful to be able to cut to the chase and simply demand what you need directly. Persuasion hasn't failed me often."

An uneasy sensation crawled down my back. That was one more way she'd aligned herself with the Nightwoods —with Malcolm's father and his domineering cruelty. Did she have any idea he'd turned that cruelty on me, repeatedly?

That was one of the subjects I'd most wanted to bring

up with her during this visit. I could have had an opening there, but before I could say anything else, Eloise, the house manager, slipped into the room with a fresh pot of tea on a small tray.

Normally one of the maids would have handled basic tasks like that, but Eloise obviously felt the newly returned lady of the house required a more thorough level of attention. From what I'd gathered, she'd already been hired on as assistant to the previous house manager in the last few years before my mother's disappearance. Most of the current staff wouldn't have worked under my mother at all.

Eloise nudged aside the older pot and set the new one in its place at the end of the coffee table. She tweaked the handle as if to set it at just the perfect angle for my mother's reach. My mother's eyes narrowed as she watched.

"That's enough," she said briskly, with a hint of an edge to her tone. "Let it be."

The older woman paled. "Yes, of course. My apologies, Baron." She scooped up the old pot and stepped back. "If there's anything else you need at the moment—"

My mother dismissed the manager with a jerk of her hand. "That's all."

I wasn't sure what to make of her apparent irritation until she leaned toward the new pot with the murmur of a casting word. Like every experienced fearmancer I'd met, she cast her spells using combinations of syllables that sounded like nonsense to anyone else—an easy way to avoid giving warning to those around you of what magic you were going to send their way.

It took more practice to use made-up casting words instead of ones that had a literal meaning that fit your intention. You had to come up with sounds that had a personal resonance with your meaning in the spur of the moment. For the six months I'd been learning how to use my magic, I'd mainly relied on literal words. Watching my mother, I couldn't help thinking it was about time I worked on disguising my own castings, for discretion if nothing else.

I might not have understood the sounds she'd spoken, but her behavior suggested the intention of the spell well enough. She brushed her hand over the pot, studying it intently, as if she were checking it to make sure it was... safe? Did she really think her own house manager, a woman who'd known her since her first years as baron and who from what I'd seen was treating her with nothing but fawning subservience would have poisoned her tea, magically or otherwise?

Had she always been that cautious, or was it an aftereffect of her imprisonment?

The casting appeared to satisfy her, in any case. She refilled her cup with a soft sigh. I took the opportunity to steer the conversation the way I'd been about to before.

"Have you spoken to the other barons since you've come back?" I asked.

My mother gave me a considering look. "They've come to give their respects and so forth, as one would expect. I'll be back at the table of the pentacle soon enough."

"I'm sure they're happy to have you back."

Her smile returned, wryer this time. "They'd better be. What's on your mind, Persephone?"

I wet my lips. "Well, I— Obviously I don't know what would be normal. But they haven't exactly been welcoming to me since I arrived here. The full barons, anyway." I wasn't going to throw Declan under the bus. My tentative phrasing didn't raise any specific complaints, but it gave me the opening to go there depending on how my mother responded.

My mother continued to study me for a long moment —long enough that the hairs on the back of my neck started to rise. I instinctively felt for my mental shields, even though she hadn't spoken a casting word.

"In what way?" she asked.

In the way that they'd given my mentor professor a deadly illness to stop him from warning me about their plans and enchanted him to try to injure me beyond the ability to cast if he were cured. In the way that they'd conspired to have me arrested and prosecuted for a murder they themselves had ordered committed. And a whole lot of other things I couldn't definitively prove if my mother needed more than my word for it. I resisted the urge to worry at my lip with my teeth.

"Baron Nightwood came by campus not long after I began classes and said some pretty harsh things," I said, figuring that was safe enough to mention as a start. "None of them stood up for me when I was accused of murder. Even when they thought I might be baron soon, they haven't seemed to want to treat me as a respected part of the pentacle." Not as long as I refused to go along with their ideas of how to rule, anyway.

My mother leaned back in her chair. "Well, we all must look after ourselves and our own. A Bloodstone doesn't rely on handouts. Given your... uncharacteristic upbringing, even though it wasn't your fault at all, I can understand why they'd have exercised some caution in their initial dealings with you. Let's not hold that against them. I'm sure you can prove yourself worthy of that respect in the years you have now before you take on the mantle of baron yourself."

That was a typical fearmancer view of the situation. It was a dog-eat-dog world with everyone out for themselves, and so powerplays and attempted manipulation were par for the course.

From what the other scions had told me, when it came to me the barons had gone beyond the scope of what even their society would consider acceptable treatment, but if I couldn't convince my mother of that... She'd grown up with the Barons Nightwood and Killbrook; considered at least Nightwood a close friend. Just as I barely knew her, she barely knew me. Counting on familial loyalty to smooth over such a huge accusation didn't seem wise this early on.

Possibly catching some of my uneasiness in my expression, my mother's gaze sharpened again. "I understand it must have been a difficult transition for you with the unfortunate lack of preparation you faced, but as a barony, we can't afford to dwell on our setbacks. You'll rule over your peers in your time as I did before and will now, and to be effective, you need to show them only strength. Any coddling offered to you would have undermined your position, even if it would have been comforting at the time."

"I know," I said automatically, although I wouldn't so much have wanted *coddling* as not being actively attacked on a regular basis. Although from a fearmancer perspective, those might be nearly the same thing. "I think I've stood up for myself pretty well."

There were a lot of other things I'd have liked to ask. Would she stand up for me if she found out the other barons were purposefully trying to undermine me? Would *she* accept the fact that I wasn't going to treat the Naries as lesser beings or demand the respect I was supposed to get by hurting people?

Those weren't the kind of questions I could expect a straight answer to, though. I'd have to figure out what sort of a mother she'd be to me as we went.

The memory of Connar's hostility flitted through my mind with a clenching of my stomach. That was a more current act of aggression against me. But again, I couldn't prove that his parents were behind it. Even if I could, it was way too easy to imagine my mother brushing that incident off as a family matter that it wasn't our business to interfere with. He'd been hostile to the other scions too, and it wasn't as if he'd hurt me in any way that showed.

Were the barons going to let up on me now that they didn't need my cooperation to run the pentacle? I guessed I'd have to wait and find that out too.

"I'm still figuring out what's normal and what's

expected here," I went on, keeping my tone casual even though I was being cautious with my words. "How do I know when someone has crossed a line? When to shrug it off and not let it affect me, and when to push back?"

My mother took another sip of her tea. "I think you must be developing a sound enough sense of that to have done as well as you have so far. If someone hurts you in any way that's obvious to onlookers, you obviously can't let that go unaddressed—but you still need to stay in control of the situation, rather than acting out of emotion. On the other hand, a failed or weak attempt at an attack can be left with just a warning, as subtle as seems appropriate. Anyone who can't manage a better feint than that isn't worthy of your recognition in the first place."

None of that answer surprised me. "All right. I think that's about the approach I've been taking anyway."

"Good. And Persephone, while I do want you to be able to stand on your two feet and manage your own affairs, especially at your age, you should also know that you can turn to me if the affront is severe enough. An assault on you would be an assault on me as well, and I'd rather no one forgets that."

She said the words coolly enough, but a momentary fierceness lit in her eyes. My throat ached for a second with the longing to tell her just how many assaults I'd already faced. Uncertainty kept it locked against those words.

No doubt Baron Nightwood would have said the same thing about his children. That hadn't stopped him from turning brutality against them when he decided it was necessary.

What if, when it was all laid out, my mother felt I'd deserved every action they'd taken against me?

CHAPTER SIX

Malcolm

Connar might have been possessed by some kind of brain-warping spell, but it hadn't altered his habits that much. I caught him out back of the kennel as he walked to cool down from his regular evening jog.

He frowned when he saw me standing there, his pace slowing, but he didn't move to avoid me completely. He came to a stop when he reached the kennel building, which would hide us from view of the main campus—but not the forest across from us.

The wind chose that moment to whip through the leaves on the nearby trees with a frantic rustling. Connar glanced over, and I forced myself not to tense. Rory had hidden herself well enough in the brush that I hadn't been able to make her out when I'd checked a few minutes ago, and I'd *known* she was there.

He shifted his gaze back to me, swiping his forearm across the gleam of sweat on his temple. In the fading sunlight, his bulky form looked more ominous than I usually found it, his eyes shadowed. Connar might not *like* to fight, but he could do a hell of a lot of damage if he wanted to. I'd never really thought I had to worry about him turning those protective instincts against me before.

We should be okay as long as I didn't mention Rory. She was definitely the primary trigger for the spell. And I was hoping I could still push on those instincts to my benefit. I'd had Connar's back through an awful lot, and I knew how much that'd meant to him.

"Hey," I said. "I'm glad I caught you. There's something I wanted to talk to you about... without anyone else around."

His expression stayed wary. "If this is about—"

I held up my hands. "I'm not going to try to convince you or argue with you about anything. I think I might need your help, actually. If you're willing to give that."

To my relief, his stance relaxed. He took a step closer, his gaze skimming the grounds all around us to make sure we didn't have any spectators. "What's the problem?" he asked, concern warring with caution in his gaze.

A twinge of guilt ran through me even though this deception was ultimately to help him. If I could have tackled this problem directly and above board with him, I would have.

I ducked my head as if embarrassed. "Between the way my dad has been lately and some of the things you've said… I'm a little worried about how much outside influence might be able to creep into my head. I'd like to be sure my mental barriers are up to the task. If you could throw some persuasive spells at me, hard as you can, so I can test them, I'll see if there are any weak spots I need to shore up."

Connar frowned again, but this time it was more pained than suspicious. "I'm not sure I'd be much help there. Persuasion is my weak area."

The guy never recognized his talents half as well as he should. "A scion's weakness is like the average mage's strength," I said, waving off his objection. "And I'd rather not admit to our Almost-Baron-Ashgrave that I'm nervous about this or give Jude a chance to mess with me if he manages to get in. I know I can count on you to give it all you've got and not take advantage if you find a crack."

Appealing to loyalty—and showing how much I already relied on him—was the fastest way to convince Connar of anything. The current situation was no exception.

He let out a rough breath and nodded. "All right. You want to do this right now, here?"

"Yeah. I already cast a spell to make sure no one wanders over this way. Better to do it where there's no chance we'll be overheard. And I don't want to keep worrying about this any longer than I have to."

"Let me know when you're ready then."

I drew myself a little straighter as if bolstering my reserves. "Go ahead." At the same time, I made a small gesture at my side with my right hand, the one Rory would be able to see from her observation point.

For Connar to launch a persuasive spell at me, he'd have to let down his own mental walls, at least for an instant. That would give Rory the chance to sneak into his head using insight. With luck, it wouldn't take her long to find the impressions of his parents' machinations.

"*Come here*," Connar said, in a casting tone firm enough that I'd imagine nearly any other student would have responded to it. The impact of the spell smacked into my inner shields hard enough that I willed them steady instinctively.

"Is that all you've got?" I said, letting a teasing note enter my voice. Might as well give Rory another opportunity if I could. "Really hit me, Conn. Tell yourself my life depends on it—because maybe it does." Or at the very least, his did.

Connar's face tensed with concentration. "*Come here*," he said again, power ringing through the command. The magic in it careened into my shields, and a tiny pinching formed in the middle of my forehead. He might not be officially *strong* in persuasion, but he wasn't any lightweight either.

The Stormhurst scion shook his head. "They feel pretty solid to me. If you're on your guard around anyone who might try to influence you…"

He trailed off, both of us aware that he'd suggested Rory might have been one such person. I wasn't sure if he thought she'd actually manipulated us with magic or with her womanly charms or something along that line… He'd started ranting about her so quickly after I'd tried to broach the subject last time that I hadn't been able to make much sense of it. His mother probably didn't care whether his animosity sounded reasonable, only that he spewed it as adamantly as possible.

"Thanks," I said. "I'm definitely not letting down my guard around my parents any time soon."

Connar let out a halting chuckle. "Yeah."

It was hard to look at him and keep my mouth shut about everything else. I considered this guy my closest friend. I should have been able to say to him, "Stay away from *your* parents so they don't fuck things up for you even more, all right?" or even, "Don't you remember that the one time you stood up to me and told me I was wrong, it was for the girl you're now attacking?" But I didn't think either of those comments would really get me anywhere.

Instead, I settled for cuffing him lightly on the arm and saying, "We'll get this figured out. All of it." Leaving it vague exactly what I was including in that "all."

"Of course," Connar said, but for a second he looked uncertain. Then the set of his mouth went so rigid I knew he must have thought of Rory. His mother had dug her spell in deep.

He walked on toward Ashgrave Hall, and I stepped into the kennel to release my familiar from his mandated school-day confinement. As Shadow trotted out with me, I glanced toward the hall in time to see Connar disappearing through the main door. The coast was clear.

"Go on," I said to my wolf with a pat on his shoulder, and he sprinted toward the trees with an eager pant of breath. By the time I reached the edge of the forest, he'd already found Rory and was nuzzling her face where she was crouched amid the brush.

"All right, all right," she said quietly with a little laugh, scratching behind his ears. "It's good to see you too."

Months ago, I'd been pissed off when I'd found out the Bloodstone scion was getting friendly with my familiar. Now, the sight of that shared affection sent a quiver of warmth through my chest. Give her enough time, and Rory had proven she could win just about anyone over. Including me.

And damn if I didn't wish I'd let her get through to me sooner.

At least the effects of the way I'd treated her those first few months were finally fading. When she stood up to meet me, it was with none of the apprehension that I'd come to expect. I could tell the sadness in her smile was about the situation with Connar, not anything to do with me.

"Did you get what we need?" I asked.

She dipped her head. "The images were kind of a jumble, like they usually are, but I think I picked out an impression from the casting. There was a point when he was in a room with his parents caught in a spell preventing him from moving, and his mother cast something that set off a bunch of pain before it was over. Like a jabbing right at the base of his tailbone."

My mouth went crooked, remembering Jude's off-the-cuff remarks. "They embedded their spell on his ass."

A faint flush colored Rory's cheeks. "As far as I can tell. We probably don't need to *see* it to try to break the spell, right?"

"Having a visual is generally easier. But we'll find a way, somehow or other."

Shadow bumped his muzzle against Rory's hand, and she gave his ears another rub. "I don't think the forest is a good place for a game of catch," she told him. "And it's better if your master isn't seen hanging out with me right now."

"Go get your hunting in," I said to my familiar with a wave toward the deeper woods. Rory watched him as he loped off. The hint of pain that crossed her face sent a jab through me on her behalf.

"How are you holding up?" I asked. God forbid I ever lost Shadow as suddenly and violently as she'd lost her familiar. I'd like to have eviscerated the joymancer who cast that spell.

"You know. It just takes time. It's strange being back here without her."

Dealing with Connar's turnaround on top of that, even if he wasn't in control of himself, had to be making matters even worse. I eased closer, tracking her reactions to make sure I wasn't overstepping her boundaries, and brought my hand to her cheek.

"I can't do anything about that, as much as I wish I could. But we *will* get Connar back to his old self—as soon as possible."

She looked up at me with a hint of dry amusement in her dark eyes. "I'd have thought you'd be happy to have a little less competition."

I made a face at the remark, even though, fair, I hadn't been especially keen on sharing her with any of my fellow scions even before I'd had a chance with her myself. She was everything I could have wanted in a partner, in a lover, so I couldn't be blamed for wanting sole dibs on her attention, could I? But watching her and the other guys over the past month had adjusted my perspective.

"He's not competition," I said. "However much being with him makes you happy, which it obviously does, that doesn't take anything away from whether *I* can make you happy. It just means you're even happier than I could make you on my own. I sure as hell don't deserve you if I can't learn to appreciate that."

Her expression softened. "I'm glad you can see it that way."

She looked so gorgeous and so tempting in that moment that I had to lean in for a kiss. Rory tipped her head up to meet my lips, her hand tucking around the back of my neck, and I couldn't imagine how *I* could have been happier than having her body against me, the heat of her mouth blooming against mine.

Okay, maybe there were a few things that would have made me even happier. None of which would be wise to initiate at the edge of the woods beside a totally open campus field. Right now I should really just appreciate that she'd welcome this kiss at all.

She pulled back with a rueful smile. "I guess I should

see when Declan and Jude can meet us again to work out our next steps."

"I can't see anything good coming out of waiting," I agreed. "Let me make sure Shadow's got all he needs, and I'll catch up with you at the hall. It wouldn't be good for anyone to see us walking back together anyway, in case Connar hears about it."

"I'll see you soon, then."

As she picked her way out of the forest, I whistled for my familiar. He came trotting back a few moments later with a rabbit clutched in his jaws. That was dinner taken care of.

"I'll leave you to that," I said. "Run in the morning?"

He perked up with a cock of his head that said he was definitely on board with that idea.

On my way back to the dorms, my phone rang. It was my little sister, Agnes, calling.

A jolt of worry raced through my gut as I answered. I couldn't remember the last time she'd wanted to talk to me urgently enough that she hadn't just waited until my next visit home. At thirteen, she didn't yet have any magic to defend herself with, and our parents saw her more sensitive nature as a reason to harass her as often as possible in the name of toughening her up.

"Hey," I said, keeping my tone even as I answered. "What's up?"

"Hi." Agnes's voice came through slightly muffled, as if she was trying to speak covertly. "I, um…"

She fell into silence for long enough that my concern surged up in full force.

"What's going on, Agnes?" I asked. "Are you okay?"

"Yeah. Yeah. I just— When Dad got mad at you last week, it was because you spoke up somehow for the Bloodstone scion, right?"

My worries snapped in a totally different direction with those last words. "Why are you asking?" I said cautiously. It wasn't outside the realm of possibility that my parents might have put her up to placing this call to test *me* somehow.

"I heard him talking to Mom today," Agnes said in the same hushed tone. "I thought maybe you would want to know. They sounded really serious, but also kind of excited, not like I've really heard them before. It was something about plans they were finally putting in motion. I couldn't hear the whole thing, but he definitely said something about Bloodstone in there."

Shit. More attacks from my dad was just what Rory needed right now. "You don't know what the plans were?"

"I'm sorry. They weren't being specific. And I didn't want to keep listening too long in case they noticed me. I just thought… it might help you to know. Maybe you'll be able to see what they were talking about."

"Okay. Thank you. You really didn't need to stick your neck out—it's fine that you didn't hear more than that." I didn't know if she thought I'd want a chance to get in on those plans or to counteract them, but I'd take the heads up either way. "I won't breathe a word about you calling me to Mom or Dad."

"Thank you," she said with a terrified-sounding giggle.

As I hung up, my stomach sank. Rory might have an

even bigger threat looming on the horizon—and I didn't even know enough about it to give her a halfway decent warning.

CHAPTER SEVEN

Rory

My new mentor, Professor Viceport, never seemed all that happy to see me, but on this particular morning she was giving off an even terser vibe than usual.

"Well," she said, dropping into her chair across her desk from me with a tap of its legs and a shake of her wispy blond pixie cut, "you must be facing a lot of catching up after all the classes you've missed."

With that edged voice, she made it sound as if I'd chosen to be arrested and then to discover my mother was in joymancer custody. I had to take a slow breath to stop myself from bristling.

Viceport, who was also my Physicality professor, had seemed to hold a grudge against me from the moment I'd arrived at Blood U for reasons she'd never made clear. I wasn't sure why Ms. Grimsworth had assigned her to me after Professor Banefield's death, but I tried to make the best of the situation. No matter how difficult *she* made that.

"Only a little more than I already had to catch up after missing the first four *years* of my schooling," I couldn't help pointing out. I wasn't exactly a stranger to being behind my peers. "I've completed all the assignments I missed."

She looked at me skeptically through her rectangular glasses. "I hope your professors haven't been lowering their expectations, regardless of your circumstances. Letting you skip by necessary training won't help anyone."

You certainly haven't cut me any slack, I barely restrained myself from saying. I clasped my hands together on my lap so it wouldn't be as obvious I was clenching them. "I believe I'm doing the same work as everyone else in the class. I've arranged a couple of sessions with the teachers' aides to make sure I'm totally up to speed."

She let out a sound that was almost a snort and shuffled the papers on her desk, though I didn't know what any of those had to do with me. She was probably counting down the minutes until I was out of her hair. I certainly was. Not that I was particularly looking forward to the rest of my plans for this morning.

"Have I been progressing in Physicality at the rate you'd have expected even with the absences?" I asked, since that was the one area she could comment on directly.

"Your performance has been adequate," Viceport said stiffly, which was about the highest praise I ever got from her. From the awed stares from a few of my classmates during our last conjuring session, I was pretty sure I'd handled myself more than "adequately," but arguing with my mentor about it wouldn't do me much good.

"You have the benefit of a wide range of strengths," she added. "That will allow you to increase your skills more quickly, but you shouldn't let yourself become complacent simply because some of the basics come easily to you."

Did she really think anything I'd worked for since coming here had been *easy*? For what felt like the hundredth time, I bit my tongue against a snarky remark.

"I won't," I said, and moved to stand up. "I didn't have anything I needed advice on. If that's all we have to talk about—"

"Hold on a moment, Miss Bloodstone," Viceport said, raising her thin hand. "We only have these sessions once a month. There's no need to rush out before we have a chance to cover every concern."

What other concerns did she have? I sank back down, watching her quizzically, but she simply gazed back at me with her icy eyes. Did she want *me* to continue the conversation? I'd just said I didn't have any other questions.

"Was there something else you wanted to go over?" I prompted after several seconds of silence.

She steepled her fingers in front of her. "You seem very confident in yourself."

I wasn't sure about that. It was probably just that I'd gotten a lot less willing to ignore other people's bullshit over the last couple months. And yeah, I now knew that I could accomplish quite a bit with my magical abilities. That didn't mean I was *over*-confident.

"I've been here almost half a year now," I said. "I'm adjusting, getting used to how things work. That's normal, right?"

"I suppose it depends on where that confidence leads. Your position is certainly more secure now that you don't have the pressure of the barony looming over your graduation."

"That's true." Where was she going with that, though? I still didn't understand what she was trying to get at.

"Perhaps you'll request a different mentor, since you don't seem entirely satisfied with the guidance I can offer," Viceport said. "No doubt you'll get what you ask for too."

I stared at her for a second, speechless. Then my tongue loosened, a little more than was probably wise, but I'd had it with all her passive-aggressive comments and insinuations.

"The only reason I'm at all 'unsatisfied' with your mentoring is that you keep taking jabs at me like that. I've been trying my best to live up to being the mage everyone thinks I'm supposed to be in all my classes, including yours. I can't help that I wasn't better prepared. I really don't know what it is you want from me that I'm not doing or why you have such a problem with me, but I can't do anything about it if you won't actually tell me."

My mouth snapped shut, and heat crept up my neck, but everything I'd said was true. Professor Viceport blinked at me, apparently lost for words herself. Well, this meeting had turned into a bit of a disaster, hadn't it?

I grabbed my purse and stood up. "Sorry. I shouldn't have said it like that. I think we're done here."

"Miss Bloodstone—"

I met her eyes, my jaw tight. "Do you actually have anything you want to talk to me about, or are you just going to make more vague comments that don't seem to really lead anywhere? Because, as you pointed out, I do have plenty of work to catch up on."

She faltered and then flicked her hand toward the doorway. "Off you go, then."

I walked out with a knot in my stomach. I'd rather she *had* told me what her issue with me was rather than just send me off, honestly. But right now I had bigger things to worry about.

As I crossed the green, a group of students meandered by—half of them with gold scholarship pins winking in the mid-morning light, the others fearmancers. That was strange. Maybe one of the general instruction courses had just let out?

They stuck together as they headed past Nightwood Tower toward the west field, though. And there was Professor Crowford, my Persuasion instructor, ushering them along from behind. He might have taught one of the general instruction courses as well as his magical ones, of course. I didn't have time to dwell on that either.

I'm out, I texted to Declan and Malcolm as I headed into Ashgrave Hall. I hurried down the stairs to the scion lounge and found Jude waiting for me there as planned.

He motioned me over to the far side of the bar cabinet. "I figured this would be the best spot for you to be staked out. The cabinet will partly hide you, and there's nothing on the wall there to interfere with the illusion, but you'll still have a clear view of the action."

"Yeah." My gut clenched all over again at the thought of what that "action" would entail.

I stepped back against the wall. The bar cabinet was a tall one, looming about half a foot over my head, but it was so shallow no one could have missed me standing there if I had no magic on me. A faint sour odor tickled my nose from the bottles of alcohol.

Jude stopped in front of me, his dark green eyes searching mine. "Are you ready?"

I nodded. "I just… really hope this goes okay."

"As we all do, Ice Queen," he said, using his old nickname for me with such tenderness that it softened the edge on my nerves.

I touched the front of his shirt, and Jude took that cue to ease closer, dipping his head as his mouth found mine. For a second, I lost myself in the feel of his lean body and the peppery coriander scent of him. Jude knew how to kiss as if he were pouring his whole heart into the gesture, as if no one in the world existed but the two of us. My heart was thumping when he drew back, but it wasn't just from anxiety then.

There wasn't time for anything else. He murmured his casting words under his breath with waves of his hand to help direct the magic. My skin tingled as the energy settled over me. The spell he'd cast was one I'd used on myself to blend into my surroundings, but it was based on illusion, and no one could do a better job with that than the guy in front of me.

When he was finished, he stepped back and glanced over me and the space around me with critical consideration. His gaze didn't quite meet mine, probably because he couldn't see anymore where my eyes were.

"That should do it. Stay still, and we'll make sure he doesn't come over too close. I don't think there's any chance he'll catch on, no matter how cautious he's being with us."

"Got it," I said, willing my breath to stay even and calm.

Jude texted the other guys to let them know we were ready. He poured himself a drink—just a Coke, whether because he'd decided it was too early in the day for liquor or he just wanted his head as clear as possible, I wasn't sure —and sat down on the sofa with it. After a few restless shifts, he clicked on the entertainment system's audio and started a playlist of classic rock playing at a low volume. I could see his own tension in the set of his shoulders.

It was another few minutes before footsteps rapped against the stairs outside the door. Malcolm strode in first, with Connar and Declan right behind him. Connar stopped just inside, crossing his brawny arms over his chest, his pale eyes taking in the room with a sharp wariness that wasn't at all like the guy I knew.

My heart squeezed as his gaze passed over me. He obviously didn't see me at all, but the thought of how he'd react if he did was unsettling enough.

Jude clicked off the music and stood up. Connar studied him too and then turned back to Malcolm. "What's this really all about?"

The Nightwood scion held up his hands in an appeal. "It doesn't have to be a big thing. I'm just a little worried about you, Conn. When we talked the other day, I got a sense of something I didn't like. We know that various people have been targeting our pentacle in different ways. I wanted to make sure there aren't any hostile spells acting on you right now."

Connar's jaw tightened. "I think I'd have noticed if there were."

"Not necessarily," Declan said in the measured tone that had served him well as a teacher's aide. "Our enemies have a lot of skill—enough to work magic it'd be difficult to detect if you're not looking for it. But between the three of us, we should be able to tell for sure. It'd just take a minute to check you over for spells."

The Stormhurst scion didn't budge. "If you really think someone's been casting on me, I should go to my parents. A baron will be able to deal with that kind of treachery better than anyone."

Connar in his right mind would definitely never have said *that*. I thought I saw Malcolm restrain a grimace. "Your mother also has lots of other things to occupy her," he said smoothly. "I might just be paranoid. I haven't seen anything definite, but I want to be sure. If we pick up on something, you can have your parents handle the rest. Including the punishment for whoever thought messing with you was a good idea."

Jude swept his floppy dark copper hair back from his eyes. "We could already be done by now if we just got on with it," he said in a bored tone, as if none of this mattered all that much to him.

Connar glanced at each of them, clearly debating what to do. Then he scanned the room again. The spell working on him made him wary of anything that could have to do with me, but in the absence of any signs that I was involved with this request, his shoulders started to come down. His parents would have wanted him to keep a decent relationship with the other guys where I wasn't involved.

He took a couple steps farther into the room. "Fine. Just make it quick."

The other three scions formed a loose circle around him. Thanks to my earlier insight work, they knew where the construct holding the spell was probably located, but they had to make a show of an overall examination. I braced myself where I stood by the wall.

We wouldn't have risked having me present at all, except I was the only one in the group who'd ever unraveled a bodily-bound spell like this before. Once the guys confirmed its location, we'd want to tackle it as quickly as possible. My experience would hopefully speed that process along. Then all we'd have to worry about were any aftereffects that might be triggered by the spell's destruction—like the violent rage Professor Banefield had flown into after I'd cured him of his magically induced illness.

Each of the guys intoned a casting word, and Connar held stiffly still. I waited for the signal that they'd identified the spot. The seconds slipped past, and then Malcolm started to raise his hand. "There's somethi—"

Connar jerked away from the three of them with a sudden ragged breath. "What the fuck?" he said. "Get the hell away from me!"

The guys stared at him, obviously as startled by his reaction as I was. "I hadn't done anything," Malcolm said, his smooth voice gone outright cajoling. "But I'm sensing—"

"*You're* trying to screw me over," Connar snapped, shoving himself even farther away from them. Shit. His parents must have included an aspect of the spell that would set off his defensiveness if any other magic touched that spot.

Unfortunately, he'd shoved himself toward the bar cabinet. I cringed back, flattening myself against the wall as well as I could. Jude's eyes had widened. All three of the guys moved tentatively toward Connar, Malcolm circling to the right so he could usher him in another direction, but Connar was backpedaling too quickly, his face flushed with anger.

"You tell me you want to help me, and then you try to pull something like this?"

"We weren't pulling anything," Declan said. "I swear it, Connar. We're just trying to help you."

Connar spun around without warning, just a couple feet from where I was standing. His gaze jarred against my form. His expression went rigid, and he spat out a casting word that shattered the magical quivering that had been clinging to my body.

At the rage that wrenched across his face, I scrambled off to the side. I opened my mouth and hesitated, not sure if speaking would only make things worse, no matter what I said.

"What the fuck is she doing hiding away in here?" Connar whipped back around to face the other scions. "Did you know? Is that part of the whole plan? You fucking assholes."

"Connar," Malcolm started, his mouth slanting at a pained angle, but the Stormhurst scion didn't give him a chance to say anything.

"You can all go to hell," Connar said, and stormed out of the room with enough fury and thunder to more than live up to his name.

"Well," Jude said with an expression as sickly as I felt inside, "I think we can safely say this attempt was not a success."

I hugged myself, just barely stopping myself from shaking. Malcolm and Declan exchanged a wince of a glance. After this, what were the chances Connar was going to trust any of us again, let alone enough to try to break through that spell?

CHAPTER EIGHT

Rory

As Declan pulled into the small parking lot next to the handful of other cars already there, I peered through the windshield at the building ahead of us. A craggy structure of dark stone rose from the wild grass, three stories high and narrow enough that you could almost have called it a tower. The gray clouds congealing overhead gave it a gloomy cast, but I had the feeling it'd have looked ominous in any weather.

"Welcome to the Fortress of the Pentacle," Declan said grimly.

So, this was where the barons held their meetings. Seeing it didn't make me feel any more at ease about the current pentacle. I couldn't imagine how Declan must have felt every time he'd needed to walk into that place to face the three older barons who saw him as more of an obstacle than a colleague.

I couldn't make too overt a gesture when there was no telling who might be watching, but it seemed safe enough to scoot my hand across the seats to grasp his, just briefly. Without looking at me, Declan ran his thumb over my knuckles in a fond caress.

"Whatever happens with your mother, the other barons should back off now," he said. "They'll see it as her responsibility to set you straight where they assume you need it—and if she doesn't, they'll focus on her, not you, since she's their peer. I don't think they'd dare to outright attack you behind her back, no matter what Malcolm's sister overheard."

"Small comforts," I said, but that knowledge was a bit of a relief. As cruel as fearmancer parents could be, it had to be better to only be dealing with one baron, even one with familial authority, rather than three who definitely had it out for me. "I'm not even sure why she wanted me to come."

"I suppose she'll tell you once we get in there. We probably shouldn't spend too much time talking first."

He let go of my hand with a note of regret in his tone. Declan had been the first of the scions to really support me, and thinking of the risks he'd already taken on my behalf made my heart ache. The barony wasn't even that important to him—he'd fought to hold onto it not out of a desire for power but to keep the heavy responsibility and the dangers that came with it off his younger brother's shoulders.

If the other barons found out he wasn't just a neutral party in the conflict between them and me but intimately involved with me, the backlash he'd face might be severe. Even though our relationship didn't break any official rules, we were keeping it quiet. My mother had wanted all the barons present for my visit to the Fortress, though, and it'd made sense for Declan and me to drive together when we were coming from the same place.

"How's your brother healing up?" I asked as I stepped out of the car into the damp air.

"No permanent damage from the prank. A few hours of magical intervention, and his leg was almost good as new, just a little sore. Not the way I'd have wanted him to learn that lesson about how much to trust his supposed friends, though."

"Yeah." None of us got off easy at Blood U. If that was how his brother got treated when he wasn't even the scion himself, no wonder Declan was worried about protecting him from the role.

I walked up to the front doors with him without allowing myself to show any further hesitation. A crawling sensation ran over my skin alongside the impression that this building might swallow me whole, never to release me again. We were just a few feet from the door when it swung open to reveal my mother.

She looked as steady and composed as she had when I'd called on her at the main Bloodstone residence not long ago, with an extra glint of energy in her eyes. She was glad to be back at her work, obviously.

"Persephone," she said, brisk but pleased. "Right on time." She inclined her head just slightly to Declan in acknowledgment. "Thank you for giving her the drive, Mr. Ashgrave."

"I was happy to help," Declan said with a careful smile. He wouldn't be fully Baron Ashgrave until he graduated from the university in a few months' time. I wondered if the aunt he'd mentioned would be here today too. She'd served as his regent when he was younger and still had a place at the table until he took complete control of the barony.

He stepped inside past my mother and headed off to wherever the barons usually met, I guessed. My mother touched my arm to guide me with her. "I understand this is your first time coming out here."

"Yes," I said, with a flash of memory back to the one time Baron Nightwood had requested my presence at a meeting of the barons. When I'd declined, he'd magically frozen me in place and warned me about my lack of respect. Good times. "I wanted to get a better handle on how fearmancer society works and on my own magic before I dove into the politics."

"Wise to have some patience about it," she said with obvious approval. At least she was on my side in that one case. She led me down the high-ceilinged hall, pointing out rooms as we passed. "Each of the barons has their own small office space here, although it's generally more convenient to hold our private meetings on our own properties, unless we want to particularly emphasize our authority."

She shot me a quick grin with that same gleam in her eyes, and I realized she wasn't just glad to be back here in the role she'd been born for. She was enjoying introducing me to more of that role too. How many times would she have imagined guiding me to follow in her footsteps even in the two years she'd had me before the joymancers' attack? And how many times afterward had she mourned that opportunity? No wonder she was excited now.

"That makes sense," I said to encourage her and to show I was paying attention.

"We also keep records from all our meetings going back through all the pentacles, although digging through the library is more drudgery than anything else," she went on. "And there's a store of essential supplies, regularly updated as need be by the staff. This building is meant to serve as a final hold-out if our society ever faces a major attack, to ensure the barons' safety."

It was hard for me to imagine some kind of magical war breaking out in this day and age. Maybe it'd been more of a concern in the past, before the mages on both sides had needed to be quite so wary of Nary observation.

She stopped by a room near the end of the hall and pushed the door all the way open. A faintly dusty smell trickled out. The space on the other side held a slim bookshelf with neatly ordered rows, a glass-topped desk with office chairs on either side of it, and an overstuffed armchair that filled one corner.

"This is my office, and it will be yours." My mother's gaze took on a distant quality. "I'll need to reorganize it some. I haven't had a chance yet. I'm told your grandfather used it from time to time while he was standing baron in our absence, up until his death…"

It hadn't occurred to me before to really think about how my mother had not just been wrenched away from me but the rest of her family too. She'd missed both of her parents' deaths during her imprisonment. Lost any chance of last regards.

Whatever she was feeling about that fact, she shook it off a moment later. We walked on to the window at the end of the hall next to the stairs. It gave a view of a broad, fenced field, the grass stirring with the breeze.

"If we'd been here as we should have been, you'd have grown up playing with the other scions out there while the barons talked," she said. "The joymancers stole that opportunity to bond from you too." She paused, and her gaze slid to me. "From what I understand, your associations with the heirs of the other families have been rather... intense."

How much exactly had she heard? I tried to will down my blush, but my cheeks heated a little anyway. "Any problems between us, we've worked out," I said. Except for the current one with Connar, which wasn't really *him* but his parents. "As for anything else... I know how the inheritances work. I haven't been making promises neither of us will want to keep."

My mother looked satisfied with that answer. Had she enjoyed her own dalliances with the scions of her time when she was younger? Ugh, I didn't want to think about that.

She turned back to the window. "Our position in this society comes with a lot of responsibilities you won't be as prepared for. Every fearmancer out there relies on us to make the decisions that will keep our community strong. The barons must show that we're capable of fulfilling that responsibility with a united front, even if we have our occasional disagreements behind the scenes. That goes for the scions too. Your first loyalty is to the Bloodstones, but your second must be to the four other barons waiting for us up there."

As she motioned toward the stairs, she started to climb them. I followed with a sinking sensation in my chest. Was she just referring to the small, somewhat public conflict I'd had with Baron Nightwood—or did she know that there'd been other, stealthy conflicts and was blaming them on my own lack of loyalty?

"I understand," I hedged, waiting to see if she'd go on, maybe to chide me for a specific action I'd taken. When she didn't, I risked pushing the subject a little farther. "I haven't had any chance to interact with most of them one way or another so far. I hope they haven't expressed any concerns about how I've handled my time so far at the university."

"It's simply something to remember," my mother said without really addressing the implied question in my comment. "They'll certainly see who you are now."

At the top of the stairs, she motioned me to a room a few times larger than the offices downstairs. I slowed as I reached the threshold.

Most of the space was taken up by a circular table etched with a pentacle. Figures were seated at all but one of the five points—Declan, of course, and the man who was an older, colder version of Malcolm, and the two barons I'd never met face to face before.

A prickle of rancor ran through me at the sight of the thin, sharp-faced man with sandy hair who must have been Baron Killbrook, Jude's supposed father. The man who'd treated Jude like dirt for years over his own decision and now was spying on him with probably malicious intentions. I didn't feel any friendlier toward the wiry woman with flinty eyes sitting across from him. She'd be Baron Stormhurst, Connar's mother and the mage currently responsible for addling his mind.

They all smiled at us as my mother came to stand behind the chair at the fifth point on the pentacle. I stopped beside her, forcing myself to smile back, even though I thought I sensed a chill behind three of those expressions.

"You already know the soon-to-be Baron Ashgrave," my mother said in a light but careful voice. "It's about time you met Barons Killbrook, Nightwood, and Stormhurst. If not for the efforts of our blacksuits, you might have been sitting among them sooner rather than later." She set her hand on my shoulder. "Barons, my daughter and scion, Persephone."

There was something vaguely possessive in both her touch and her tone, as if she were staking a sort of claim over me. Reminding them that I was hers as much as she'd reminded me downstairs to respect the four figures in front of me.

"We're glad to finally have a proper meeting," Nightwood said without a hint of emotion. "I'm sure you'll learn all you need to know to join this table from your mother."

Declan nodded to me, and Killbrook and Stormhurst offered quiet greetings.

"Thank you for having me attend," I said awkwardly. "I definitely want to be properly prepared to take that place, even if I'm glad it won't have to be soon."

My mother patted my shoulder as if she approved of that sentiment and reached down at the buzz of her phone. "Ah," she said. "I asked Lillian to come around so we could discuss some matters relating to my incarceration. Persephone, go down and meet her, and let her know I'll just be a few minutes."

It was a command, not a request, delivered coolly with the obvious expectation that I'd accept it immediately. I didn't really *want* to be in the room with the three barons who'd made my life hell anyway, so I bobbed my head and slipped out without a word. It only occurred to me as I reached the stairs that she'd been making another sort of statement in that moment.

She'd made it clear that I was hers—and then she'd demonstrated her authority over me. I wasn't sure how much it was for my benefit and how much for the barons, but possibly a little of both. If they'd expressed any concerns about her ability to… discipline me, or whatever, I suspected that gesture was meant to answer those.

Wonderful.

I didn't have much chance to dwell on that, because as I reached the lower hallway, a staff person was just holding open the door for Lillian. The blacksuit, gracefully powerful with her leonine looks, stalked inside. Her assistant, Maggie, bounded at her heels with a swish of her chocolate brown curls. I went over to greet them, trepidation expanding through my chest.

I didn't need any more reasons to distrust Lillian. She'd murdered Imogen. She'd set me up to take the fall for that murder. Would her intentions toward me change now that my mother was back?

Maggie I wasn't sure about. She didn't seem to act outside of Lillian's orders often, if at all, but now and then in the last month she'd asked me questions and made remarks that felt unexpectedly barbed. I wasn't sure whether she'd simply realized my intentions were at odds with her employer's or she had some other hostile agenda. Or maybe I'd just gotten paranoid considering how many other people had turned out to be looking to squash me.

"My mother said she'll be down in a few minutes," I said to Lillian with a smile I couldn't stop from feeling stiff. A different sort of uneasiness tremored through me as I reached her.

I'd promised Mr. Wakeburn I'd bring his daughter's murderer to justice if I could. Here she was right in front of me. I didn't have the faintest idea how I could go about it from there.

Well, I had this moment with her to myself. Maybe Lillian could tip me off without even knowing I'd use the knowledge against her.

"What do you think of the place?" she asked me.

"Hard to believe I'll be working here someday myself,"

I said with a little laugh. "Um, before my mother comes down, could I ask you a couple things?"

Lillian cocked her head. I felt Maggie studying me from just behind her. "Of course. What about?" the blacksuit asked.

I scrambled for a plausible excuse. "I just—you know how the students at Blood U are." I rolled my eyes for effect. "I'm still working on making sure my dorm room is as secure as possible and all that. I was wondering—is there any magical technique that would let me detect who's been in a specific space before, in the past? Even what time they were there?"

Lillian rubbed her jaw as she considered. "If they left some sort of trace, like a hair or even some flakes of skin, you'd be able to establish their presence and identify them from that. It'd be difficult to tell the timing with any accuracy unless it was very recent, though."

Okay, scratch that possibility. I couldn't imagine Lillian would have been careless enough to leave any sign of her presence at the murder scene anyway, and the maintenance staff had cleaned the dorm room thoroughly since then.

"Okay, good to know," I said. "What about—if you know a specific spell was cast in a room, is there any way to tell who cast it?"

"You should be learning about caster identification in your classes," Lillian said with a raise of one eyebrow. "Surely they're covering that still."

The basic concept had come up at least once, just not in any way that was useful to me. "Oh, yeah, of course.

For a spell that's currently active. I mean if the spell is already over. Like, if someone cast something in my room last week, would there be any lingering traces of that I should be able to pick up somehow to figure out the caster?"

Lillian's lips pursed as she shook her head. "Unfortunately, once the energy dissipates, it fades very quickly. It'd certainly make our jobs in the blacksuits a lot easier if we could work with magic that way." She gave me a thoughtful look. "Have your classmates been harassing you excessively? If you need some sort of intervention—"

I held up my hands quickly. "Oh, no, it's nothing that extreme, and nothing I can't deal with. I'm just figuring out the most effective way how. Believe me, most people have realized it's better not to mess with the heir of Bloodstone."

Lillian grinned at that, and footsteps sounded on the stairs behind us. I couldn't think of anything else to ask in the last moments before my mother joined us. I stepped to the side, my chest tight.

I'd only promised Imogen's dad that I'd do what I could, not that I'd definitely be able to help him. But even so, I couldn't help feeling I was failing him.

CHAPTER NINE

Jude

In the past few days, I'd gotten in the habit of making some of my jaunts across campus in short dashes followed by a leisurely stroll. I tried to fit those in when there weren't many spectators around, but anyone who spotted me probably thought I'd been hitting the bottle a little too hard again.

That was fine with me. My fellow students could think whatever they wanted. *I* just wanted to know whether my recent chat with my not-actual-father had gotten him off my back.

I lingered now for a moment outside Ashgrave Hall, watching to see if any concealed stalker would hustle over to see where I'd gone when I'd made my hasty way to the green. It should be easier to see through an illusionary disguise when the person behind it was moving quickly.

Nothing blurred or shimmered around the area I'd

passed through, even when I watched from the edge of my vision. Either "Dad" had decided to back off for now... or his lackeys had figured out better tricks. I wasn't sure whether the lack of an obvious pursuer made me feel better or worse. Maybe I shouldn't have confronted him or his underling after all.

It was done now, though, so I'd just have to live with the uncertainty. I took one more surreptitious scan around and headed into the scion lounge.

Declan and Malcolm were already there, Malcolm glowering at the pool table as if it'd challenged his status on campus somehow and Declan sitting in one of the armchairs reading something on his phone. The Ashgrave scion lowered the device as soon as I came in, and Malcolm sauntered over from the table to drop into the other chair. I tipped my head as I considered the vacant sofa.

"We're not looping Rory in on this meeting?"

"Her mother wanted to have dinner with her," Declan said. "Besides, she's been through enough stress in the last month. There isn't much she can do for Connar while he's set off just by the sight of her. If we can figure out a way to snap him out of that spell without her needing to be involved, we should do that."

"And we should snap him out of it sooner rather than later," Malcolm said. "Man, the way he snapped yesterday..." He grimaced.

"It's not going to be easy." Declan sat a little straighter with that authoritative air he put on so easily. "His parents obviously worked protections into the spell itself so that he'll defend himself—and it—against any interference."

I flopped onto the sofa, wishing the firm cushions were airy enough to swallow me up. My fingers itched for a glass, but I didn't really want a buzz right now. I drummed them on the arm instead. "If we can't pick it apart directly, then what *can* we do? I don't really fancy getting into a wrestling match with the guy."

"If we could manage to convince him that we really are trying to help him, maybe his own mind could overcome some of the effects of the spell," Malcolm said. "You can fight persuasive effects."

"But you can't magically persuade someone to do or think the opposite of another persuasive spell that's already working on them," Declan said.

"And he's not likely to give you a shot at cracking into his head any time soon after yesterday." I waved toward Malcolm. "You've always been the most buddy-buddy with him. If anyone's going to talk him down the regular way, it'd be you."

I liked Connar all right, and it was excruciating watching him treat Rory in ways I knew he'd have hated if he'd been in his right mind, but we'd never been close. I had too much wary respect for that temper of his and the muscle mass he could bring to bear with it.

"I'll see what I can do." The Nightwood scion glanced at Declan. "We might be able to at least moderate some of the effects of the spell. Tackling them directly might not work, but if we could plant our own spells in his room or somewhere else he'll be near regularly to encourage him to be calmer in general, or to want to reach out to friends—something like that, it should still take hold, shouldn't it?"

"To some extent. I suspect the current spell will override any of those effects in the moment, so that'll only do us good for approaching him in a more round-about way." Declan's expression turned thoughtful. "I'll see what I can come up with that might ease along your attempts to reconcile."

It didn't sound as though there was a whole lot for me to contribute. No surprise. I'd always been more the comic relief than anything else among the scions. It was easier that way, anyway. Fewer chances for them to notice that my skills weren't actually on par with their own.

"I'll look into illusionary distraction techniques," I said, since I did want to make myself slightly useful. The sooner we were all back on Rory's side, the better for the whole pentacle of scions, especially her. "There might be a way I can interrupt the effects of the spell at least partially."

Declan nodded. "Good idea." He considered me for a moment, with an intentness that made my skin twitch. Before I could throw out a quip to break whatever train of thought he was on, he drew in a breath. "I'm wondering if we have to worry about threats from more than just the Stormhursts. It came up at one of the recent baron meetings that you've moved off of the Killbrook properties to your own apartment, Jude."

Damn it. Now I wanted to crawl right out of my skin. I settled for sinking as deep into the sofa as I could, which wasn't very far. "You know my father and I have never gotten along very well. I was tired of his attitude. Why shouldn't I have my own space?"

"That's fucking ridiculous," Malcolm said hotly. I was about to bristle in my defense when he added, "You're his son and his heir. He can't just drive you out. How the hell does he expect to ease you into the barony like that?"

He doesn't, I thought, holding my tongue tight, but at the same time a waft of relieved surprise hit me. Malcolm wasn't upset at me; he was pissed off at Baron Killbrook for how he treated me. Of course, he'd probably change his tune if he knew the real reasons my "father" didn't want me around.

"I got the impression that might be part of the problem," Declan said. "You have a sibling on the way, don't you? Has he threatened to cut you out of the barony?"

"He hasn't said that much to me," I said, which was true. "I wouldn't put him past it, though."

"What?" Malcolm's hands clenched on the arms of his chair. "You've been part of the pentacle your whole life. He brought you up for this, and now he's going to tear it away from you? For a kid that's not even *born*? Maybe someone should check *him* over for mind-altering enchantments."

"I appreciate the vote of support," I said, summoning as much dryness as I could, "but my father knows exactly what he's doing. I'm in the pentacle because I was his only heir, not because he liked me for the job."

"At this point, he'd be an idiot to upend everything," Malcolm muttered.

Declan was watching me carefully. "Is that all it's been?

The insinuation that he might remove you as heir? If you left because he was actively attacking you in some way—"

I shook my head. "No. It was nothing like that."

"Well." He paused. "I suppose no one can control what he decides for the Killbrooks other than him. But I agree with Malcolm that it doesn't seem like a wise move at all. If it does come to that—you know *we're* not going to push you aside, don't you? If the situation escalates, whether you're the official heir or not, we'll stand up for you. Taking away a title doesn't change what we've been through together."

As I blinked at him, trying to stop a fresh wave of surprise from showing, Malcolm nodded his head with a jerk. "You're part of *our* pentacle. Fuck him. You need backup, you just have to say the word."

My throat constricted. I wouldn't have thought anything these guys could say would get to me—but then, I'd never have thought they'd express sentiments like that to begin with. Apparently they'd seen me as more than just a sometimes irritating source of witty remarks.

What would they say if they'd known my presence in the pentacle of scions had been a lie all along, though? Would the loyalty they were announcing now survive that? Somehow I found it hard to believe.

I didn't think Declan had used that insight skill of his on me, but those alert eyes saw too much on their own sometimes. Something in my reaction must have struck him as off. His brow knit for a second.

"Unless…" he said slowly. "Do you *want* out of the barony?"

Panic clanged through my body. That was too close, rubbing right up against the full truth that would change everything about the way they looked at me. "That'd make *me* the idiot, wouldn't it?" I said with a laugh that came out stiffly. "What the hell would I do with myself then?"

Declan didn't look horrified by the idea, only concerned—about me. "I'm not saying there'd be anything wrong with that. Lord knows there are days… You have a right to decide how you spend your life."

Not really. Not from the moment my false father had convinced my mother to carry another man's child for his own security. Not when my mere existence was treason.

I lost my tongue for an instant, and then I was scrambling to my feet as if that would help me find it.

"I didn't ask to have *my* mind dissected," I snapped, which probably wasn't fair, but at least it gave me an excuse for an abrupt exit. "Obviously we've covered everything actually important that we're going to talk about."

I marched to the door. "Jude," Malcolm called after me, but I just walked faster—up the stairs, down the hall, into the library where I didn't expect they'd look for me if they happened to come searching.

My feet carried me on what seemed like an aimless path until I arrived in an aisle between two of the tall shelves in the mages-only section. I'd sat across from Rory here once. Teased her about her reading material. Managed to make her laugh.

I eased down to the floor in the spot where I'd sat then, remembering her startled grin. I was good for that—

for making that girl happy. Why the hell couldn't that be enough to build a life around? Why did I have to care what any of the other scions thought of me?

Closing my eyes, I tipped my head back against the shelf behind me. The uneven spines of the books pressed against my skull and the smell of old paper filled my nose. Then my phone chimed with an incoming text.

It was Declan. *I'm sorry,* he'd written. *I shouldn't have pushed, especially with a difficult subject like that.*

That was decent of him, anyway. I wavered and then wrote back, *Apology accepted.* Hopefully I didn't need to tell him that I'd rather he steered clear of that subject in the future.

Are you free to talk a little more right now? he sent next. *There's something I wanted to discuss in regards to Rory.*

A jitter of a different sort of panic ran down my spine. Were the barons acting against her again after all? Why hadn't he led with that?

I typed out my answer as fast as my thumbs would fly. *Of course. What's going on?*

CHAPTER TEN

Rory

The text from Declan simply asked me to come out to the garage. I walked over, my shoes dampening in the morning dew, with a mix of anticipation and uncertainty. Knowing Declan, it was more likely he wanted to see me about something serious than anything else. The garage was an odd choice, though. Did he need to take me somewhere to show me evidence of more of the barons' wrongdoings or to find something that could help Connar?

I stepped into the dim concrete space to find not just Declan but also Jude and Malcolm standing around the Ashgrave scion's Honda. From the sly grin on Jude's face and the slow smile that crept across Malcolm's at the sight of me, this might not have anything to do with business at all.

"What's this about?" I asked with an arch of my

eyebrows as I reached them.

Declan studied me for a moment as if waiting to see if I'd clue in—to what, I had no idea. Then he gave me a crooked smile of his own and said, "Happy birthday."

I stared at him. "What? My birthday's in…"

I faltered, realizing I couldn't actually make a statement about that with any certainty. Mom and Dad had always celebrated my birthday in mid-November, more than a month from now, but they couldn't have known when I'd actually been born. They must have just made their best guess based on how old I'd appeared to be.

"It's in the barons' records," Declan said gently.

"It never occurred to me to look it up," I admitted. My mother hadn't mentioned anything yesterday—but then, she might not have known she needed to tip me off. Maybe yesterday's dinner had been meant as a birthday celebration and I'd simply missed the cues. "Wow. Okay. So I'm twenty now."

"A whole four months older than me," Jude said with a playful tsk of his tongue. "Turns out you're quite the cradle-robber."

I rolled my eyes at him, but I couldn't stop the corners of my lips from twitching upward. "Is this my surprise party, then?"

"Something like that," Malcolm said. "You were talking about getting away from campus the other day. I know it would have been better with all four of us… but we'll do our best to make up for that. My present is the little talk I had with Ms. Grimsworth yesterday evening to get us out of today's classes. We have the whole day."

"We wanted you to know that *we're* all here for you through this, no matter what," Declan added.

A bittersweet pang ran through me at the sentiment and the thought of the scion who wasn't with us, but my pulse sped up with an eager beat at the same time. It would be so nice to get away from all the pressures of this place. "Where are we going?"

"That's my present. You'll see when we get there." Declan motioned to the car.

"*My* present is in the trunk," Jude informed me as we got into the backseat together. "No peeking."

"I'm surprised you're lowering yourself to riding in a regular sedan," I teased. His Mercedes was one of his most beloved possessions, and he'd fawned over my Lexus more than once.

Jude chuckled and reached across the seat to take my hand. "I'm willing to make occasional concessions to my dignity. This arrangement means I get to sit here with you."

Malcolm let out a snort. Jude kicked the back of his seat in retaliation. "It could have been you if you didn't insist on sitting up front, Your Highness."

"It might not be the flashiest ride ever, but I'd still appreciate it if we can get there with my car in one piece," Declan said, sounding amused.

I settled back into the seat with a rare sense of contentment washing over me. This might not be exactly how I'd have wanted to spend a day with the scions, without Connar and not knowing when we'd have him by our side again, but there was something a little magical about being surrounded by these guys and their friendly hassling, with all the familiarity I could feel in it. They really were a sort of family, closer than maybe they were with their siblings by blood.

And I was a part of that family now too. I definitely preferred spending the day in their company to being constantly on my toes around my birth mother.

I kept my hand around Jude's as Declan drove the car down the road out of campus. He turned west in town, taking a route I'd never been down before. I studied the signs and buildings we passed for some sort of clue.

The guys were all keeping very quiet about their secret. Malcolm told a story about a ridiculously over-ambitious spell a classmate had attempted—and flubbed—in his last Physicality seminar, which set Jude off on a tangent about the most embarrassing illusions he'd seen cast. Declan pitched in comical stories of student spells he'd read historical records of.

It hardly felt as if a whole hour had passed when the Ashgrave scion turned down a narrow, shadowed drive between leaning trees. The lane meandered on for another five minutes before ending at a simple wooden gate. Declan got out and pressed his hand to the side of the gate so it would swing open.

"This is one of your family's properties?" I asked him as he drove us through onto the grounds. "You never told me you had one this close to school."

He let out a wry laugh. "I forgot it was here. This... used to be one of my mother's favorite spots to come and center herself. Somehow, the way my dad used to describe it, I ended up thinking it wasn't much more than a little cabin in the woods. I stopped by the other day just to see how it's been kept up and realized it's a little more extensive than that."

The Ashgraves were, after all, still a barony. He parked at the edge of a neatly trimmed glade surrounded by fading fall flowers. A delicately sweet scent hung in the air as we stepped out. A gazebo stood at the far end of the glade next to a sparkling stream that burbled softly by. A small stone bridge led over that to a log-lined building that *could* have been called a cabin, although it was more on par with the fancy ski chalets I'd seen pictures of.

Jude had hopped out and was already opening up the trunk. He pulled out an immense basket and a blanket, shooting me a grin. "I seem to recall that you're a picnic fan."

The first sort-of date we'd ever gone on had been a picnic he'd arranged. I hadn't been sure what to make of his overtures back then. Remembering that outing, from the banter I hadn't realized was covering up so many fears to the way he'd accepted my criticism and offered an honest apology, brought a swell of emotion into my chest.

"I seem to recall you're very good at supplying them," I said, beaming back at him, which turned his expression twice as bright.

The other guys helped spread out the blanket, which was more than big enough for the four of us, and we each took a corner with the basket in the middle. Jude laid out the contents with pride and an announcement of each one. "Lemonade and beers. Roast duck legs. Prawn-filled rolls. Deviled eggs. Wild rice salad. Fruit salad. Ginger cookies. And of course, lemon tarts." He caught my eyes. "Happy birthday. I paid close attention to what you went for the most last time."

He had indeed. My mouth was already watering. Even Malcolm looked impressed.

"What are we waiting for, then?" I snatched up one of the deviled eggs, and the guys took my cue to dig in too.

Every dish was delicious, the perfect mix of savory and sweet, creamy and spicy. I had no idea where Jude had procured the stuff—I couldn't imagine he'd turned to the Killbrooks' chef now that he'd moved out of his father's home—but I wasn't going to risk embarrassing him by asking. I was happy enough to immerse myself in the symphony of flavors.

Far too soon, I was licking the last traces of lemon tart filling from my fingers. Malcolm leaned back on one hand, draining his beer. Jude tossed the bone from the final duck leg into its container, and I lay back on the blanket. The crisp but warm autumn breeze washed over me.

"Well, this has already been a very excellent birthday," I said.

"It could get better," Declan said. "You haven't seen what's inside yet. Why don't you relax, and I'll get everything set up that the staff couldn't handle in advance?"

Intriguing. I resisted the urge to tag along to see exactly what he was getting up to. My full belly would appreciate the time to digest anyway.

Malcolm sprawled out with his head by my feet, tucking his hand around my calf with a stroke of his thumb. Jude ran his fingers over my hair in a soft caress. I settled more deeply into the blanket. Maybe I should look into having birthdays more often. Once a month sounded nice.

Declan's shoes whispered over the grass as he returned. "Capable of moving yet?"

"I think curiosity will be enough motivation." I pushed myself up, and we all helped pack up the remains of the picnic. After we'd returned the basket and blanket to the trunk, Declan led the way to the "cabin."

Warmth and a woody scent washed over me as we stepped inside. The place had the feel of an elegant ski chalet too. Leather sofas with a faint patina surrounded a wool rug in front of a crackling fireplace. A lilting instrumental melody carried from speakers I couldn't see.

"The Ashgraves have apparently used this space mainly as a meditation retreat and spa of sorts," Declan said, leading us through the room. "There's a dry sauna and a steam room around back, and also this."

He opened a sliding glass door at the other end of the room. Currents of heat mixed with cool outdoor air in the screened-in sunroom on the other side. The wooden boards of the floor surrounded a pool maybe ten feet square, its water bubbling from jets beneath the surface and gleaming with wall-mounted lights.

Jude let out an approving whistle. "Now *that's* a hot tub. I won't say no to an after-lunch soak."

It did look incredibly appealing. But— "I didn't bring a bathing suit," I said automatically.

Jude waggled his eyebrows at me. "Suits have no place in a hot tub anyway. If you're not going nude, there's no point." He reached to strip off his shirt without hesitation.

A different sort of heat tickled over my skin at the thought. He and Declan had seen me naked before, and after the interlude we'd shared in his hotel room last week, Malcolm might as well have. What did I have to be shy about?

I reached for the zipper at the back of my dress. Malcolm moved to my side. "I can help with that," he said in a voice that sent a tingle straight to my core. A streak of anticipation shot down my back with the motion of his hand.

He drew back to pull off his own shirt and slacks. I kicked off my shoes and tugged my dress over my head. Jude hadn't wasted any time, already tossing his boxers into the heap with the rest of his clothes. I couldn't help admiring his lean body in the few seconds before he leapt into the water.

He went under and came up with a blissful sigh. "Oh, this is the life. Maybe I'll just move in here if you're not really using this place, Declan. What are you all waiting for, you slowpokes?"

I scrambled out of my undergarments as quickly as I could, trying not to feel self-conscious, and slipped in at the side of the pool. The hot water enveloped me. There was a ledge along the side of the pool that let me stand in it up to my shoulders—farther out, Jude treaded water where it must have been over his head. Bubbles gushed against my side from one of the jets.

Declan and Malcolm slid in too, before I could really ogle either of them. Malcolm crossed the pool with a couple powerful strokes and propped his arms along the side. Declan stayed next to me, the water lapping around his slim but toned chest.

"I definitely regret not coming out this way sooner," he said.

"You were probably too busy working yourself into the ground," I suggested.

"Yeah. That does seem to be a common theme." He shot me a smile. "No work today, though."

"Mmm." I shifted to the side so the jet would massage my back, which conveniently brought me nearer to him as well. The shifting of the water against my naked body was heating me up more than I could blame on the spa. "Any other particular ways you were thinking of staying occupied?"

A gleam lit in his bright hazel eyes as he gazed down at me. "I can think of a few."

He dipped his head to kiss me, his hand coming to rest on my shoulder. The knowledge that there was nothing between us but a few inches of water—not even a shred of clothing—gave the meeting of our mouths an electric zing.

It hadn't been very long since Declan had started to feel comfortable kissing me at all, let alone with witnesses. But he wanted me, *loved* me, enough that he'd decided it'd be more painful holding himself back than having to part ways when we needed to think more seriously about our futures.

The tang of the lemonade he'd drunk lingered on his lips. I kissed him harder, my fingers tracing over his bicep, and the currents shifted around me. Another hand, not Declan's, touched my waist.

"Getting started on the real celebration, I see," Jude murmured. As he leaned in to press his own mouth to my neck, his fingers skimmed up over my ribs to trace the side of my breast. I reached back and urged him closer to me. In that moment, all I wanted was to feel encompassed by the guys who'd come to mean so much to me and who'd shown with this day and so many other things how much I mattered to them.

Jude's hand teased over the curve of my flesh until his thumb grazed my nipple. The shiver of pleasure made me whimper against Declan's lips. The Ashgrave scion cupped my other breast with a swivel of his fingers over the peak. My next breath turned into a gasp.

Declan eased toward me, his already rigid cock brushing my belly. A jolt of excitement sparked between my legs. As both of the guys continued drawing bliss through my chest, I turned my head to steal a kiss from Jude. He leaned over my shoulder to meet me, his mouth hot and slick from the water. He tweaked my nipple hard enough that I nearly bit his lip.

Malcolm was watching us, still in his languid pose at the other end of the pool. When I caught his eyes, his gaze smoldered into mine, but he stayed where he was. Did he think I wouldn't want him joining in? Or did *he* not want to share me quite this openly? The most we'd done with any of the other guys in the mix was kiss once.

But we'd done a whole lot more since then, even if we hadn't consummated our relationship yet. He'd proven he was so much more than the guy who'd tormented me during my first couple months at Blood U. I couldn't hold those actions against him anymore, not when he'd worked so hard to make up for them. Not when I understood him so much better now.

I would have beckoned him over, but at that moment, Declan tugged me upward in the water. He tucked one of my legs around his back, and the other joined it instinctively to steady my body there as he lowered his mouth to my breast.

His tongue worked me over even more thoroughly than his fingers had, leaving me quivering. Jude took the opportunity to claim my mouth again, *his* hand trailing lower. He teased his fingertips over my mound until they could press down on my clit.

Another graze of pressure found me—a determined current that licked over my unattended breast and then down my belly. I didn't need to look to know it was Malcolm using his magic to join in.

A giddy pulse raced through me. The current raced over my core alongside Jude's fingers, and his mouth captured my moan. I arched into Declan's body automatically, in just the right position for the base of my thigh to graze his erection. His breath shuddered against my breast.

My fingers tangled in Declan's hair, damp and in

perfect disarray. I loved it when he got messy in his passion.

"I want you," I said. "Please."

Jude continued to stroke my clit at a steady rhythm that was already building a wave of pleasure inside me. More currents swirled around me, teasing every sensitive inch of my skin. Declan dipped his hand lower to trace my slit. He mumbled a casting with his lips grazing my sternum, hooking his forefinger up inside me. I couldn't help bucking against him.

"You'd better give our girl what she needs," Jude said in his usual careless tone, but he gave my shoulder a tender peck a moment later. He was telling Declan in a roundabout way that he wouldn't resent the other guy taking the lead in this moment. My heart swelled with affection for him as well.

Declan kissed me one more time, so thoroughly it left me breathless. As his lips left mine, he shifted me to align with his cock. The long, hard length of him slid into me inch by inch. Bliss crackled through my core. My fingers curled against his scalp, just shy of scratching the sensitive skin there. The Ashgrave scion groaned.

"Happy birthday to me," I murmured in a singsong tone, and Jude chuckled behind me. He gave my clit one last caress and then smoothed his hand over my ass. His erection grazed my outer thigh. I reached back to grip him with a careful pump as Declan started to ease in and out of me. Malcolm's current throbbed more firmly against the nub between my thighs, amplifying the sensation.

Jude pressed his cock into my hand, his teeth nicking

my shoulder. He squeezed my ass. "You know," he said, roughly and unusually hesitant, "if you think you'd like it… we could see how you'd enjoy being doubly satisfied."

His finger traced down the line between my cheeks, leaving little doubt about his meaning. Oh, God. I'd never really thought about having sex that way before. When I'd first come to Blood U, I'd only had sex *any* way once. But after opening up so much to these two guys, the idea that might have made me balk back then now felt perfectly appropriate. I could have them both inside me at the same time. Just imagining it made me twice as giddy.

"Yes," I said. "Let's just—let's try."

Declan stilled against me, as deep as he could get, as Jude traced his fingers right around my other opening. The nerves there quivered with a different but no less heady pleasure. He murmured a casting word and pressed one finger inside me so smoothly it was hard to imagine I wasn't simply built for this. I made an encouraging sound.

Jude spent a few minutes simply working me over and making sure I was relaxed. My head tipped against Declan's shoulder with the waves of sensation, and he kissed my temple. Just when I started to feel I would die if we didn't get on with it, Jude brushed the head of his cock over the space he'd made ready.

"Good?" he asked even more raggedly than before.

I hummed almost desperately. "So good."

He edged into me even more carefully than Declan had, but all the new rush of pressure brought was more bliss. They held me between them, one hand on my waist and another on my thigh, keeping the perfect balance.

And then I was filled twice as much as before, and it was more heavenly than I could have imagined.

But our joint embrace didn't feel quite complete. I turned my gaze toward Malcolm again, and this time I didn't wait. I wanted *him*, not just his magical tricks. I reached my hand across the surface of the water to call him over.

In the first instant, he tensed against the pool wall. His eyes practically scorched me, they held so much heat and hunger. Then he pushed himself toward us in one brusque movement.

"Even two isn't enough to satisfy you?" he teased in a voice gone raw.

I held his gaze through the pleasure singing all across my body. "Not when I can have three."

He caught my chin to draw me into a kiss, holding himself on the end of the ledge. Through some unspoken communication, Declan and Jude started to move at the same time. They eased back and plunged deeper into me in unison with a crash of ecstasy. I cried out.

Malcolm captured the sound, kissing me like a command. He stroked one breast and then the other, urging even more bliss from my body the way he had when he'd brought me to release with just his hands the other morning in the hotel.

I hadn't repaid him for that pleasure at the time—he hadn't let me. I couldn't bear to be that selfish now. I *wanted* to touch him, to feel him give himself over as much as I was to all three of them.

My hand drifted down over his well-muscled chest to

his jutting erection. My fingers closed around its solid girth. A growl grumbled in Malcolm's throat. His body went still, and for a second I thought he was going to pull away from me. Then he was kissing me even harder with a thrust into my grasp.

"Fucking hell," Jude managed to say with an awed laugh. He kissed the back of my neck, and Declan nipped my shoulder, both of them speeding up their rhythm. With the pleasure skyrocketing through me, I knew I wasn't going to last long.

I kept my own rhythm, gripping Malcolm's cock as steady as I could even as I careened toward my release. I twisted my wrist and flicked my thumb over the head, and it twitched against my palm. His mouth devoured mine hard enough to bruise, leaving me dizzier.

"Rory," Declan murmured. "God. I'm going to—"

He jerked his hand between our bodies to fondle my clit, and then I was falling and soaring all at once, tumbling into an ecstasy that shook me down to my bones. Jude let out a choked sound, and Malcolm's breath broke, and somewhere in the collision of our four bodies, we all reached our peak.

Malcolm kept his hand by my jaw, his head close to mine, as the other two guys withdrew. He pressed his lips to my cheek as gently as his kisses before had been fierce. Right then, I felt what Declan had said earlier with every ounce of my being.

The three of them were here for me no matter what came our way. And I intended to be there for them and Connar just as much.

CHAPTER ELEVEN

Rory

I checked my phone for the hundredth or so time as I crossed the green to Nightwood Tower, as if it were at all likely I'd have missed the alert of an incoming call or message. It was mid-morning the day after my birthday, and I hadn't heard a thing from my mother.

Maybe birthdays weren't much of a thing in the fearmancer world? Although the scions had thought it was worth celebrating mine. If the dinner the night before had been intended for my birthday, I'd have expected some acknowledgment on the day of.

It could be that she'd been out of the loop for so long that any important dates from before her imprisonment had faded away. She'd only been back for a week. It was amazing she'd gotten herself together as much as she already had.

Anyway, I had bigger things to worry about. Like the

fact that I was heading to Persuasion class for the first time since Connar's mind had been warped against me, and it happened to be the one class I shared with the Stormhurst scion.

I climbed the stairs with growing trepidation. I'd just reached the last flight before the right floor when a bunch of Nary students came flooding down toward me.

The dazed expressions on all their faces made me stop in my tracks. I pressed myself off to the side to give them room to pass, watching them as they went by. Some of them were outright stumbling. The vagueness in their eyes reminded me uneasily of Shelby's odd spaciness the other morning. Where were they coming from?

I touched the arm of one of the girls to get her attention, and she flinched with a jerk of her head to face me.

"Sorry," I said quickly. "I was just wondering—what class are you coming out of?"

She stared at me blankly for a few seconds. "Class?" she said, sounding puzzled. "I was— There were— We just wanted to take a look around upstairs."

That was one of the least plausible excuses I'd ever heard. She didn't give me the impression she was purposefully lying, though. I frowned as she walked on and then murmured my insight casting word under my breath. "Franco."

As a Nary, she had no defenses. My awareness tumbled right into her head. Flashes of impressions darted by me— a muffin she'd particularly enjoyed at breakfast, a boy she was hoping to see on the green… and a haze far more blurred than any memories I'd encountered before.

I tried to focus on it, and my attention jittered away as if repelled. Then the girl slipped out of view, and my connection with her broke.

That was strange. If I'd been asked, my best guess would have been that someone had magically interfered with *her* mind.

I continued on up the stairs in time to encounter several fearmancer students leaving Professor Crowford's classroom. They were talking amongst themselves in hushed voices, their gazes flicking warily over those of us just arriving at the classroom, but most of them were smiling in a way that unnerved me even more than the look of the Nary students had.

What were *they* all wrapped up in? Did it have anything to do with the Naries? I had seen Professor Crowford with a class of both Naries and mages the other day.

The seminar was starting in just a few minutes, but I hesitated outside the door and then drifted back down the stairs after the previous students. I hadn't gotten very far with my peek into the Nary girl's thoughts, but this bunch might offer more.

"Franco," I whispered, training my eyes on the back of the head of a boy who'd been smiling particularly gleefully.

My attempt smacked into a wall of magic around his mind. His head twitched as if he'd noticed. I stopped and pretended to be searching for something in my purse in case he looked right around. If I put any more power into

the spell, I'd probably be able to break through his shields
—but he'd almost definitely notice I had too.

One of the girls said something, and the others
laughed. They went around the bend in the staircase out of
view. I slipped after them, thinking maybe I could try the
spell again with someone else, but by the time I'd reached
the bend, they'd picked up their pace and were already
disappearing around the next landing.

It'd get obvious if I started outright chasing them—
and I did have to get to class. My jaw clenched in
frustration as I hurried back up to Professor Crowford's
room.

I stepped through the doorway just as the professor
was coming over to close it, and found I'd set myself up in
a situation that might be even worse. All of my classmates
had arrived, filling every desk except the one in the back
corner. Next to Connar.

"You *are* joining us, Miss Bloodstone?" Professor
Crowford said at my hesitation, the corners of his heavy-
lidded eyes crinkling to match his smooth but lightly
teasing tone. With his classically handsome features and
his suave demeanor, it was easy to tell that in his earlier
years he'd have been able to charm plenty of people
without needing any magic at all. Hell, he probably
still did.

"Sorry," I said, and hustled across the room to the
vacant desk. Connar glowered at me as I came, but he
didn't say anything or move. Apparently the spell was
flexible enough to allow him to stay in the same room as
me if his schooling demanded it. I guessed if his parents

had made him *too* reactive, he'd have ended up looking like a problem to more than just us scions. Lucky me.

As Crowford started his lecture, I tried not to notice the stiffness of Connar's stance or the way he tensed even more with every shift I made in my chair. It was too easy to remember the way just a couple weeks ago he'd have glanced over at me with a smile here and there, to share a subtle joke or just because he could. My throat tightened.

In my distraction, I didn't catch everything the professor said, but the gist sank in. He was talking about internal forms of persuasion today—altering people's thoughts and beliefs rather than their actions. Did he have any idea that the guy sitting next to me was the victim of that kind of magic?

Crowford had been on Professor Banefield's list of the older barons' allies. My mentor had left a packet of documents for me in case of his death, since the spell the barons had cast on him had prevented him from giving me more than a vague warning directly. In his last few words to me, he'd called the people who worked with Malcolm's and Connar's parents and Baron Killbrook "reapers."

I had no idea how that term fit in with their plans or how involved Professor Crowford had been with their schemes. It didn't seem likely that Baron Stormhurst would have publicized what she probably saw as familial discipline even to her allies. But I started listening more closely, staying wary, anyway.

Unfortunately, Crowford didn't touch on how you'd go about snapping someone out of a thought pattern they'd been persuaded into. He described some techniques for subtly shifting a person's attitudes without outright commanding them to think a different way, and then clapped his hands together.

"Let's pair off and see if you can make a go of this. Write down the thought you want to place in your partner's head, and after ten minutes, my aide and I will come around and check whether each of you has been successful. Work with the person sitting next to you. I'll spare the rest of you the challenge of facing off against one of our scions."

He winked at the class, but I couldn't appreciate his good humor. My stomach sank as I looked at Connar. His mouth had twisted.

I turned gingerly to face him as the students around us began to chatter with their attempts to work their persuasive spells into casual conversation. "Well," I said, and didn't know how to continue.

"Forget it," he said, low but harsh. His shoulders were outright rigid now. "I'm not even going to try, because there's no way I'm risking giving you an opening."

"Okay. Fair enough." I curled my fingers around the notepad on my desk. "We should probably at least pretend that we're doing the assignment, even if we're both going to fail it?"

He made a disgruntled sound that must have been some kind of agreement, because he pulled out a notebook and pen of his own. I tore a page out of mine and looked at it uncertainly for a moment. I knew what I'd have wanted to try to plant in his head. *I'm not the enemy. You care about me, and I care about you just as much.* But I wasn't writing that down for Crowford or his aide to see.

I settled on a random innocuous idea about buttered pecan being the best ever ice cream flavor. When I looked up, Connar was folding his paper, having already written his own theoretical goal. I wet my lips.

Who knew when I'd next get a chance to talk to him without him totally exploding at me? I had to take advantage of the classroom sort-of truce while I could. I just… had no idea what I could possibly say that might sink in through the magical clouding of his mind.

"I know you don't trust me right now," I said quietly. "And I'm not going to ask you to. I've got no idea what you're remembering or seeing that's convincing you I'm out to hurt you or the other scions."

Connar scoffed before I could continue. "And I'm supposed to believe *that*?"

I held in a wince at the derision in his tone. "Maybe not. I just— I hope sometime when I'm not here and you're not feeling so angry with me, you'll really look at those impressions and consider how… real they actually feel. Whether they line up with other kinds of impressions that might rise up too."

The Stormhurst scion managed to keep his voice down, but his expression hardened. "Are you trying to suggest that I'm somehow *deluded*? *You're* trying to mess with my mind right now, aren't you? For fuck's sake."

I ducked my head, trying to give every appearance of meekness. "You don't have to listen to me. I only wanted to ask. Just… think about it."

Connar turned away, muttering to himself. "Why the hell would I listen to a bitch who's out to bring the whole pentacle down?"

Pain prickled through my chest. For a second, I could hardly look at him, it hurt so much to compare the hostility on that chiseled face to the fondness that had shone through it so many times before. A lump filled my throat, but I couldn't help letting one last attempt slip out, even if it was a long-shot, even if it got me nowhere. A simple appeal straight from my heart.

"I miss you," I said, the overwhelming emotion of that fact quivering through the words.

Connar's head jerked back around, his eyes searingly chilling. "Fuck off," he snapped, loud enough this time that several other heads turned to look at us around the room.

Professor Crowford strode over to us with an expression so puzzled it convinced me that he had no idea what was going on with Connar. "Well," he said, "it sounds as though we've already reached an impasse over here. Let's see how well you've done."

He held out his hand for our papers. I offered mine with a hopeless sensation swelling inside me, vast enough to squeeze my lungs. I'd tried to get through to Connar because I'd *had* to, but I might have only made things even worse.

CHAPTER TWELVE

Connar

These days, the Blood U campus felt more like a cage than a haven. I was secure enough in my dorm bedroom, knowing my magical wards were powerful enough to keep any other student out or at least to tip me off if someone broke them, but the last thing I wanted was to sit around in that cramped box for hours on end. The scion lounge had already been used as a trap against me. Anywhere else I roamed, I could run into one of the guys I'd thought of as my friends or into… into the Bloodstone scion without warning.

Part of my mind wanted to call her by her first name. But every time the name Rory passed through my thoughts or into my hearing, a surge of jagged emotion came with it. Memories, too: images of her smirking at me as the other guys hung on her every word; veiled insults whispered in her soft voice. The knowledge that she'd shown her true, malicious intentions, even if I seemed to be the only one who'd escaped her spell disguising them.

I found myself walking aimlessly across the outer fields where fewer and fewer people wandered as the weather turned cooler. It gave me solitude to go over the teachings I'd most recently absorbed and plenty of clear ground so I could see before anyone came too close. The grass rustled under my feet, and the breeze nipped at my face, but otherwise it wasn't so bad.

This afternoon, though, I couldn't quite keep my thoughts on track. Every time I started to consider today's persuasion lesson, my mind immediately went to that brief conversation with the heir of Bloodstone. The simple way she'd asked me to look closer at my impressions of her. The plea in her voice when she'd told me she *missed* me, that had struck a chord somewhere deep inside even as the attempt to soften me up had annoyed me.

It was all more manipulation. That was what she did. That was what she'd always done, even if I wasn't totally sure I'd always seen that. There *were* other impressions floating somewhere beneath the clearer ones at the surface. I only caught hints of smiles and laughter and warmth before they flitted away under a jab of revulsion. She'd won me over, before, but I'd woken up.

I wouldn't feel this awful around her if that wasn't true, would I? If she'd had good intentions, she and the other guys wouldn't have snuck around and tried to work magic on me without telling me the whole story. That was all the evidence I needed right there.

A few juniors, no one I knew, drifted out of the

Stormhurst Building with towels slung over their shoulders as I came up on it. I had the brief urge to go in for a workout myself, but the idea sent an immediate unnerving sense of vulnerability through me. If anyone cornered me in the changeroom, I wouldn't have as many avenues to get away from them.

Better not to risk it.

I strode on past the building to circle around by the lake. I'd just come into view of the boathouse when my phone vibrated in my pocket.

It was my mother. The twist of emotion that wrenched through me at the sight of the call display must have been more unconscious meddling. Why else would I feel relieved and horrified at the same time?

The Stormhursts stood together. If Rory or the guys tried anything, my mother would notice something was off. And they should know better than to try to take on a baron.

"Hi, Mom," I said with a twitch of my jaw.

"Connar." Her blunt voice filled my ears, and everything except an overwhelming calm fled my body. "I wanted to make sure you're keeping up all right. Are you still under the weather?"

I didn't remember being sick recently, but I'd probably used that as an excuse to explain the grouchy mood recent events had put me in. The constant uncertainty even within the pentacle of scions had left me out of sorts.

"I'm fine," I said. "Whatever it was, it wasn't serious. I'm just focusing on getting as much out of my classes as I can."

"Good, good," she said approvingly. "You haven't run into any more troubles with your colleagues, have you?"

I hadn't told her about the incident in the scion lounge. The other scions hadn't gotten the chance to actually influence me with any spells before I'd caught on. No need to worry her about that. I had to show her I could look after myself.

"Nothing serious there either," I said. "At this point, I can hold my own pretty well."

"I'm glad to hear that. If you do run into anything that makes you more concerned than usual, you know you can always turn to me for advice. I'll let you get back to your studies."

The calm that had come over me faded as I lowered the phone. A twinge of nausea ran through my stomach. She hadn't said anything strange or upsetting. Maybe that was only guilt over not telling her everything. I didn't think she'd *want* me complaining to her about minor disputes, though…

A flicker of memory passed behind my eyes—a sneer, a cutting tone, something about *what I expect from my heir*. A chill rippled through me with it. I shook it off, pulling my jacket closer around me.

No, I didn't want to disappoint her. I was her *only* heir. I was a Stormhurst. I had to live up to that role. Even if the people around me were trying to drag me down.

I miss you.

My stomach lurched again. I shook my head, but that didn't stop a tiny ache from forming in my brow. Whatever the Bloodstone scion had done to me before, she must have sunk her claws in deep. I had to just… just put her completely behind me.

I found myself ambling toward the woods by the east end of the lake. I had my spot there that I'd kept to myself, that no one else at school had bothered exploring enough to stumble on. The trees closed around me, shutting out most of the sun. The smell of damp earth filled my nose, as soothing as it'd always been. I veered off the path automatically at the spot I knew well, twigs cracking under my feet as I climbed the slope to the cliff.

I stepped out into the rocky clearing with its expansive view over the lake ready to let the fresh watery breeze wash over me. It ruffled my hair—and stirred up more of those glimpses. Stars reflected on the water. Soft skin under my fingers. The core-deep recognition that I'd been *seen*—for myself, not just as an icon of authority.

Nothing in that jumble made sense. I rubbed my forehead as if I could swipe the uncomfortable fragments out of it. How could *they* be anything real when I could barely hold onto them to really take a look at them in the first place?

I walked right to the end of the clearing and sat down at the edge of the cliff. There, where I couldn't see anything but water and the dark line of trees around the distant shoreline, couldn't hear anything but the hiss of waves hitting the rocks below, my thoughts settled again. After a while, I leaned back with my arms behind my head and let the sky swallow up my view instead.

I wasn't sure how long I'd lingered up there, lost in the present, when footsteps crunched through the brush behind me. I sat up with a jerk. When I turned, Malcolm was just emerging from the trees.

He didn't look at me at first, taking in the landscape around us instead with his confident consideration. "Quite the place you've got for yourself up here."

"What are you doing here?" I said, but not quite as forcefully as I might have otherwise. If anyone else could shake off Rory's influence, it'd be Malcolm. I'd never known him to let anything get the better of him. If he understood how much she'd tried to hurt us—to hurt me—

The ache in my forehead came back. I did my best to will it away as the Nightwood scion shifted his gaze to me.

"I saw you head up this way," he said. "It seemed like it might be a good place to talk, away from everything else. We obviously *do* need to talk."

"About what?" I hedged. Just because I wanted to trust him didn't mean I could. He'd been part of that ambush in the lounge.

Malcolm glanced around again and walked over to hunker down on the log that stretched across one end of the clearing.

"Will you listen to me?" he asked. "I know… there's been a lot going on. I haven't had your back as well as I should have, and I'm sorry about that. But I swear to you on my position as scion and my name as a Nightwood that I'm trying to make up for that now, to make sure you don't get screwed over any more than you already have been."

The comment about listening to him gave me a

prickling reminder of Rory's similar words. He sounded like he meant it, though, and I couldn't imagine Malcolm swearing that emphatically if he didn't believe what he was saying.

"If you cast any magic at all at me," I started.

"You don't even need to say that. I just want to talk. Properly, like friends."

God, I could use an actual friend right now. My chest constricted with the loneliness that had gripped me the last several days.

"I don't want to talk about anything to do with... her," I said. "Unless you're ready to admit you see what she's doing to us."

"Subject taken entirely off the table." Malcolm made a sweeping gesture to go with that promise. "I'm guessing from some of the things you've said and how you've been acting that you're probably at least a little confused. There's some stuff in your head that isn't totally gelling. Am I on the right track?"

I bristled instinctively. "If you're going to try to convince me that what I know isn't actually real—"

"I'm not here to convince you of anything," Malcolm said. "You know what you know. I think there might be a few blanks there that I can help fill in, if you'll let me talk and hear me out. You can decide what to make of it afterward."

The balking part of me wanted to tell him to get the hell out of here regardless. I swallowed that impulse down. The truth was, I *had* been confused. Maybe something Malcolm would mention would help me get my thoughts more in order, even if it wasn't the way he was hoping for. I'd keep my mental shields strong—I'd know if he came at me that way. And in the end, it'd still be me deciding what to believe.

"Okay," I said. "I'm listening."

CHAPTER THIRTEEN

Rory

I was sitting at my dorm room desk working on a paper for class when my phone chimed from where I'd left it to charge. I tugged it over.

Malcolm had texted the group chain that included me, Jude, and Declan. *Had a decent chat with Connar. Not sure how much real progress I made, but he was at least willing to have me around, and he didn't yell at me when I told him how odd his random disappearance and the excuse about the tournament looked to us.*

How did he respond? Declan asked.

He didn't show much, but he didn't argue either. I brought up a couple things that've happened in the past too. I think I managed to sow a little doubt about his parents' intentions, anyway. He couldn't handle me bringing up Rory at all, so I couldn't get into anything very specific there.

My stomach twisted, but I hadn't really expected anything different. *That's okay*, I wrote. *The spell is obviously mainly focused on me. That'll be the hardest part to tackle.*

I'd still try if I thought there was any chance of it not just pissing him off more, Malcolm replied.

I glanced up at my window, larger than most of those in the dorm bedrooms because as scion I'd been given one of the corner rooms. It looked out over the north end of campus toward the lake—a pretty view, even if most of the time I'd been faced with it, I'd rather have been anywhere but here.

The afternoon sun glinted off golden hair across the field. Malcolm was just making his way back to the center of the campus. He knew exactly which window was mine —it was directly across from his, and he'd once spent the better part of a term sending nightmarish magic toward my bedroom. It was hard to reconcile those memories with the guy who tipped his head to me now as if suspecting I was watching, though I'd have been hidden behind reflected daylight to his eyes.

We were all in this together. The much more recent memory of our hot tub encounter rippled through my mind with a rush of heat. The peace of that interlude away from everything hadn't lasted long, but the sense of the four of us as a united front had held firm. Baron Stormhurst was putting us all through the wringer with her warping of Connar's mind, but if she'd hoped to tear the rest of us apart, she'd be disappointed.

I had to do my part too. I sucked my lower lip under my teeth and tapped out the message to Declan that I'd been considering since my conversation with Connar this morning.

Can you still get access to student files even though you're not an aide anymore? Or maybe you already know this without checking—I want to find out when Connar has his next Insight seminar.

He wrote back as quickly as he had to Malcolm. *I don't know off the top of my head, but I can find out pretty quickly. What are you thinking?*

I want to take another look inside his head if I can. I figured while he's letting down his shields to practice his own insight spells would be the best time, if I can arrange to be nearby without him realizing. It could be useful to find out exactly what's happening in there when his mother's spell activates.

That's a good point. Maybe I should have held on to the TA position a little longer so I'd have had an excuse to peek in there myself. He ended with a grimacing emoji.

You couldn't have known we'd end up in this situation, I pointed out.

No. And I have enjoyed the benefits that've come with being free of those rules.

I warmed all over again, knowing exactly what he was talking about. *As have I.*

A few moments passed without a response. Then Declan said, *I'm sure I could find a moment if I'm watching for it. You don't have to take this on. I know just being around him, the way he is right now, has got to be painful for you.*

I swallowed hard with a sudden prickling behind my eyes. I'd managed to get through the day after my talk with Connar without any tears, but somehow that short expression of sympathy had cracked the self-control I'd been holding onto.

It couldn't hurt for us both to see what impressions we can pick up, I replied. *But I still think it'd be good for me to be involved because of my experience with Prof. Banefield. I'll be okay. I've faced worse.*

I wish that wasn't so true. I'll let you know as soon as I have the info.

Knowing Declan, I could probably expect the follow-up text within the next few hours. He was nothing if not diligent.

I sat back in my chair with a squeak of its wheels. I wasn't sure I could summon the concentration to do much more schoolwork at this exact moment.

The urge ran through me to call out to Deborah so I could talk through the situation with her—and shattered against the fact that I couldn't. Just to list one in the many horrible events I'd faced recently. My gaze slid toward the wardrobe drawer that'd been her first home in this room, and the prickling behind my eyes came back.

The ache of the broken bond eased more with each passing day. I barely noticed it now unless I was thinking about it. The grief, I suspected, would take a lot longer to fade.

A knock on my door snapped me out of those gloomy thoughts. I straightened up in my chair. "Yes?"

An all-too-familiar voice filtered through the door. "It's Victory. There's something I wanted to talk to you about."

I hesitated instinctively. Victory might have backed off after Malcolm had ordered her to, but I had no illusions about her enjoyment of my company. She might still decide to take a jab at me if she thought she could get away with it without the Nightwood scion finding out... or she might have decided she wasn't going to win however much good favor she'd wanted with him anyway, so she could go back to taking out her frustrations on me. She'd certainly never come to me with anything like friendliness before.

On the other hand, at this point I could take care of myself. I had twice as many magical strengths as she did, and I wasn't half bad at using them by now. If she messed with me, she'd have *me* to deal with. I might as well find out what was going on.

"Okay," I said, getting up. "I'll come out."

"No," she said quickly. "I'd rather—I think we should keep this private."

Even more mysterious. And even more unnerving to welcome her into *my* private space. Although the thought of going into her room where she could have set up any sort of spell unsettled me twice as much.

I touched the dragon charm on my necklace to reassure myself. As my prize for winning the summer project competition, one of the professors had imbued it with a spell to distinguish illusions from reality. If she did anything with illusionary magic, I had that tool as well as my own skills. I could handle her.

"Fine." I removed my magical defenses from the door with a couple words and a wave of my hand. When I opened it, Victory was standing stiffly on the other side as if she didn't want to be having this conversation any more than I did. Curiosity tickled through me.

"Well, come in," I said.

There wasn't a whole lot of space to sit. It seemed most appropriate to offer my desk chair to Victory, who sat on it primly as if she didn't want to risk absorbing too much of my essence that might have been left there. I sank down on the edge of the bed a couple feet from her, which was still a little too close for comfort.

Thankfully, the other girl had no problem getting to the point. "You've always been a fan of the feebs," she said.

The comment rankled enough that I had to hold back a glower, even though it was technically true. "I don't think Naries are lesser human beings than mages, if that's what you mean."

She flicked her hand through the air as if what we'd said was exactly the same. "I have some... concerns about the way the staff have decided to handle the current batch. I finally found out the details of what Sinclair was babbling about."

And she'd come to me. My apprehensions shifted in a new direction, more for my fellow students than for me. "What are you talking about? How are they being 'handled'?"

Victory gave me a narrow look. "Ms. Grimsworth has

been convinced to loosen the school rules. I think you know how much shit I got in when *someone* set me up to look like I was talking about magic in front of the feebs. Well, now some of the professors are leading some of their students to reveal exactly what we are to the Naries, to terrify them out of their wits with magic, and then to put some kind of spell on them so they won't remember after. Until they do it all over again, I guess."

Every inch of my body went cold. "*What?*" I said, but the question was more horror than disbelief. The pieces clicked into place far too easily—the Naries mingling with the fearmancer students, the daze I'd seen them in, the blur in the one girl's thoughts.

"I know," Victory said with a sniff. "It's ridiculous. One stupid show-off doesn't handle the memory wipe properly or decides to go for extra points in the wrong place, and we could all be exposed. Lord knows what'll happen to the school or the rest of us then."

Of course she'd be more worried about how it'd affect her life and not the immediate torment the Naries were going through. My hands balled in my lap.

"Why are you telling me?" I had to ask. "Why not go to Ms. Grimsworth or whoever?"

Victory appeared to stop herself just short of rolling her eyes. "Who do you think they're going to listen to more—me, or everyone's favorite four-strengths scion? I'd rather not get involved at all."

Sure, why not stand back where she wouldn't face any consequences and let me rain down hell on those involved? I couldn't exactly argue with her logic, as self-serving as it was.

I rubbed my brow. "Do you have proof of this? They're obviously keeping it somewhat quiet. I'm not going to get very far if I confront Ms. Grimsworth and she denies the whole thing."

"I'm sure an outstanding mage like you can figure out how to tackle that problem," Victory said, unable to keep a hint of a sneer from her tone even while she was coming to me for help. "I overheard a couple of the idiot students who are in on it talking about it. Use that story if you want—let them know how badly people are keeping the secret already."

Yeah, that would probably be enough. If I made it clear I knew rather than suspected what was happening, Ms. Grimsworth might not want to risk lying anyway.

Did the other scions— No, if they'd been aware of what was going on, we'd have talked about it already. Declan and Jude knew how I felt about the Naries' safety here and had shown they shared my concern. They wouldn't have hidden something like this from me.

Malcolm's attitudes in that area I was less sure of, but even if he wasn't all that worried about looking after the Nary students, he'd realize it'd matter to me. I couldn't see him jeopardizing the still-tentative partnership we were developing over a change in school policy.

So, the staff had kept the development secret from all the scions, unless Connar was aware of it in his addled state. I'd definitely have a lot to say to the headmistress on *that* subject.

Victory got up and made for the door. "Now you know," she said in a tone that washed her hands of the matter. Then she looked back at me, and her lips curled with what might have been the first genuine smile she'd ever aimed my way, sharp as it still was. "Bring all that righteousness down on them, and for once it'll be put to good use."

CHAPTER FOURTEEN

Rory

Shelby didn't get back to the dorm until just before six, lugging her cello case beside her. The second I saw her, I sprang off the sofa where I'd been waiting. I was supposed to meet the guys downstairs in a matter of minutes, but I'd been hoping I could check on my Nary friend first.

"Hey," she said to me, at least looking more alert than she had at breakfast the other day. She set down her cello with a thump so she could open her bedroom door.

"Hey." I picked up the case so I had an excuse to follow her in. A couple of my other dormmates were eating an early dinner in the common room, and I wasn't sure it'd be a good idea to show my concern in front of them. For all I knew, they were in on this terrorizing-the-Naries scheme.

"How are you doing?" I asked as the door swung shut behind us. I set the cello against her desk where I'd seen her leave it before, and Shelby tossed her book bag onto her bed.

"Oh, same old. The non-music classes are kind of a drag, but we're starting a new unit in orchestration that I'm loving."

That gave me the perfect opening. "Have you had any classes with Professor Crowford? Tall guy, mostly gray hair, very smooth talker?"

Shelby tipped her head as she considered. "I think I've seen that guy around, but he doesn't teach any of my classes. Why?"

He probably wasn't the only teacher involved in the new approach to the Naries... or she might simply not remember. "I thought I saw you with a bunch of other students he was taking somewhere off campus the other day," I said. She hadn't been in the group I *had* actually seen heading off the green, but there could have been other occasions. "Just wondered where you all were going."

Shelby's gaze went abruptly distant, her mouth jerking into a frown. A tremor ran through her. Then she was laughing, if a bit shakily, as if nothing had come over her. "Mustn't have been me. All my classes have been in the tower. I wouldn't mind a few more field trips."

A shadow of uncertainty lingered in her face despite her jokey attitude. She'd experienced *something* that had affected her, even if she had no conscious awareness of it. My teeth gritted with the thought of all the hell I'd *like* to rain down on Professor Crowford for messing with my friend and the other Naries this way.

There didn't seem to be any point in pushing her harder on that subject. I'd only stir up more uncomfortable reactions.

"No kidding," I said with a laugh of my own that probably came out a bit weak. "Well, I've got to get back to work. Lots of catching up to do."

"Of course. Let me know the next time you're up for going down to town for lunch or dinner."

My smile at that suggestion came more easily. "Let's see if we can make that happen next week."

My horror and anger over what had been done to her and the others chased me down the stairs to the scion lounge. I burst in right behind Malcolm, who turned at my arrival. His expression darkened as he took in my expression.

"What are the assholes up to now?" he asked, his stance shifting as if he meant to go tackle whoever might have attempted to hurt me this exact second. I hadn't wanted to try to explain what Victory had told me through texts, so I'd only told the guys that it was urgent that we talked.

Declan and Jude hustled over from where they'd been talking by the espresso machine. Declan's forehead furrowed. "Did you have a bad run-in with Connar?"

Jude made an elaborate show of cracking his knuckles. "Whatever's gone wrong, they'll have to deal with a lot more than just you."

Their automatic show of support steadied me, even

though they weren't at all on the right track. "It's not about me, actually," I said. "I just heard a disturbing story from Victory about why the extra Nary students have been brought on campus."

I related what she'd told me and added in my own observations that lined up with the story. By the end of it, Jude was holding my hand with a reassuring pressure, Malcolm's expression had turned even darker, and Declan was pacing the area in front of the TV.

"That's incredibly disturbing," the Ashgrave scion said. "It's bad enough the way the staff allow some of the students here to treat the Naries, but to be messing with their heads in ways that are causing long-term effects… There's no way it won't harm them to be continually memory wiped, not to mention the terrorizing beforehand."

"Why the hell didn't anyone notify us—or our families, anyway?" Malcolm demanded. "Secrecy about our magic is one of the fundamental tenets of fearmancer society. Playing around with the Naries like this could hurt *all* of us. Who gave Ms. Grimsworth or the professors involved permission to throw caution to the wind?"

"So none of you had any idea this was happening?" I said. It was a relief to know my instincts had been correct.

Jude shook his head. "They've obviously been keeping it very hush-hush. And they must have known if any scion found out about it, we'd bring it up with our parents."

"I was getting the impression earlier this term that a few of the other families were encouraging their kids to push back on the secrecy issue," I said. "We had a debate about it in one of my classes because this one guy brought it up. Maybe those families somehow convinced—or forced—the staff to go along with it, and they're planning on using it to prove their point once they've been at it for a while."

Declan stopped his pacing, his narrow eyebrows drawing together. "You said Professor Crowford is definitely involved. He's on the list you got from Professor Banefield—the people he said are plotting against you. *With* the barons."

"Yeah." I paused. "But—if the barons were in on it, even if they wanted to keep it from us, wouldn't *you* at least have had to be part of that conversation? They couldn't make a change that big without all the barons being on board, could they? I thought that was the whole reason they were so set on getting control over me."

"You're right. They couldn't have made any official changes in policy without my go-ahead."

"Who says Crowford isn't playing more than one side?" Jude pointed out. "That's hardly unusual in this community. In the end, he'll have his own interests at heart before anyone else's. And apparently he's especially interested in tormenting Naries."

"He's not going to be very happy with where that lands him when the barons *do* find out," Malcolm muttered.

"Should we bring it up with them?" Jude's hand squeezed around mine, his tone doubtful. I couldn't imagine he was in any hurry to go running to his supposed father, even with a problem that had nothing to do with his own life.

"No," I said. "Crowford might be an asshole, but Ms. Grimsworth has always seemed to at least try to look out for me. I don't think she's happy about the situation. If the staff have been pressured into this, we should find out the full story before we set them up to face sanctions or whatever."

Declan made a face. "Fair. We know the barons aren't always careful to make sure they're bringing down their brand of justice on the people who actually deserve it."

"We can all go and confront her," Malcolm said. "She can't lie in our faces when she's got four of her future barons in front of her."

Or maybe that would be so intimidating the headmistress would be *less* inclined to tell us the truth. People didn't make the best decisions in a panic.

"I think that might be overkill," I said. "We don't need to terrorize *her*. She's seen me work on behalf of the Naries before. She'll know it's them I'm concerned about—that if she's concerned too, she can be honest about it. Why don't I see what I can get out of her before we bring out the big guns?"

"I don't know," Jude teased. "I think you're selling yourself short if you figure you're not a 'big gun' yourself."

I wrinkled my nose at him. "You know what I mean."

"Rory has a good point," Declan put in. "This is a fraught situation and a potentially precarious one for everyone involved. But I don't think we should leave it any longer than we already have. Lord knows what damage they've already done."

"I'll see if I can speak to her tonight." I glanced at the time on my phone. "I'd better go right now before it gets any later. I'll let you all know how it goes as soon as I've gotten what I can out of her."

"I wouldn't want to be our headmistress right now," Jude murmured as I headed for the doorway.

Night was starting to fall when I made it outside. Lights gleamed around the doorways of the buildings that bordered the green. I hurried through the swiftly chilling air to Killbrook Hall, which held the offices and living quarters for all the teachers and administrative staff.

Ms. Grimsworth's office stood at the end of a long corridor past those of the professors. I knocked once and then again, harder. Even if she wasn't on her office hours, that room connected to her personal apartment. I'd just have to make enough noise to bring her back to work if she wasn't on the job already.

I didn't need to escalate the situation any farther. A few seconds later, the door clicked open. The headmistress peered out at me, her graying blond hair loosened from its usual tight coil to hang across her shoulders. Her slightly beady eyes fixed on me with a flicker of worry.

"What brings you to my door at this hour, Miss Bloodstone?" she asked in her usual prim way. "Out-of-hours visits from you haven't boded well in the past."

I guessed this time wasn't any different. "I wanted to talk to you about something that's been happening on campus. Something I think has already been going on for too long, so it didn't feel right to wait."

Her face tensed, partly exasperation but I thought there was some guilt in there too. Nevertheless, she stepped back and opened the door wider. "Why don't you come in and explain what this is about?"

I found myself sitting in the same chair where I'd perched almost six months ago when I'd first arrived at Blood U—where Ms. Grimsworth had explained who I was and why six people in black had slaughtered my parents and brought me here against my will. The girl I'd been then felt incredibly far away right now. What would Mom and Dad have made of me if they'd seen who I'd become as I'd caught my stride with my magic?

I didn't want to think about that. At the very least, they'd have been proud of me for taking this stand on behalf of the people who couldn't defend themselves from the threats this school posed.

"It's come to my attention that there's been a change in school policy regarding Naries," I said. "I understand that at least a few of the professors are allowing some of their students to reveal their magic to groups of Naries with the intent to frighten them as much as possible and gain power from them, followed by tampering with their memories so they won't be able to share what they've seen. I've got to assume you're aware of this, since you had to be involved in accepting more Naries to the school this term in the first place."

Ms. Grimsworth pursed her thin lips. She looked down at her desk and then back at me. "I have some say in how the school is run, but I'm hardly the final authority," she said. "The adjustment in policy wasn't my initiative."

"Well, whoever's it was, there's got to be some way to stop them," I said. "A change this big affects everyone in our community. I might not be a baron yet—and maybe I won't be for a while now that my mother has returned—but I know there are certain standards for what—"

Ms. Grimsworth cut me off with a raise of her hand. She studied me appraisingly for a moment before she spoke.

"I'm afraid there's been a misunderstanding. The decree to alter our handing of the Nary students came from the *highest* authorities. It was a decree from the barons themselves. Frankly, Miss Bloodstone, as one of those baron's heirs, you're in a much better position to challenge it than I am, but you'd need to take it up with them rather than me."

I blinked at her, my thoughts stalling before they could catch up. But—without Declan—without breathing a word to any of us scions... My own mother hadn't said anything about major changes during the time we'd spent together. How *could* they?

I didn't sense any deception in the headmistress's demeanor, though. It certainly couldn't help her to tell a lie like that. And she couldn't answer any of the questions now racing through my head as my gut sank.

"I see," I said, reaching for the implacable air of calm that had gotten me through more than one shaky situation in the past. "Thank you for telling me. I'm sorry for bothering you unnecessarily."

As I stood up, I tensed my legs so they wouldn't wobble. The enormity of this transgression gaped wider with each passing second I thought about it.

If the barons had gone this far, this quickly… what else might they be planning? What else had they already done?

CHAPTER FIFTEEN

Rory

Spying on someone in one of the Nightwood Tower classrooms wasn't the easiest thing. Most of the rooms were small, holding no more than a dozen students, and contained little furniture other than the desks and chairs and possibly a storage cabinet that wouldn't have made an ideal hiding spot. To avoid curious Nary eyes, the doors were solid and windowless.

My one saving grace was that Connar's insight seminar was being held on the fifth floor—farther than I'd have liked to climb, but not so high it was impossible. I'd ended up getting a lot of practice at climbing to and from windows over the last few months.

I'd already slunk out to the tower early in the morning to compel a couple of the stones beneath the window into growing wider so they'd make a decent foot ledge once I got up there. I'd also conjured most of the rope I'd climb up and cast an illusion that would show only the plain wall to anyone looking that way, other than the lower several feet so that no one would stumble on either by accident just walking by. Right before the seminar, all I needed to do was surreptitiously draw the illusion and the rope down to the ground.

Not too many people were hanging around on the green between classes in the cold mid-morning air. I thought I managed to work the magic without being noticed. Still, I felt vaguely ridiculous as I slipped beneath the illusion and grasped the rope.

I was doing this for Connar. He needed us—needed me—to do whatever we could to free him from the spell that was clutching his mind. If I had to pull a few stunts to accomplish that, who was I to complain? At least I wasn't the one who'd been brainwashed.

As I hauled myself upward, the burn in my muscles made me grateful for the chilly breeze. I planted my feet one after the other, setting them as quietly as I could, the rope digging in my palms. A bird called out as it swooped toward the forest. More voices carried up from below as students started to leave the building after the earlier classes. I pushed myself faster. I'd hoped to be in place before Connar's class came in.

My shoulders and calves ached by the time I reached the ledge I'd created for myself. I settled my feet there, still clutching the rope for balance, and eased up to peer through the window pane.

For this part, I was counting on Jude's magic as well as my own. Last night, after a lot of snarky commentary about the duplicity of the barons that I'd discovered, we'd hashed out this plan. Jude had popped into the classroom before any of the seminars started and created an illusion that would replicate the view anyone would expect to see when looking out. It was more detailed work than I could imagine carrying out, but he'd seemed confident he could pull it off. As long as no one had opened the window, his spell shouldn't have been disturbed.

I held my breath as I looked into the classroom. The teacher, Professor Sinleigh, was standing behind her desk, gazing right toward the window. My pulse stuttered before I realized that she hadn't reacted to my presence at all. She just kept up her reverie for a few seconds longer and then turned back to the pages of notes in front of her.

She hadn't seen me at all. Jude's illusion was holding.

I slid my elbow onto the rough stone of the window ledge to help my balance and tried to relax into my awkward pose. With luck, I wouldn't need to stay here *too* long. It'd better not take them the whole class to get around to actually casting any insight spells of their own.

Students started trickling in and taking their seats with nods to the professor. I was just starting to tense up again with the fear that I'd gotten this all wrong when Connar finally joined them. He sat at the back of the room like he had in Persuasion, but at the far end from the wall with the window, so I had a decent view of him when I shifted to peer past his classmates.

He looked… sad. That was the only way I could put it. There, surrounded by peers he couldn't really call friends, without any of us scions provoking him into anger, a haunted sort of distance came into his eyes. The set of his mouth softened, the corners curled down. Somewhere under his mother's influence, he was suffering. Seeing it wrenched at my heart.

I braced myself, my gaze flicking between the professor and the three rows of students, watching for a sign that they were getting into their spellwork. Professor Sinleigh talked for a while, her lips moving but her voice not loud enough to penetrate the glass. My legs started to stiffen from holding me in place. The students nodded and a couple raised their hands with questions. Then, finally, Sinleigh made a few gestures toward them and they turned toward each other to pair off like we had in Persuasion.

I trained my gaze on Connar's profile, on his broad temple beneath his chestnut crew cut. At the same time, I watched for the parting of his mouth. There—he said something that I assumed was his casting word. My own rolled off my tongue as fast as I could propel it out.

Like when I'd watched him and Malcolm talk from my hiding spot in the forest a few days ago, my consciousness shot straight through the gap he'd opened up in his defenses. I hadn't used a specific question this time, though. I just wanted a sense of his recent impressions, which should include some to do with me.

The sadness I'd caught in his expression rang through me with a pang of loneliness. I got a glimpse of Malcolm's face on the clifftop where I'd told the Nightwood scion he might find Connar, along with a mix of hope and dread. Wanting to trust his friend, but afraid that he shouldn't.

There was Connar's dorm bedroom, flavored with a

welcome aura of security. There, a snippet from a class with Professor Viceport, the confidence of forming something solid with his hands. And there—there was my form in front of him, my voice reaching his ears.

I focused on that moment as well as I could, and the image shifted. Not his feelings about me, but what he actually saw and heard. My plaintive smile curled into a malicious smirk; my eyes narrowed. A remark echoed through Connar's thoughts as if from an earlier memory of my voice: *Do you really think an idiot like you can stop me from getting what I want?* My tone was so caustic I winced inwardly. With that, my concentration shattered.

I came back to myself on the makeshift ledge, shivering and tangled up inside. God, no wonder he hated me. If those impressions rose up every time he talked to me, every time he even thought about me…

It wasn't persuasion. That fact had come through crystal clear. Maybe his mother had used some small element of that too, but the thrust of the spell was all illusion. Clouding his mind, making him believe I'd done and said and shown things I never really would have. Painting over the closeness we'd shared with a mockery of it.

How could I shatter *that*?

Jude might have an idea when I talked to him and the other guys about what I'd found out. Of course, it'd probably still require getting at the construct that was filling Connar's head with all that garbage. Which was going to be awfully hard as long as his parents' spells kept doing their work.

Unless…

The answer hit me as obvious as anything. I had the perfect tool against illusions hanging around my neck. If I could get Connar to put on the necklace or maybe even hold the dragon charm with the illusion detection magic activated, we could prove to him that he'd been deceived without needing to break the construct on him first. And once he could see what was happening, surely he'd let us help him?

I just had to pull off the first part of that equation. Hmm. Somehow I didn't think he'd trust me enough to accept the necklace as a gift. And I couldn't just have one of the other scions talk him into taking it—he'd recognize it as mine. He'd commented on the dragon charm in the past.

I wasn't going to convince him of anything while I was perched up here—that was for sure. Carefully, I released my stance and edged one foot and then the other down the wall. It was a long climb and a whole lot of pain if I lost my grip.

When I reached the bottom, my muscles quivering and my breath short, I stopped for a moment to gather myself and then glanced around to make sure no one was looking my way. Stepping out from the illusion, I said a few words and sent up a waft of magic to dissolve the spells I'd cast. Jude would have to come around to take care of his when he had the chance.

While the classes continued inside the tower, I meandered around its base, debating my best course of action. In the end, the only solid approach I came up with was to wait and see what Connar did when he came out. I'd decide my next step then. I didn't think confronting him in the middle of the green would go well for either of us. The more witnesses who saw his hostility, the more impact his mother's spell would have even after we broke it.

It took more time before students started to trickle out of the building. I lingered in the shrinking shadow beside the tower, hugging my jacket close. Connar emerged— and veered off in the opposite direction, around the tower and onto the west field.

He walked alone. No one else was ambling around over there at the moment. I hesitated, but I couldn't have asked for a better chance. With my heart thudding at the base of my throat, I hurried after him.

He heard my footsteps before I reached him. The second he started to turn, I picked up my pace even more. I might only get one chance to say something that would catch his attention and make him listen.

His gaze connected with mine, his eyes already flaring with fury, and I forced the words out. "You blame yourself for what happened to Holden, even though your parents set the whole situation up. Even though you never wanted to hurt him."

It was the most personal thing he'd ever told me, in a raw, unguarded moment when we'd been figuring out where we stood with each other. I hadn't gotten the sense he told that story often or to many people.

Connar's mouth had opened to hurl some insult at me, but he halted, his expression twitching as if startled.

"What the fuck are you talking about?" he said, but he didn't sound quite as aggressive as he had the other times I'd tried to talk to him outside of class.

I stopped too, leaving five feet of grass between us. My chest felt as tight as if I'd run a marathon. "You told me the story of what happened between you two because you wanted me to understand how other people see you. And I think because you know I don't see you the same way. You trusted me enough to open up like that. And I've never broken that trust."

"You—" His mouth twisted. Lord only knew what illusions were flooding his mind now. "You probably dug inside my head to find that. Or else you persuaded me to tell you. It doesn't mean anything."

I swallowed thickly. "I've seen you in your dragon form. I've watched you fly over the trees—I've felt how much you love that freedom. We flew together one—"

"Shut up!" Connar rasped, cutting me off. "Don't throw all these lies at me. You jerked me around and used me, and I'm not letting it happen anymore."

He was still standing there, though. He hadn't marched away. I dragged in a breath and made the best plea I could.

"I swear to you that none of the things you think I did really happened. They're illusions. You're being manipulated, but not by me. Those memories never really happened, and they've got to be blurring out the things that did. I can prove it."

I clutched my necklace and undid the clasp behind my neck. "Take this. There's a spell on it to react to illusions.

It'll clear your head. Don't you want to be able to sort out all the conflicting impressions you must have in there? Professor Burnbuck did the casting. You don't have any reason to think he'd want to hurt you, do you?"

Connar stared at me and then the glass dragon charm in my hand. I held it out to him. He tensed and shook his head with increasing vehemence.

"I have no idea if any of that is true. You're probably going to use it to get me back under your sway. Do you really think I'm going to be that stupid again?"

I looked straight at him, willing all the honesty I could into my voice. "I've never thought that you're stupid. We can go to Professor Burnbuck right now, and he'll confirm it. Please."

He wavered. I saw it in his face, in the slight but noticeable sway of his body toward me. Then he jerked himself backward, all but baring his teeth at me.

"Stay the fuck away from me, or next time I'll have to make sure you do."

He took off without a backward glance, heading toward the lake. I stayed where I was. My feet felt leaden under me. What good would there be in following him? Even if every particle of my being wanted to call after him, to lay my heart at his feet, to make him see how much he mattered to me.

I knew what the solution to this horrible problem was now. I just had no idea how to make it happen.

CHAPTER SIXTEEN

Malcolm

I could tell the second I saw Rory coming out of the Ashgrave Hall stairwell that she was on a mission. She had that look, her jaw set and her eyes alight with determination, that sparked a flicker of desire in me even as I pitied whoever she was about to take that fire out on.

Then it occurred to me who it was most likely she was planning on confronting, given recent events. My stomach flipped over. Even the heir of Bloodstone had her limits.

She nodded to me with a tense smile as she moved to pass me by the front door, and I caught her arm.

"Where are you going all fired up, Glinda?"

She wrinkled her nose at the teasing nickname, but it did suit her, even if I'd developed an appreciation for her righteousness. A couple other seniors brushed past us on their way to the library, and she pitched her voice low.

"Declan can't meet with the rest of the barons until tomorrow. I figured I'd go talk to my mother now."

Of course she'd figured that. "To try to change her mind about the new Nary policy?"

"What else?" She crossed her arms over her chest. "Or to fill her in and get her to lay into the others, if she wasn't part of the decision in the first place."

I could tell from her expression that she didn't believe my father, Killbrook, and Stormhurst would have taken a step like that without including the newly restored Baron Bloodstone. In fact, the timing suggested they'd gone ahead with it *because* she'd returned. When the four of us had discussed Rory's discovery last night, I'd realized and pointed out to the others that this change at the university was probably the plan Agnes had overheard my parents talking about—a plan that had required a Bloodstone's participation. They hadn't meant Rory but rather her mother.

The only real question was how the other barons were going to justify keeping Declan out of the loop. If they'd wanted to do this before and didn't have any qualms ignoring the near-barons in their midst, I didn't know why they'd have waited.

Rory wouldn't want to believe her mother had immediately jumped on board to hurt the students the Bloodstone scion had so often championed, though. That was her biggest problem. She understood in theory what the barons could be like—she'd seen how brutal our parents could be. But she'd never experienced it herself.

I didn't want to think her mother would come down

on her the way my father did on me... but I wasn't so naïve to think it was unlikely.

"Come here," I said, tugging her with me away from the door. When she balked, I gave her my most cajoling look. "Please. Just to talk for a minute."

"Fine." She followed me past the library windows around the curve in the hall. No one generally ventured as far as the stairs to the basement except us scions and the occasional maintenance staffer. I stopped there, deciding I was better off not trying to drag her all the way to the lounge when she'd already been in mid-quest. With a few quick words and a thrum of magic from my chest, I ensured this spot would be private enough for the time being.

When I looked at her again, for a second it was difficult to remember why I'd hauled her over here. Because I'd called her over to this exact spot before, months ago—I'd confronted her and accused her of ridiculous things because I'd been pissed off about the other scions taking her side over mine in the feud I could now admit had been my fault.

Something had come over her in that moment, something assured and powerful and so goddamned delicious my groin stirred at the memory. That was the first time we'd ever kissed—because *she'd* kissed me. It'd been a power play, not a gesture of affection, but fuck, it'd been hot all the same.

If she'd never taken that step, pushed me that way, I wasn't totally sure we'd have ended up where we were now, with the forgiveness and trust she'd managed to grant me.

"Here we are again," she said, with a probably unconscious flick of her tongue over her lips that made me suspect she was remembering the same moment.

"You made a good show of telling me off that last time." Telling me how I was the last guy she'd ever want to be with. Somehow I couldn't stop myself from adding, boneheaded as the comment might be, "You really thought you meant everything you said back then."

Rory let out a huff of breath. "I *did* mean everything I said. If you were still acting like you were back then, we probably wouldn't even be talking right now, let alone... anything else." She paused, and a hint of a softer smile crossed her lips. "I'll admit that didn't stop me from noticing you were a very good kisser."

Well, fuck it all, now all I wanted to do was push her up against the wall and remind her of that fact for as long as humanly possible. With the self-control I'd gotten a lot of practice at in my time around Rory, I kept that urge in check. "It helped that I was particularly inspired by the girl I was kissing," I said with a smirk I couldn't hold back.

She rolled her eyes at me, but she was still smiling. For a brief time, anyway. A shadow crossed her expression, and she looked away.

"You know, the way you were talking back then, it was a lot like the things Connar's saying now. Accusing me of manipulating the other scions for some kind of malicious purpose."

My stance tensed at the pain in her voice. There was nothing I could do to make sure that pain went away—it wasn't even because of me this time—and that was driving me crazy.

"I wasn't in my right mind when I said that crap," I said. "Connar isn't either. We'll snap him out of it too."

"But no one was magically warping *your* memories. It was only you we were dealing with, not some awful spell." She rubbed her forehead. "We can get back to work on figuring that out after I talk to my mom. At least Connar isn't outright hurting anyone as long as he's nowhere near me. And I can handle it better than the Naries can cope with the torture they're being put through."

There she was, being Glinda the Good Witch again. Putting people she barely knew ahead of herself.

"Look," I said. "The whole reason I pulled you over here is to say—maybe you should leave this to Declan. One more day isn't that long. He's got years of practice maneuvering around the other barons, and if your mom didn't know, then she'll find out when he brings it up and be able to tell them off at the same time."

Rory frowned at me. "Why shouldn't I talk to her now? She's my *mother*."

Yeah, that was the problem with her thinking right there. As if the blood relation was any guarantee of mercy or even an open ear. "This is politics," I said. "Major politics. You can't just march into the middle of it and start making demands, or you're giving them an excuse to come down on *you*, openly this time. If you want to change this without screwing yourself over, you need to handle it carefully."

"I still have to handle it." Rory's brow knit as she

studied me. Something in her expression made my stomach knot. "I remember how you talked about the 'feebs' before. Do you even think they deserve better than what the professors like Crowford are setting them up for?"

I opened my mouth and closed it again. I didn't think all those random kids were worth risking her safety over, but I'd have said the same about any group of fearmancers too. The Naries were just there. For us to work on and work around as need be... But after all the ideas I'd challenged myself on over the last couple months, maybe I should take a closer look at that instinctive reaction too.

"I don't think they deserve to be terrified or to have their memories scrambled," I said. "Maybe I haven't seen them as worthy of making friends with or whatever, but I never went out of my way to torment them myself. Picking on people who don't have the slightest chance of keeping up with you is lazy and pathetic, not impressive. I think the mages who terrorize their familiars to fuel their powers are jackasses too."

Rory arched one of her eyebrows. "So you see Naries as on the same level as animals."

"That's not what I meant." I dragged in a breath, willing my thoughts into some kind of order. It was my own fault for walking into this conversation, but I wasn't going to fail the test it'd turned into if I had any say in it.

"I can't give you a perfect answer right now, Rory. I honestly hadn't given it much thought. The way I see them is mostly based on the attitudes I picked up from people like my parents, so obviously I need to re-examine those. I know—I know *you* were a force to be reckoned with before you even knew you had magic, let alone how to use it. Magic isn't all that matters. And not having it shouldn't consign someone to be kicked around. I just…"

I couldn't bear the thought of the girl—the *woman*—in front of me setting off to do battle and returning broken. I'd already lost my best friend in every way that counted until we could figure out how to save him. If I lost Rory too…

I couldn't find the words to express any of that in a way I could stomach. The best I could settle on was, "I don't want anything else happening to you."

Rory's posture had relaxed as I'd spoken. "Okay," she said. "That's fair. I *will* be careful. I just can't stand back and not try when I'm one of the few people who has a chance of making a difference."

"Of course you can't." So much affection rose up inside me as I gazed down at her that I couldn't hold myself back any longer. I slid my fingers along her jaw to the soft fall of her hair and leaned in to kiss her.

It was so much better than that first time—having her melt into me rather than stiffening against her desire, the hot press of her lips matching mine. I lost myself in the embrace just like I had back then. To be honest, the moment her mouth had brushed mine in the midst of our argument, everything I'd wanted to prove, everything I'd been accusing her of had flown out the window, and nothing had mattered but provoking all the passion I could from this stunning woman.

That thought stayed with me as I forced myself to pull

back, with an itch of inspiration. Rory had been right that during that argument I'd been looking at her with nearly as much hostility as Connar was now... with more attraction than I'd wanted to admit underneath. Maybe there was something in that we could use.

I'd have to poke at the possibility some more and see where I could take it. We didn't have time to discuss it right now. Rory stepped away from me, and I groped for anything concrete I could offer.

"I'll talk to Crowford this afternoon and see what I can find out," I said. "He's my mentor. I don't need much of an excuse to call on him."

Rory nodded, her cheeks still lightly flushed from the kiss. "That sounds like a plan. You can tell me how that goes when I get back—in one piece, I promise."

"You'd better be," I muttered, but I flashed her a smile before she set off again.

I didn't have to wait long to call on the Persuasion professor. After five years, we didn't have regular mentor appointments scheduled anymore, but I knew his office hours. I spent the last little while mulling over my approach and trying not to agonize over the trouble Rory might be getting herself into, and then strode over to Killbrook Hall.

Another student, a junior, was just leaving Crowford's office when I reached it. I gave the kid a mild glower just to make sure he knew who I was and where respect was due, and let up the second a flicker of nervous energy flitted from him to me. "I'm guessing you have class to get to," I said mildly, and he scampered off with a bob of his head.

Professor Crowford looked up as I came in and blinked with obvious surprise. Gratifyingly, he stood up to welcome me. This man certainly knew to defer to his future barons. The problem was more how much he was already deferring to the ones currently in charge.

"Mr. Nightwood," he said. "It's been a while. What can I help you with today?"

I propped myself on the arm of the chair across from his desk, tipping my head with an air of total confidence. "I've heard you've got a special program that just started running. Something about getting more juice from the Naries. Only a select number of students involved. I assume it was simply an oversight that I wasn't included in that number?"

Crowford stayed standing, giving me his usual slick smile, but his hands had tucked into his pockets as if to stop them from fidgeting. He could tell he was on shaky ground.

"I didn't realize word had gotten out," he said. "Who did you hear it from?"

"I'm not here to get anyone in trouble. I just want in —and to know why I wasn't included in the first place."

"Well…" He shrugged, all casual. "The barons requested that we run the initial sessions without any involvement from their heirs. The concern was, I believe, that having any of you present might bias the reactions we got from the other students, who'd look to you for cues as authority figures. They wanted clean runs so we could count on the responses being genuine."

I supposed that excuse made a decent amount of sense, at least enough for the barons to avoid it looking odd that they were hiding the policy change from their own heirs. If we acted like the whole thing was a great idea—or a horrible one—a lot of the other students would fall in line no matter what they'd have thought otherwise. A fact which could work in our favor later on.

"The cat's out of the bag now," I said. "You've had time to gather a decent amount of data."

"I'm sure you can understand that I'd prefer to stick to our agreement with the barons," Crowford hedged.

I had to get something useful out of this meeting. I sighed as if the whole thing was carrying on too long for my liking. "I'd like to at least see how it all works. I can keep out of the way, out of sight, and simply watch. Unless you doubt my abilities."

I said the last bit just pointedly enough to provoke a slight but noticeable tensing of the man's shoulders. Crowford shifted his weight from one foot to the other. He had to contend with my father now—but he'd have decades of dealing with me coming soon enough.

"I suppose in that case it wouldn't be breaking from the agreement," he said. "It would be awkward in the classroom setting, but we do have an outdoor session planned in a short while."

"Perfect," I said. "Just tell me where and when."

CHAPTER SEVENTEEN

Rory

When I'd contacted my mother to ask to see her, she'd directed me to a small city about halfway between Blood U and the main Bloodstone residence. Apparently we had a business property there.

I parked outside a mirrored building in the middle of the downtown core and gazed up at it for a moment, gathering my resolve. Malcolm's warnings were still lingering in my head.

I didn't really know my mother yet. She might think exploiting the university's Nary students this way was a brilliant idea. She might not care at all that I disagreed. But I could at least find that out and make the best case I could.

She wanted a strong heir. I'd show her I was one—and that I wasn't afraid to tell her when I thought she was wrong.

The company it appeared the Bloodstones had a major stake in was on the fifth floor. I took the elevator up and walked through the door just down the hall with the right sign next to it.

The room I stepped into had probably used to be a bustling modern office. Several glossy white desks were spread throughout the space, brightened by sunlight streaming through the broad windows along one wall. The sight was made eerie by the fact that none of those desks were occupied except the one my mother was sitting at toward the far end of the room.

Lillian sat kitty-corner to her, flipping a paper they must have been going over, and Maggie lingered near the windows. Otherwise the office was utterly vacant.

My mother's voice nearly echoed through the emptiness as she beckoned me over. "Persephone. Not the most impressive setting, I realize, but we're working on restoring operations here. Hard to keep businesses running with no one around to oversee them."

"Of course." As I crossed the polished floor, my shoes squeaked so loud that I had to restrain a wince. A lemony scent hung in the air. She'd made enough progress that someone had already come through to give the place a thorough cleaning, anyway.

What kind of business was she setting up that she needed advice from a blacksuit? Or was Lillian here acting only in her best-friend, non-professional capacity?

"How have you been?" my mother asked as I reached the desk. It occurred to me that she still hadn't mentioned my birthday in any of our communications. Had she still not remembered, or was she waiting to see if I'd bring it up? I wasn't sure it'd be wise to mention that failing when I had a much more serious problem to tackle.

"Good," I said. "There's just something I wanted to talk to you about. Preferably in private." I shot a quick smile at her companion. "No offense."

Lillian had been working with Baron Nightwood on his other illicit plans. I doubted I could count on her supporting my complaints.

The blacksuit eyed me consideringly, but she kept her tone light. "Don't worry about me. Family comes first."

"Indeed." My mother stood up. "We can use the president's office." She tipped her head to Lillian. "Give that one aspect of the proposal some more thought and see if you can't find a simpler strategy."

Lillian bobbed her head in agreement, and I bit my tongue against asking what strategies they were working on. Yet another thing that would distract from my main purpose. But I couldn't help commenting, as my mother led me over to a walled room in the corner, "I guess as you're getting things back on course, you'll let me know how this all works? I haven't really had a chance to look over all of the family's properties or anything like that."

"Of course you haven't," she said easily. "Your schooling was naturally your top priority, as it should be. We'll have plenty of time to discuss the various pies we have our fingers in as I get settled in myself."

She opened the door to the supposed president's office with a casting word and a twist of her fingers. The space on the other side had the same tall windows along one wall, a glossy desk nearly twice the size of those in the outer room, and a couple of cabinets in pale gray. There was nothing else, not even a chair. The emptiness there felt more claustrophobic than outside. Maybe that was why my mother had been working in the larger room.

She propped herself on the edge of the desk, looking trim but no longer gaunt in her long-sleeved sheath dress. "Well, then. What's on your mind? You look rather serious. This obviously isn't a mere social visit."

"No," I acknowledged. "I—" I'd thought I'd known exactly how I wanted to approach this, but faced with her cool eyes, my confidence faltered. Any dissembling I tried, she'd probably see through in an instant. Maybe it was better to cut to the chase.

"There's been a recent change to how the Nary students at the university are handled," I said. "Allowing students to reveal their powers to them. Were you involved in making that decision?"

My mother chuckled, a low melodic sound. "The other barons could hardly have gone ahead in approving that large a shift *without* involving me."

But somehow they did without Declan, I thought but didn't say. At least she was admitting how big a deal the change was. On the other hand, she was obviously totally on board with it. My throat tightened. I couldn't be surprised by that, but I still wished it wasn't true.

I kept my voice as calm and steady as I could to match her bearing. "I've been seeing the effects on the Nary students firsthand, and I think they're more extreme than the barons must have anticipated. Their memories might be altered so they don't remember that magic exists, but the emotional impact is lingering. And that's with only a few exposures, I have to assume."

"All the better," my mother said. "Any fear that continues to rise up because of the students' actions will give those mages even more energy. That's the primary reason we've taken this step—so that you all will have more magic to work with and be able to do bigger and better things with it. I don't see a problem there."

Right. Because to her it obviously didn't matter what distress the Naries were feeling. Or occur to her that I might not want to do greater magic if it meant torturing innocent people in the process.

I groped for the practical reasons I could offer that didn't require saying, *Treating other people that way is really shitty even if they don't have magic.* "I'm not sure how sustainable it could be. If they all end up having nervous breakdowns within a few months of starting school, pretty soon no one's going to send more Nary students to Blood U at all. There could be investigations."

My mother waved those concerns off before I could go on. "You haven't been in our world long enough to see how efficiently we can handle the Nary authorities. They don't pose any threat. And this stage is merely the first experiment to evaluate how it goes. If we find we're pushing them too hard, we'll have the students adjust their strategy so it can be sustained for the entire period of enrollment."

And then what? They'd all have nervous breakdowns

within months of leaving Blood U? It'd really have earned the name Villain Academy then.

My throat had constricted even more, but I forced another argument out. "If we want to avoid exposure to the larger world, it's also going to be a lot harder when the fearmancer students start feeling like it's okay to openly use their magic on Naries. It wouldn't take many slips for word to get out no matter how hard you try to control things. They couldn't keep the secret even just at school for more than a week."

"Persephone." My mother pushed herself off the desk and came over to rest her hand on my shoulder. "You really don't need to worry about all of this. We *do* have the situation entirely under control. I appreciate how much thought you've put into this and how you're looking out for the school and our society in general, but I assure you, we've put even more thought into it. We're certain this is the best way forward."

The best way forward toward *what*? I didn't know how to ask that in any way that wouldn't sound accusing. Or how to explain that I wanted to look out for the Naries too. My heart was sinking with the suspicion that if I mentioned that, she'd laugh in my face.

Before we'd even rescued her, I'd been prepared that she might share the common, callous fearmancer attitude toward Naries. It'd taken a hell of a lot for even Jude and Malcolm to start to see things differently. I'd just have to work on this over time—and find other ways to show the problems with the new policy back on campus, until the barons would have to admit that it couldn't continue.

Arguing with my mother any further didn't seem likely to get me anywhere.

"Okay," I said, forcing a smile. "I'll see how it ends up working out. I'm sorry I bothered you with this. Thanks for talking it through with me."

"Of course. I can hardly give you proper guidance if I don't know what's on your mind. I can't imagine how you managed all those months here without anyone to properly turn to."

I'd had my fellow scions, as slowly as it'd taken some of them to come around. I'd had my first mentor before the other barons had ripped him apart to put me off balance. If the guidance came with swift decisions to institute cruel policies… that wasn't a deal I'd have wanted to make.

I walked with her out into the main office space, doing my best to ignore the churning in my gut. Lillian got up from her chair when she saw us, holding some of the papers in her hands.

"Everything sorted out?" she asked, her gaze sliding between the two of us.

"Quite satisfactorily," my mother said.

Lillian motioned with the papers. "I think I can find some additional leniency when it comes to that one ruling. I'll need to talk with a couple people when it comes to the others, but there are always options for exerting more sway. I'll get on that right away, unless there was something else you needed me for right now?"

I suspected she was being purposefully vague because of my presence. It didn't seem to faze my mother at all.

"The faster we can move on this when we're ready, the

better," she said with an air that felt more momentous than if they were just talking about setting up some kind of workforce here. A prickling ran over my skin.

They exchanged a brief clasping of hands that I guessed was as warm as a high-level fearmancer friendship got, and Lillian strode out with Maggie at her heels. I expected my mother to dismiss me too, but instead she went straight to the windows to peer down at the street. She murmured a few casting words under her breath, her gaze going intent, her posture tensed as if expecting some kind of attack.

"What's going on?" I asked with a skip of my pulse. When I came over to the window, I couldn't see anything concerning on the street below.

My mother held up a hand in a request for silence. Her gaze stayed fixed on the street.

Lillian and Maggie emerged and headed to one of the blacksuits' sleek black cars farther down the block. My mother murmured again, her eyes following them. They narrowed, and then she pulled herself back with a sharp exhalation.

"Have any of your interactions with Lillian made you uneasy?" she asked, searching my expression with uncomfortable intensity. "I understand she involved herself quite a bit in your life before I returned."

Pretty much *all* of my interactions with Lillian had unnerved me, but not for reasons I could easily explain to my mother. Where the hell had that question come from anyway?

"Mostly she just told me a little more about the family

and then, obviously, got my help in finding you," I said. "I didn't see her that often."

I thought the baron might bring up the murder charges, but apparently she had other things on her mind that didn't have to do so much with me. "Was there anything unusual she mentioned about the family, or specifically me? Did her approach to my rescue seem at all unconventional?"

I had no idea what a conventional rescue would look like. But those questions made understanding click in my head.

My mother was having trouble trusting *anyone* around her, from her longtime house manager to her supposed best friend. If anything, she seemed more paranoid now than she had about Eloise back at the house.

Seventeen years in captivity must have taken quite a toll—one she wasn't shaking off all that quickly.

"I—I don't think there was anything strange," I said, not sure what she'd consider strange but not wanting to give her false reassurance either. For all I knew, Lillian did have malicious intentions toward my mother and was hiding them as much as she'd hidden her scheming against me. "I'm not really sure how to judge."

"Hmm," my mother said, and turned back toward the window. In that moment, she didn't look like the cool and collected ruler of mages she'd presented herself as so often. Right then, all I could see was a nervous, worn-down woman.

A nervous, worn-down woman who was nonetheless

making decisions that affected not just our society but the Naries' as well.

It only lasted for a second, and then her expression snapped back into its authoritative calm. "It was good to see you, Persephone," she said. "I'm sure you have to get back to your studies, but we'll have to find time to grab another dinner soon and talk more."

"That would be nice," I said, and hurried out of the office as quickly as my feet could take me.

CHAPTER EIGHTEEN

Rory

Malcolm's text had only asked me to come to his dorm. When he answered the door, the common room on the other side was totally empty, the space silent. He motioned me inside.

"I've… encouraged my dormmates to be elsewhere for the next little while," he said, his voice low. "I might have a way to get through to Connar, but we'll want our privacy." He hesitated, his dark brown gaze holding mine. "Do you trust me?"

Four simple words that held so much weight after the history between us. I looked back at him, and found that after what we'd been through in the last few weeks, it wasn't even hard to say, "I do. What do you have planned?"

"I was thinking that the illusions he has of you are probably set off by triggers his parents were able to observe themselves to work into their casting—your voice, your face. But he's been a lot more intimate with you than that. So maybe, if we focus on re-establishing *that* type of connection, it'll override at least some of the brainwashing."

Intimate. A tingle passed over my skin at the word and the hint of heat that had come into Malcolm's expression. I could follow his reasoning, even if I wasn't sure the scheme would get us very far. "Is he even going to be willing to try?"

"I've talked with him. And there are certain conditions that should help him relax. I'll be right there the whole time in case he gets messed up again—if you're all right with that."

"Yeah." The thought of Malcolm watching only made the idea more tempting.

"It'd be best if you don't say anything to him, I think, to make it less likely he'll be set off before we get anywhere." Malcolm tipped his head toward a door at the far end of the common area. "He's waiting in my room."

I nodded, my lips pressing tight together. My hand leapt to my dragon charm. "I should take this off. He associates it pretty strongly with me, and especially after I tried to get him to use it, it might set him off."

"I'll take care of it for you." Malcolm accepted the necklace and tucked it into his pocket.

Anticipation and nerves jittered alongside each other through my body as we walked over. Making appeals through both logic and emotion hadn't worked to shake Connar out of his magic-induced delusions. Maybe this wouldn't either, but if the Nightwood scion thought it was worth a try, I couldn't refuse. All we needed was to restore enough trust with *Connar* for him to let us do the rest of the work to break the spell.

Malcolm's bedroom looked nearly identical to mine, only with a slightly different mahogany bedframe and a midnight blue bedspread that was neatly tucked over the mattress. The aquatic scent of his cologne lingered in the space.

Connar was leaning against the desk. His posture tensed the moment we came through the door. I stopped just inside, keeping my mouth shut as Malcolm had suggested, waiting to see how he'd handle this.

"We're going to unearth those memories I think have been buried," Malcolm said to his friend. "Rory wants to be a part of this. I know you're wary, and we both understand that. There's no way she'll be able to work any magic on you." He turned to me, his eyes even darker than before. His voice dropped even lower than before. "You'll need to take off your shirt and your bra first."

A heady shiver traveled down my spine. I was really doing this. I pulled the silky blouse up over my head, my skin cooling as I bared it, and set the shirt at the base of the bed. A flush crept through my cheeks as I unhooked my bra.

Connar watched the proceedings without stirring, still tensed, but a flicker of desire crossed his face. It was progress just that he wasn't telling me off or marching out.

When I'd set down my bra on top of my shirt, I crossed my arms over my chest instinctively. Malcolm motioned me over to the bed. I sat down, and he produced a pair of handcuffs from the drawer on the bedside table. They didn't look like police ones but like the wide silver ones I'd worn when the blacksuits had first taken me into custody for Imogen's murder. The ones that had suppressed my ability to cast.

My body balked instinctively with the memory of the powerlessness I'd felt back then. No wonder Malcolm had asked if I trusted him. I glanced up at him, and he gave me a crooked smile, waiting patiently without any pressure.

I could manage this. If it would reassure Connar enough for him to get past his hostility, it was more than worth it.

I held out my arms. "She won't be able to cast anything at all while she has these on," Malcolm said as he clicked the cuffs into place.

Nothing changed about the hum of energy behind my collarbone. The cuffs did nothing but add a faint, cold weight around my wrists. I suspected with one word I could have unlocked them. Understanding clicked in my head. He wasn't really confining me, only convincing Connar that he had.

My anxiety faded a little. Malcolm touched my shoulder, his fingers hot against my naked skin, to ease me farther up the bed. He pulled up one of his pillows to cushion the frame and guided my hands over my head to hook the cuffs' chain over a little spire in the center of the headboard. I tried to relax into the bed, even though I was totally exposed now.

Malcolm moved around me on the bed to sit at my left and nudged my knees down so my legs were sprawled straight in front of me. He beckoned Connar over. "Touch her. She *wants* you. See what you feel, what you remember."

Connar stiffened for a second, but then he pushed himself toward the bed. As he looked down at me, I tipped my head back in the hopes that I could make it easier for him to keep his attention away from my face and whatever illusions that sight might trigger. He lowered himself tentatively onto the mattress beside me. My heart thumped faster.

"Take your time," Malcolm said, low and smooth as ever. His voice teased over me like a caress in itself. "Some part of you remembers what she likes, doesn't it?"

He trailed his own fingers over my ribs to the base of my breast, sparking heat in their wake. My nipples pebbled at the contact.

Then another hand came to rest on my torso. Connar's, broad and solid, and so familiar I had to choke back words of encouragement. He traced his thumb in a slow arc over my skin, and I closed my eyes, remembering the times we'd come together before. At night in the clifftop clearing. In the lake, with Jude. In the back of his car after our first real date. Back on the cliff with Declan. And that last time, right before I'd left for California, the two of us melding together in the darkness of the Shifting Grounds.

His fingers edged up inch by inch to stroke the base of my breast. They followed the curve and just barely grazed the nipple. It hardened even more with a pulse of pleasure that made my breath catch.

"Just like that," Malcolm said encouragingly, the hunger in his tone turning me on even more. He'd made it clear more than once how much he wanted me, but bringing me back together with his friend was more important to him. He flicked his thumb over my other nipple. I just barely held myself back from arching into their combined touch, not wanting to scare Connar off.

The Stormhurst scion cupped my breast more firmly. He rolled my nipple under his thumb, and I did arch a little then, with a fresh stutter of breath.

"I do remember things," he said to Malcolm. "But I— She could have persuaded me into going along with it, or—"

Malcolm was shaking his head. "Sink into those memories," he said. "Give them all room to rise up. You weren't with her in some mindless haze of lust. You cared about her, and you wanted to show her that. You wanted to offer her all the affection and passion she'd shown you."

He caressed me again, the backs of his fingers rippling over the peak of my breast to provoke a wave of bliss. There'd been a rawness to those last words that made me wonder how much he was speaking for himself too. What it would mean to him when he and I finally came together.

Connar gazed down at me for a long moment, working over my other breast with a gentleness that was becoming more assured by the second. Then, to a skip of my pulse, he leaned over. As he continued to fondle my chest, he brought his lips to the bare skin just below my collarbone in a ghost of a kiss.

His smoky smell flooded my nose. My own lips ached to meet his, but that might break the counterspell of pleasure we were creating between our bodies.

He lingered there with a few more tentative kisses, and then he dipped lower, pressing my breast upward with his palm the way he had when offering them to Jude weeks ago. This time it was his mouth closing over the peak, his tongue slicking over me so hot and forceful I couldn't contain a whimper. The giddy heat radiated through me to pool between my legs.

"That's right," Malcolm said with a rasp in his voice. As if sensing my longing, he bowed his head too, pressing his lips to my cheek. Longing thrummed through me to have his mouth claim mine, but he held back, maybe worried Connar would feel usurped. The slow path he charted over my jaw and down my neck was blissful enough.

The Nightwood scion eased back as Connar shifted closer to me. Connar reached for the other side of my chest as he continued to nip and suckle my breast. My fingers itched to run through his hair and tease out an answering pleasure, but I didn't dare move my arms from where they were hooked above me. A tremor of pleasure ran through me, and I bit back a moan.

Malcolm let his hand drift lower to the waist of my pants. I sucked my lower lip under my teeth as he snapped open the fly. He tugged the fabric off me, exposing my dampening panties. Connar raised his head to take me in with a shakily eager breath.

Malcolm grazed his fingers along the top of my panties. "Look how wet she is for you. Are you going to leave her wanting?"

He eased his hand over to tease up and down my thigh as Connar trailed his fingers downward. I was practically dying by the time the Stormhurst scion reached that thin scrap of fabric. He brushed lightly over my mound and below to the evidence of my arousal. Then he pressed harder, right on my most sensitive spot.

Pleasure shot through me like an electric shock. I couldn't hold back the cry that tumbled from my lips. "Oh!"

Barely a word, one mere syllable. But just like that, Connar's hand jerked back. His stance tensed all over again.

"No," he said, wrenching himself away from the bed. "I can't— This isn't— It's all part of her fucking plan."

He stumbled and spun around, grabbing at the door. I stared after him as he slammed it behind him. A sense of failure coiled through me despite the longing that hadn't faded.

"Damn it," Malcolm muttered. "I'm sorry. I was really hoping... I don't know."

He sounded so repentant, as if Connar's departure were somehow his fault, as if his idea hadn't gotten us closer to some kind of reconciliation than anything else any of us had tried before had. My heart squeezed. I murmured to the cuffs, and they clicked open with a quiver of my magic as I'd expected. Sitting up, I tucked my arm around Malcolm's.

"It might still have helped," I said. "He let down his guard—he was remembering things. Maybe he'll have those real memories stronger in his mind now to challenge the false ones. This wasn't likely to cure him all in one go."

Malcolm let out a rough laugh. "True. But I wish I could have given you that."

A lump rose in my throat. I didn't know how to answer him, other than by touching his face and drawing him into a kiss.

Malcolm turned so he could fit his mouth against mine at an even better angle, his arm sliding around my waist to tug me against him. So much wanting radiated through the kiss that my body lit up in answer.

I wanted this too. I wanted *him*, just as much as I'd wanted Connar. I'd wanted him for what felt like forever, but the selflessness with which he'd urged his friend to rekindle what we'd once shared sharpened that desire even more.

Instead of carrying the kiss into something more, Malcolm pulled back with a look of regret as if he thought that was the end of it. I caught his shirt before he got very far, searching out his gaze until it met mine. "There are lots of other things you could give me. You've got me practically naked in your bed—isn't this exactly what you've been waiting for?"

His eyes turned outright smoldering, his fingers curling against my back. "Rory, you don't have to—"

I leaned in to shut him up with a kiss, short and sweet.

"You really should know by now that I don't do things just because someone else expects me to. Did you think I wasn't wet for you too? I want you, all of you. Or are you going to make me beg now?"

Malcolm inhaled raggedly. "Fuck, no." Then his mouth crashed into mine with all the passion I'd been waiting for.

He tipped me over on the bed without breaking the kiss, devouring me in the most blissful possible way. His hand stroked over my breast as he braced himself over me. Every movement of his fingers reignited the flames he'd stirred up before, twice as hot now that he wasn't holding himself back.

I fumbled with the buttons on his shirt. I'd only managed the first couple when he sat up just long enough to yank it off. Before I could do more than briefly run my hands over the sculpted muscles of his chest, he lowered his head and sucked the tip of my breast between his teeth with such blissful force I gasped.

"I've been waiting so long for this," he murmured as he moved to the other side of my chest. "You can have the other guys, but I'm going to make you come so hard you forget you've ever been with anyone else."

A tremor of anticipation raced through me. I dug my fingers into his short curls with an encouraging sound that turned into a moan with the swivel of his tongue over my nipple.

My hips lifted toward him of their own accord. He slid one hand down to my ass and massaged the curve of it while he sent another wave of pleasure through my breast.

Then he eased up over me to kiss me on the mouth again, fitting me against him at the same time so my core met the bulge in his slacks. I couldn't hold back my moan. It was a good thing he'd cleared the whole dorm.

I rocked into him, reveling in the pleasure that flared with each moment of contact, kissing him hard and dragging my fingers down his back. Malcolm groaned and ground into me in turn. In a mess of spilled breath and rough kisses, we peeled his slacks off him with only a few breaks in our rhythm. I palmed him through his boxers, and a growl reverberated from his chest.

He caught my hand and pushed it up against the pillow, sliding his hardened cock against me. The friction between those two thin layers of fabric made me shudder with bliss. I raised my hips, urging him onward, already lost in the haze of feeling.

When he reached down to tug my panties off me, I dipped my hand between us for just an instant to murmur the protective spell Declan had taught me. Malcolm's gaze caught fire, watching. He kissed me again so thoroughly it left my head spinning and sat back on his heels, urging me up with him.

As I sat up to meet him, he turned me at the waist and pulled my back flush against his chest. One of his skilled hands molded to my breast and the other slipped between my legs. He teased his teeth against the top of my shoulder, each press of his fingers above and below sending me soaring.

He pinched my clit lightly to earn himself another moan and tested my opening with a careful touch. I shifted my legs farther apart automatically at the graze of his erection. He slid into me from behind so fast and sure that I lost my breath.

With that one thrust, he hit the perfect spot inside me. His hands worked over my clit and my breast as he plunged into me again, and that was all it took to tip me over into a rush of ecstasy.

Malcolm didn't stop with my orgasm. He didn't even slow his pace. Again and again, he filled me to the brim, propelling the pleasure already flooding me to even greater heights. His fingertips kept circling my clit and my breast.

I reached back to grasp at his head where it bowed over my shoulder, and he nipped me harder. A sound that was more whine of need than anything else escaped me. He was making me feel so fucking good already, and somehow I craved even more.

"Tell me what you want, Rory," Malcolm said around broken breaths. "All you have to do is say the word."

I leaned into him, and his cock penetrated me at an even more perfect angle. My body trembled with another building surge of bliss. "Faster," I managed to say. "Give me everything."

He bucked into me even faster and deeper than before. I felt ready to split in two, but only in the best possible way. The brilliant burn seared up through my chest, and stars spun behind my eyes as I clenched around him all over again.

Malcolm's arms tightened in an embrace made slick by the sweat that had formed between our bodies. He eased in and out of me, letting me ride out the aftershock of my second release, not yet having found his own. He really was determined to give me everything, wasn't he? Every bit of pleasure he could coax from my body, before he took as much for himself.

A much more tender sensation filled me. I twisted to bring my mouth close to his. "I want to be with you, face to face."

Malcolm hummed low in his throat and lowered me to the bed. I almost cried out in protest when he pulled out of me, but it was only for the time it took him to help me roll onto my back. He bowed over me, I lifted my knees to cross my legs behind him, and he plunged back into me as if there was no place in the world it made more sense for him to be.

I gripped his shoulder, his side, gazing up at him. His golden hair had dampened along his forehead and his face had flushed, but his eyes were as alert as ever, focused completely on me. The divine devil I'd met half a year ago looked at me with such reverence that I'd have melted if I hadn't already been nearly boneless with pleasure.

I touched his cheek, longing to tell him how much I treasured the fact that we'd found allies and so much more in each other despite the odds, too absorbed in that same moment to form words. All that slipped out, more a sigh than anything else, was his name. "Malcolm."

"Fuck," Malcolm said hoarsely with a tightening of his features. Whatever control he'd been holding onto must have snapped. His hips jerked against mine, but the feeling of him losing himself to the moment tipped me right back over the edge alongside him. We came together, my cry mingling with his groan. Right then, it was a miracle I even remembered my own name.

When we'd rocked to a stop, Malcolm stayed braced over me, still inside me. He brushed a few strands of hair back from my damp forehead with his thumb. While he didn't speak, the reverence had only intensified in his expression. An ache formed around my heart.

He'd said in so many ways what I'd come to mean to him—that he adored me, that as far as he was concerned I was perfect... I could offer this one thing first. The truth of it pealed through me from head to toe.

"I love you," I said.

Malcolm blinked, looking so startled that for a few painful seconds I thought I'd misjudged, that he hadn't even been interested in sentiments like that. Then he ducked his head and kissed me, hard and deep with his tongue tangling around mine. I hugged him to me, echoing what I'd said in the squeeze of my arms and the returning press of my lips.

"I love you too," he said a moment later against my cheek. "God, Rory. So fucking much, sometimes I don't know what to do with myself."

"I'm sure I could make a few suggestions," I said.

He chuckled and kissed me again. "No doubt. I'll let you know when I need your guidance, Glinda."

There was nothing but affection in that nickname now. He rolled onto his side, still holding me to him. I snuggled against him, lingering in the love I had that would surely be powerful enough to bring back the love I'd lost, even if we hadn't quite gotten there tonight.

CHAPTER NINETEEN

Declan

I arrived at the Fortress of the Pentacle early with the intention of getting a read on my colleagues one by one as they arrived for our meeting. It appeared they'd anticipated that move—or they'd all been particularly eager to get talking this morning. I recognized the cars belonging to the Barons Nightwood, Stormhurst, and Killbrook in the parking lot, along with a gleaming gold Lexus styled similar enough to the family car Rory had inherited for me to assume it belonged to her mother.

Wonderful. I got to face them all at once, already united against me. I dragged the damp autumn air into my lungs and set off for the building.

The air inside wasn't much drier, with a cool edge that the ancient heating system could never quite touch once the weather started to turn. As I climbed the stairs, I straightened the sweater I'd thrown on over my dress shirt.

Looking as professional as possible wouldn't make that much of a difference, but I had to make use of every tool at my disposal.

My first glance into the meeting room confirmed my assumptions. The four older barons were already sitting at the table. A couple of candles lit in the middle added a warmer glow and a thin waxy smell to the otherwise dim space—and made the planes of their faces shift eerily. All four of those faces turned toward me as I stepped inside.

There'd been times in the past when I'd wondered what it would be like to have a full pentacle of barons. I probably should have expected it'd be like this. Instead of that vacancy at the Bloodstone point providing additional awkwardness, now I was the only odd one out. I was met with what felt like a united front of wariness and unstated disapproval.

"Ashgrave," Baron Nightwood said in that smooth tone Malcolm had picked up a long time ago, "so good of you to join us." As if I were late instead of the rest of them being incredibly early.

Baron Stormhurst let out a guttural chuckle that sounded too loud for her sinewy frame. "Especially seeing as you're the one who demanded this meeting."

Demanded might have been overstating the case, but they wouldn't have shown up at all if I hadn't been firm about it. "I appreciate you all coming on relatively short notice," I said as I took my seat, grateful that at least the second chair Aunt Ambrosia had so often occupied was currently empty. Now that I was nearly of age, the barons preferred to deal with me without her grasping presence. Small mercies.

Baron Killbrook said nothing, his mouth set at a sour angle in his sharp-edged face. How did *he* feel about the new arrival in our midst, who'd immediately usurped any extra authority the Killbrooks could have claimed before?

Technically, the Bloodstones had always been considered the greatest presence in the pentacle and the Ashgraves the weakest, with the other three shifting in power depending on their family's current situation, although the Nightwoods tended to lord it over the others. This Killbrook had never been able to stand up to Stormhurst when the chips were down, though. Now he'd been bumped even farther down the ladder of consideration. The current Baron Stormhurst had overthrown her brother and claimed that position in the pentacle years after Rory's mother had been taken, but from the rapport they'd already developed, the reinstated Baron Bloodstone clearly recognized certain types of strength when she saw them.

She watched us now with dark blue eyes that would have reminded me of Rory's if not for their piercing quality. She was leaning back in her chair in a causal pose that looked studied, and I didn't think her gaze missed much. She was cataloguing our dynamics and our missteps for her future use, no doubt. And possibly trying to determine how much of a thorn in her and the others' side I was going to be.

They had to know what this meeting was about. Even if they couldn't have been sure before, Rory's talk with her mother yesterday would have tipped them off that their secret was out. I still had to be careful in how I broached the subject without undermining my own authority.

"I understand that the Pentacle has given staff at Bloodstone University permission to retract the longtime policy about keeping our magic completely secret from Naries," I said. "A decision that momentous should have required a consensus between all of us. I'm hoping you can explain why you moved forward without consulting me."

None of them looked bothered by the question. Killbrook even produced a thin smile. Nightwood cocked his head with an expression I suspected was meant to be slightly pitying, to imply it was sad that I was even concerning myself with this.

"Of course you should have been," he said. "We made every effort to include you in the discussion. Unfortunately, we had a limited window where it would be convenient to have more Nary students brought into the university to study the effects in full, and when we reached out to you, we got no answer."

"We did have an Ashgrave weigh in on the matter," Stormhurst put in with a flinty gleam in her eyes. "Your aunt Ambrosia was able to fill in in your absence."

So, this once having her around had been convenient for them. Of course she'd have gone along with anything they suggested to try to curry their favor. I was supposed to get precedence, though. I opened my mouth, about to protest that there hadn't been any time in the weeks before the change that I'd have been unreachable, and a thought struck me with a sudden chill.

"When exactly did you have this discussion?" I asked instead.

"It was an afternoon last week," Nightwood said carelessly. "I'm sure you could find the date in the records." He nodded to Bloodstone. "We convened at the blacksuits' headquarters so we could include every member, since one of our number was in recovery at the time."

"My first day back and already hard at work." Rory's mother sounded amused.

My heart sank. I remembered the day Rory had first gone to visit her mother—the first day Baron Bloodstone had been awake after her ordeal. That afternoon we'd met to discuss how to handle Connar's situation, and I'd been called away to rescue my brother off in the woods. To rescue him from a prank that coincidentally had required I go underground where my phone had lost all reception and no one else could have reached me.

Except it hadn't been a coincidence, had it? I could hardly accuse them of some elaborate conspiracy without a shred of proof, but I'd be willing to stake my life that the barons had guided Noah's classmates in their prank, instructed them on where to trap him and when to call for my help. They'd known I'd never have agreed to the torture they were subjecting the Nary students to.

How long had they been planning this move behind my back, only delaying because they couldn't count on Rory's compliance and had no other options on the Bloodstone side? The instant they'd been able to turn to her mother, they'd charged ahead.

She hadn't hesitated at all either. Because she'd been foggy from the medical treatment still, because she didn't give a damn about Naries… or because this plan went all the way back to her past time as baron, in one form or another?

My first impulse was to demand we reopen the discussion, but I knew before I even thought that through that it wouldn't get me anywhere. I wasn't officially Baron Ashgrave until I graduated and completed the ceremony. My aunt, as regent baron, had just as much authority as I did to approve a policy change if I wasn't available. My word wouldn't be enough to overturn hers on this for another few months. I could argue about it and have them shoot me down, but then I'd just look ineffectual. Damn it.

"I trust I'll be included in any discussions about continuing developments with this new approach," I said. And I'd have to be extra cautious about any sudden emergencies that called me off campus. Now I wished twice as much that Noah had stayed in Paris, both for his sake and mine.

Nightwood's smile bordered on a smirk. "Naturally. We were planning on bringing you up to speed at our next expected meeting as it is. We were simply waiting for more data to fuel that discussion."

"I can certainly contribute a needed perspective, considering I'm on campus to observe the outcomes. What was your reasoning for making this move?"

The barons exchanged a discreet glance. "The Naries offer a particularly potent source of magical power,"

Stormhurst said. "They're so unaware, it doesn't take much to frighten them compared to setting the students against each other. That resource has barely been tapped. *We* shouldn't be the ones living in fear of them. They're allowed at the university for the regular students' benefit, not their own."

That explanation fit with what Rory had reported that her mother had said. I resisted the urge to clench my jaw. "And if we see problems arising, we'll rethink that position? More power isn't always to the benefit of the entire community." It all depended on who was wielding it and whether they could be trusted.

"The staff involved are reporting on their students' reactions and any shifts in the atmosphere on campus," Bloodstone said. "We intend to watch their progress closely. I'm sure any observations you can contribute would also be welcome, Mr. Ashgrave."

She gave the "Mr." a slight emphasis, not so overt I could have been justified in bristling at it, but clearly reminding me that I wasn't quite a baron yet. She'd barely been back a week, and she already felt comfortable holding my lesser authority over my head, when I'd spent nearly the entire time she'd been gone preparing for this role while she'd had no idea what was happening in fearmancer society.

Why should I have expected any different?

"Well," Nightwood said, getting up, "since this meeting did come at the last minute, I have other responsibilities to get to. Unless you had some other concern you needed addressed, Ashgrave?"

Not that I thought I could get anywhere with. I dipped my head. "No. Thank you again for coming."

Killbrook had stayed awfully quiet during the entire discussion. The other three fell into hushed conversation as they headed out, leaving him to trail behind them. As I followed, a tenuous idea formed in my mind.

If I was going to last as baron and not see my family torn apart or be forced to agree to policies I hated, I needed at least one ally in the pentacle. Whatever was going on between him and Jude, Killbrook was obviously the weakest link. If I could find the right point of leverage to sway him into going against the others on at least a few subjects, that could make the difference between this new dynamic becoming an outright catastrophe.

I picked up my pace so I was nearly close enough to tap his shoulder. The other three barons went out the main entrance ahead of us. As soon as the door shut and before Killbrook could reach for it, I cleared my throat.

"They shut you out fast, didn't they?"

The pale man whirled, his face turning even more pinched as he frowned at me. "I'm not sure what you're insinuating," he said with forced haughtiness.

I tipped my head toward the door. "Nightwood and Stormhurst needed you when they weren't sure what they'd be contending with on the Bloodstone side. Now that Althea is here, they don't have to play friendly at all. Do you really think they'll back you up if *you* need something that doesn't fit with their interests?"

Killbrook glowered at me. "I don't think I'm interested in taking advice from a boy who's not even old enough to become full baron yet." But he didn't move to leave. He wanted to hear what else I'd say.

I slung my hands in my pockets, affecting as much confidence as I could summon. "You should be. Neither of us has a whole lot of footing on our own, and they know that. If we stay open to supporting each other as need be, it could benefit us both."

"And what is it you're looking for 'support' with, Ashgrave?"

I knew better than to present any specific propositions on ground this shaky. I shrugged. "I don't know yet. I'm sure occasions will arise, as they will for you too. I just wanted to extend the offer for you to consider. It's not as if they won't get even more standoffish when they realize just how uncertain your line of inheritance has become."

Killbrook's eyes flashed with a frantic vehemence that made me flinch inwardly. He stepped toward me, all unexpected menace, and jabbed a finger at my chest hard enough to bruise. "What the hell stories has that idiot been telling you all? He's never cared about anyone other than himself, you know. He's not content with what I've given him, so he's perfectly happy to tear it all down. You can't listen to a thing he says."

I stared at the baron as I fumbled for my words. He was obviously talking about Jude, but with an intensity that didn't fit what I knew about the situation. "All Jude said was that things got tense enough that he's moved out, which I already pretty much knew from the talk at our recent meeting, and I gathered that you're at least considering making his unborn sibling heir in his place.

If that isn't true, you should probably talk to him about it."

My words didn't appear to register with Baron Killbrook at all. "Don't play games with me," he sputtered. "I know the kinds of stories he'd tell. You'd better keep them to yourself, or you'll have the embarrassment of repeating a lie."

He spun back around and stalked out the door without another word. I stayed where I was for a moment, still processing the sudden turn that conversation had taken.

Whatever was going on between the baron and his son, it might be a hell of a lot more complicated than even Jude knew.

CHAPTER TWENTY

Rory

The first time I had class with Connar after our encounter in Malcolm's bedroom, I couldn't stop my cheeks from flaming at the sight of him. His gaze caught on mine and jerked away so quickly it felt as if he'd slapped me. I hesitated for a second in the doorway to the Persuasion classroom and then hurried to a seat that was thankfully open at the opposite end of the room from him. This obviously wasn't a good time to try to hash anything out.

I'd had other plans for today anyway. As my other classmates trickled in, I studied each of them, watching for a face I recognized. Not him… not her… That guy. I didn't remember the messy-haired, long-faced boy's name off the top of my head, but I'd definitely seen him amid the bunch that'd been heading off campus with Professor Crowford and the group of Naries the other day. He was in on the plot the staff still hadn't revealed to the campus at large.

Declan had told me in the past that there were plenty of fearmancer families who didn't share the barons' cutthroat attitudes. That the community in general had once been much less antagonistic toward the Naries we had to live among, and the current disdain for them had grown with encouragement over recent years.

No doubt Crowford and whichever other professors were involved had been instructed to pick their initial participants from the families the barons knew were on their side. There had to be other students here who'd be horrified, and whose parents would be as well. If I could expose the situation early enough and incite them to protest, we might be able to end this experiment before it went any farther.

I'd learned enough about fearmancer politics to realize that blurting out the story myself wasn't a wise idea. Someone on the inside could spread the word for me. Knowing what that guy had willingly done to Nary students like Shelby left me with no qualms at all about using him as a tool. A taste of his own medicine.

Jude would have been proud of me for taking such a fearmancer view of the situation.

Crowford was standing behind his desk, looking through the notes on his papers, not paying much attention to us yet. I considered the exact phrasing I wanted to use. It'd be easier to cast when my classmate was using his own persuasive magic, since then his guard would be down, but I also faced a higher chance of getting caught.

The decision was made for me with the snap of Crowford's papers against the desk. He peered through the classroom with his slick smile. Too late to try to slip anything in before class started.

"I'd like us to continue working on the same concept we started discussing a few days ago," he said. "Persuading ideas and beliefs. This area of study requires particular care because it's difficult to judge the results of your spell immediately. There generally won't be concrete indicators of success."

A hand shot up at the back of the room, and he nodded to the girl there.

"I've been wondering since last class," she said, "how long would something you persuaded a person into thinking or believing actually stick before the spell started to fade? Most of the behavioral persuasive spells we cast, we don't expect to continue for all that long."

"Excellent question," Crowford said. "Internal persuasive spells often last longer than ones modifying external behavior because adjusting thoughts generally requires less energy than adjusting outright actions. That's one of the reasons this area is *worth* studying—because it gives you a way to drive a pattern of behavior without the power necessary to compel all of those specific behaviors themselves. But yes, an internal spell has its limitations too. Even a powerful mage is unlikely to see it maintain for more than a couple of days. I'd imagine all of you have shaken the ideas your partners implanted in you last time."

Yes, because none of them had constructs on their body continuing to feed those spells. I resisted the impulse to glance at Connar, even though I knew now that the magic gripping his mind was mostly illusionary.

Professor Crowford rubbed his hands as he went on. "One interesting factor is that once you've trained a mind to think in a certain way, it's easier to nudge it in that same direction again. Future persuasive spells along the same line will catch hold faster and linger longer than the first time. Those of you who were successful last time, find your partner, and why don't you see how you experience a repeated attempt?"

Well, that left me and Connar out of the game, since neither of us had even tried to cast on each other. I still needed a way to cover my casting now.

My intended target swiveled in his seat to face the guy behind him, who I guessed had been his partner before. He grinned and started to speak his casting. I braced myself, and a spark of inspiration flashed through my head. All I needed was a brief distraction to ensure no one was paying any attention to me.

I swiped my hand over my mouth and murmured a physicality spell under my breath, picturing the door for the classroom next to ours and propelling a surge of magical energy toward it.

A bang sounded from outside. Then the squeal of hinges, and a thud. Again: bang, squeal, and thud, as the door slammed open into the wall beside its frame and then closed again.

It was a simple trick and probably way more startling

to whatever class was in that other room, but all the heads around me whipped in the direction of the sound, even Crowford's. With the second iteration, I murmured the longer casting I'd been waiting to use, fixing my gaze on my target's head.

"*In five minutes, talk about revealing magic to the Naries and relate it to this lesson. Make sure everyone understands what you've been doing to the Nary students.*"

Leaving it vague gave him room to approach the subject in the way that felt most natural to him, so it wouldn't be obvious he'd been compelled. Professor Crowford had taught me that technique too, sometime in the last few months. I guessed I should be a little grateful for his expertise even if I didn't like his other uses for it.

The door fell silent again. Crowford peeked out into the hall and exchanged a few words with someone outside. He came back in with a shake of his head. "Someone got bored, apparently. All right, back to our practice. Then I'll mix up your pairs. Those of you who didn't manage to make your casting work last time, start planning a new strategy for today."

Ugh. I didn't really want to be messing with anyone's thoughts just for the hell of it. What was the most innocuous thing I could think of? Maybe shift someone's favorite color for a little while? That shouldn't hurt anything, right?

After a few minutes, Crowford clapped his hands for attention and asked the students who'd been practicing to share their observations comparing today's class to the previous one. Before he'd even called on the guy I'd worked my magic on, my target raised his voice, interrupting someone else's answer.

"This technique would be even easier and stick even longer on feebs, wouldn't it?" he said.

Crowford gave him a wary look. "Generally speaking, yes, most spells are more effective on those with no magical defenses."

"That could be an amazing way to terrify them in the new sessions," the guy rambled on, his voice rising with his apparent excitement. "Show them how we can warp their minds right in front of them. They might freak out even more than over illusions and conjurings."

"Mr. Groving," Crowford said in an unusually firm voice. "I don't think—"

"We really should get everyone in on it already, shouldn't we?" the guy barreled on thanks to my magical encouragement. "Why shouldn't we all get that extra magical boost?" He gazed avidly around at his classmates. "It's amazing!"

The guy he'd been partnered with was frowning. "What are you talking about, man?"

"Yeah," a girl piped up. "What sessions? What are you doing with the Naries?"

Crowford motioned to us all with a wave of his hand, his mouth tightening. "This isn't the time for a discussion on this matter. Mr. Groving, if you'd please—"

"We've been getting small groups of the feebs and showing them enough magic to terrify them," the guy announced to the rest of the class. "It doesn't take much. The rush you get—"

Crowford's voice crackled through the room with a smack of persuasive power. "*Stop talking now.*"

The guy's mouth snapped shut. If he'd had any defenses up, the Persuasion professor would have been experienced enough to crack them. And he'd already fulfilled all of my orders, so there wasn't even my spell to clash with it.

That was fine. He'd done exactly what I needed.

"People have been showing the Naries their magic?" one of the other students said. "Isn't that, like, breaking the biggest rule here?"

Professor Crowford could obviously tell there was no making this out to be a misunderstanding. His smile came back, smoothly reassuring. "There's been an adjustment in policy that's slowly being rolled out while a few select groups evaluate the impact. It's nothing for the rest of you to be concerned about."

Fuck that. The barons had said they didn't want their heirs to know because we might sway the other students' opinions? I was going to make use of whatever sway I had right now.

"I think we have a lot of reason to be concerned," I said, letting conviction carry through my voice. "If the Naries are finding out about magic, that affects all of us. And does it really help us learn how to use our power effectively if we're taking an easy route we could never use on Naries in the real world?"

To my relief, some of the murmurs around me sounded like agreement. Another girl raised her voice, though.

"Why shouldn't we use the Naries while we're here, if it works that well? It sounds pretty amazing to me."

A couple of the other students nodded. I reached for the arguments that seemed most likely to get through to people who didn't necessarily care about the Naries' wellbeing. One thing most fearmancers I'd met had in common was a strong sense of pride.

"Shouldn't we be better than taking a route with so many risks for the entire community, just because it's easier in the moment? I think we all have the skills to manage our power without going around flaunting our magic at people who don't have any. We're not any weaker than all the generations of fearmancers before us, are we?"

A deep, forceful voice broke through the conflicted muttering. "What the fuck do you care about the community?" Connar glared straight at me. "You've hardly been in it for half a year. You care more about the Naries you were basically *living* with than you do about any fearmancer. You want to help them, not us."

A chill shot through me. I hadn't expected him to lash out at me in the classroom, on this subject or any other. Apparently my arguments had provoked something in the spell he was carrying that overrode the need to keep the peace in class.

"It's true," someone said, just loud enough for me to hear.

I swallowed hard. Connar had clout too—more than I did, probably, because everyone here had known him for years longer than they had me.

"This is my home now," I said as firmly as I could

manage. "I don't want to lose it, and I don't want to see us go down a path that'll hurt us in the long run."

Connar snorted with so much disgust I had to restrain a wince. "Sure. You haven't even been part of these sessions, have you? You're just assuming there are problems with them. It figures." He looked around at everyone else in the room. "Don't pay attention to her. She wants to rile you all up. We know what's good for us better than she does."

What could I say to that? I *hadn't* actually witnessed the sessions with the Naries. I *had* wanted to rile the class up against them. And I didn't have any proof of my claims, just my own standards of wrong and right.

Relief had crossed the faces of the other students as they watched Connar. They didn't want to feel uncomfortable about what their professors or fellow students were doing. An established scion had just given the new policy his seal of approval. That was all they needed.

I opened my mouth and caught myself. Anything I said would just give him another excuse to insult me. Until I found the right argument…

"How do we get in on these sessions?" one of the guys was asking Crowford.

"Yeah," the girl who'd first disagreed with me said. "I want to try it out."

My hands clenched under my desk. Instead of encouraging opposition to the new policy, I'd ended up setting the stage for a bunch of new supporters. More people eager to torment the Naries.

God, maybe it'd have been better if Shelby had stayed dismissed from school. I might have done more damage to her by influencing Jude into arranging for her return than losing her place had hurt her career. How much more agony were my fellow fearmancers going to put her through before she was done here?

And Connar was now not just taking jabs at me but egging on that agony. An ache spread through my gut. We couldn't let him go on like this any longer, not unless we were prepared to see him ruin more than we could fix.

CHAPTER TWENTY-ONE

Rory

Whatever worries dogged Jude these days, they followed him into sleep. I woke up to him rolling over on the bed with a yank of the covers and a wordless muttering. The bedroom of his Manhattan apartment was still and dark around us, only a hint of city noise penetrating the walls.

Jude's shoulders twitched, a shudder running down his back. He said something else, still in the jumbled language of sleep-talk, but more urgent sounding, as if he were giving a warning. I eased upright on the firm mattress to squint at him through the darkness. His eyes were definitely closed, his brow knit beneath the mussed fall of his floppy hair.

He flinched and rolled onto his back again with another frantic mumbling, and I couldn't stand to keep watching. "Jude," I said gently, touching the side of his head.

He snapped awake, a shout escaping his lips, his arm flailing out and smacking me across the stomach. I couldn't contain a startled gasp, although the impact had barely stung. Jude stared at me, blinking blearily as he woke the rest of the way up, and then shoved himself into a sitting position.

"Fuck. I'm so sorry. I didn't mean to—it was automatic. I don't know what the hell was going on in my head."

"It's okay. I'm fine." I slipped my arm around him, leaning closer when he tensed. "Really. You didn't hurt me. And it's my fault for waking you up out of the blue. You just—you looked like you were having a pretty bad dream."

"Yeah." He returned the embrace, starting to relax into me but still partly on edge.

"Do you want to talk about it?"

He let out a hoarse chuckle. "Not really. It's all kind of a blur now anyway. And you already know about everything in my life that's likely to give me nightmares. I was hoping it wouldn't happen with you here."

So, he'd been having those kinds of dreams a lot. My heart squeezed, and I hugged him tighter. He'd put on a believable carefree front during the drive out here and our late-night dinner, but glossing over his more fraught emotions was what Jude did best.

He'd seemed to sleep all right the first time I'd stayed the night here, but that'd been weeks ago. The looming threat of his supposed father must be weighing on him even more. It couldn't help that with my mother back, there was one more authority figure who'd want to punish Baron Killbrook's crime.

There were other people who'd help defend Jude if he'd give them the chance. I dipped my head to press a kiss to his shoulder. "Declan and Malcolm know you've moved out now. Are you going to tell them why? They can help keep an eye out for any interference from your family."

Jude grimaced. "Or they could toss me out of the pentacle so fast my head'll spin. Arguing with my dad is a lot more acceptable than not even being his son."

"Do you really think they'd shun you like that? Look at how hard they're working to help Connar."

"That's different. Connar's still a scion; spells can be broken. There's nothing that'd make me a real Killbrook."

"I don't think the name is going to matter that much. Do you really think that's what's most important to them?"

Jude hesitated for a moment. "I don't know," he admitted. "But if it is, it won't be much fun finding out." He pulled me closer, tucking my legs over his lap, and nuzzled my cheek. "I have you. You know how much that matters to *me*, don't you, Rory? As long as I'm all right in your eyes, who the hell cares what anyone else thinks?"

"You're a lot more than all right," I had to say.

He kissed me, and I melted into him at the passionate tenderness of his mouth against mine. But a kiss wasn't enough to completely distract me. When our lips parted, I nestled my head against the crook of his neck and rested my hand on his bare chest.

"You know," I said carefully, "even if we got married when we're old enough to, and the other guys go on to have their own lives, and I'm just with you… I don't think it'd be a good thing for me to be the only person you can turn to. I want to be here for you as much as I can, but I *am* just one person—and what if something happens to me, or—"

Jude's arms tensed around me. "*Nothing* is going to happen to you," he insisted with so much vehemence it was like he was trying to turn the statement into a spell to ensure that.

My throat constricted. "You can't know that for sure. And even if nothing does, you deserve to have more people in your life you can open up to. There's nothing wrong with you, no matter what some fearmancer snobs might think about it."

"Too bad so many of them are snobs," Jude said with a tight laugh. He ran his lithe fingers over my hair. "I've been thinking about it. I just haven't decided yet. And whatever happens to *me*, you're not responsible for that, okay? You don't owe me anything, and I'm not in this to heap all my troubles on you."

"I know."

"Good." He paused. "Since we're awake now anyway… Do you want to see something? It might not fix all my problems, but it's a possibility for making a future that's got nothing to do with being a Killbrook."

A tingle of anxiety passed from him to me, as if he was

afraid of my reaction. I reached for his hand instinctively to give it a reassuring squeeze. "Of course. What is it?"

"I'll show you. It's not remotely definite yet... just something I've started looking into. I think it could be really good, though."

He tugged me off the bed and into the dim living room where his laptop lay on the coffee table. With a few clicks, he brought up a website with video clips. He played one, which showed a scene from a movie where two actors soared through the air as they clashed swords against each other, and another where one of those actors summoned a demonic looking creature from a jar.

"Some of the 'lesser' fearmancer families have gone in together on a movie studio," Jude explained. "Nothing huge—they might be able to pull off one or two films a year—but they're bringing on mages to handle the special effects: physicality specialists for things like that flying stunt, and illusionists to create visuals from scratch. Costs a lot less than needing a bunch of stunt-people and computer experts, which'll give them an edge."

"Wow," I said. "And you're thinking you'd join in?" They'd be lucky to have Jude. He might not have the same power at his disposal as the actual scions, but as far as I knew, no one at Blood U could top him when it came to illusions.

"We'll see. I still need to finish school before I commit to anything, and for all we know the company will have gone under by then. They're still working out some snags like whether they can manage to involve Nary actors while still keeping the secrets of their process under wraps. But

I've been chatting with a couple of the founders." He snapped the laptop shut. "Not the kind of magical work that people like Baron Killbrook would see as worthwhile, but…"

"But why worry about assholes like him?" I filled in for him. "It looks like an amazing opportunity. I had no idea mages were getting involved in industries like that."

"I think some of them are getting tired of the idea the prominent families push about high finance business ventures being the only valid career path," Jude said dryly, but his face had lit up at my approval. "Anyway, the last thing I want to do is loaf around living off money that used to be Killbrook funds. I've got to make some kind of future for myself."

"Of course you will." Contemplating the future made my throat close up again. I gripped Jude's hand harder. "Do you think we'll be able to snap Connar out of it? If the intervention tomorrow doesn't work… I don't know what else we can try." After I'd told the other scions about what had happened during my last class with Connar, we'd agreed it was time to come at the problem with everything we had. Tomorrow evening, we'd get him alone, subdue him as well as we could, and bring all our magic to bear on unraveling the spell.

If we didn't have enough power to overcome his mother's magic, then not only would we be out of options, but Connar would also be ten times as furious with all of us. How long would he have to live with his mother's spell warping his mind? What kind of future could *he* have like that?

"The four of us should be more than up to the task," Jude said, but his confidence sounded a little forced. He wrapped his arms around me. "Baron Stormhurst doesn't stand a chance with you in the mix."

Waiting for the evening to come so we could tackle Connar's spell was made only slightly easier by having something else important to occupy myself with in the meantime. Just past lunch time, I crouched in the woods around the Casting Grounds next to Declan, the sharp scent of the fallen leaves prickling my nose.

The Nary session that Professor Crowford had told Malcolm about was due to start in a quarter of an hour. I intended to make sure it was much less enjoyable for the fearmancer students than the previous ones appeared to have been. If words wouldn't convince them, then maybe it'd take some action.

"You won't be able to stop them from casting completely," Declan said quietly. He couldn't stick around, because it'd look pretty bad for a near-baron to be found interfering with his colleagues' plans, but he'd come along to offer guidance beforehand. "By watching, you should be able to tell pretty quickly who the more powerful mages are. Focus on them, and use a mix of persuasion and physicality techniques to throw off their focus or interrupt the effects of their spells. Once they're having trouble, the other students will start to notice and become unsettled too."

I nodded. "And if I can make it look as if the extra power made them lose control of their spells, even better."

"Exactly." He glanced around and tugged me a little farther to the right. "You'll have a clearer view here. I can cast an illusion to help disguise you so you don't need to drain any of your own magic beforehand."

"Thanks."

As he stood up to cast the spell, my gaze followed him, lingering on the concentration that steadied his handsome face, the confident tones with which he spoke his casting words. Declan was never grandiose or flamboyant with his magic, but the other barons shouldn't underestimate him. I could feel the controlled power in every movement he made. The subtlety of it made it even more impressive to watch.

When he'd finished, he stepped into the clearing briefly to evaluate the spell's effectiveness. "Totally hidden," he announced as he returned to me, and hesitated. "I'd stay if the politics weren't so fraught."

I waved him off. "It's totally fine. I know I'm taking a risk messing with the new policy, but I'm nowhere near baron yet now, and I'm the only Bloodstone heir, so it's not as if they could replace me. Your situation is way more precarious. I wouldn't want you to put yourself in that position."

"I still wish I could be here to see it." He knelt down and kissed me, quick but determined with his fingers tracing along my jaw. "Look after yourself. Your situation might be less precarious, but you could still get into trouble."

"I'll be watching my back."

He slipped away through the trees, and I settled into my stake-out spot, the gaps between the scrawny shrubs ahead of me giving me a decent view of most of the clearing ahead. The smooth bark of the sapling I rested my hand against was cool but not uncomfortably so. The peaceful sounds of birds chirping overhead and the faint rustle of the breeze through the leaves gave no hint of the torture that was about to take place here.

Footsteps broke that peace. Figures tramped into the clearing from the direction of the school—several fearmancers and as many Nary students, Professor Crowford at the back. He scanned the trees around the clearing, probably wondering if Malcolm was observing the way the Nightwood scion had apparently suggested he would. The Persuasion professor's gaze skimmed right over my hiding spot.

To make sure he wouldn't get the blame for my meddling today, Malcolm would be descending on the junior cafeteria right now to awe the younger students with some scion advice within full view of at least a few professors.

"What are we doing out here?" one of the Nary students asked. They all looked puzzled. The fearmancer students drifted around them with a glint in their eyes I could only describe as predatory, like a pack of wolves circling a herd of sheep.

None of them appeared to have any qualms about what they were about to do. No, I didn't see anything other than eager anticipation on those faces. It made my stomach turn.

I was supposed to rule these people someday. Didn't they realize they were proving every awful idea the joymancers had about us right by participating in something like this?

"We needed room for a little demonstration," Crowford said in a casual tone. He tipped his head to the students, and just like that, they launched into their spells.

So many casting words filled the air at the same time that it was hard to catch all of them. An illusion of a monstrous figure loomed over two of the Naries, gnashing blood-drenched teeth. One of the nearby trees leaned forward to swipe at others with a jagged branch.

"*Punch her*," one fearmancer ordered, pointing from one boy to the girl beside him, and the boy swung his fist immediately even as he cried out in protest, not having any way to fend off the persuasive compulsion.

The Naries shrieked and stumbled, spinning around as if looking for a way to flee. Someone conjured a ring of fire around the edge of the clearing, probably real from the heat that wafted from it all the way to my face.

Crowford watched it all, smirking. Some of the fearmancer students laughed, all of them glowing with elation at the fearful energy that must have been rushing into them faster than they'd ever have felt before. They'd never had the chance to terrorize anyone quite this thoroughly.

Ignoring my rising queasiness, I focused on the magic

thrumming in my own chest. They wouldn't be feeling quite so triumphant for long.

With a hushed word, I made the animated tree lurch so it smacked one of the fearmancers in the chest, knocking him off his feet. As he let out a startled shout, I burst apart one horrifying illusion and then another. The boy who'd been relying on persuasion opened his mouth to give another command, and I whispered one to him instead. *"Prevent the other mages from casting any way you can."*

He ran at the girl next to him, clapping his hand over her mouth before she could speak a spell. I was about to turn my attention onto the flames licking over the grass, but at the same moment, Professor Crowford stepped deeper into the chaos of the clearing. He was eyeing the forest again. His lips moved with the start of a casting.

Shit. I scrambled backward as quietly as I could. A wave of quivering energy rushed over me as he must have sent some sort of spell over the whole area—to detect where the opposing magic was coming from? To shatter any spells that were protecting me?

I couldn't risk hanging around to find out. I dashed through the trees, hoping I'd fled fast enough to avoid him seeing me—and that my brief sabotage had shaken up the students enough to make them question whether it'd be wise to continue using their new source of fear.

CHAPTER TWENTY-TWO

Rory

"Oof," Shelby said with a hand on her belly as we emerged from the forest path onto campus. "It's going to take a lot more walking to burn off that dinner. But totally worth it."

I laughed and licked my lips, tasting the lingering custard sweetness from the dessert we'd split. Getting it at all after the already substantial dinner might have been overly ambitious. My own stomach felt full to bulging. But the new restaurant that had just opened in town was definitely going on my favorites list.

"Gotta indulge every now and then," I said. "We work hard."

"We do." Shelby nodded emphatically. "Speaking of which, I really need to get some more practice in on that new piece. Are you coming back to the dorm?"

I'd thought I was, but as we passed Killbrook Hall, my

gaze caught on an unexpected figure waiting in the middle of the green. My mother's dark eyes took in me and Shelby, no doubt noting the scholarship pin on my friend's blouse, before she turned away as if she had no interest in either of us.

My body tensed. I knew better than to go by that gesture. She was just avoiding making any kind of a scene in front of my classmates, but she wouldn't be standing around there unless she was waiting for me.

"I just remembered something I need to grab," I said to Shelby. "I'll see you up there later."

Maybe not for a while later. I checked my phone as I walked over to join my mother. Operation: Save Connar was supposed to come together in a little less than an hour. That was, assuming Malcolm could cajole the Stormhurst scion into the lounge in the first place.

"What's going on?" I asked, coming up beside my mother. "If I'd known you wanted to see me, I'd have made sure to be around."

Baron Bloodstone's mouth slanted at a doubtful angle. Her gaze slid over me, not exactly *cold* but with a distance she hadn't shown me in the past. Before she'd even said anything, the hairs on the back of my neck had risen.

Something was wrong, and it had something to do with me.

"Come along," she said in a similarly detached tone. "We have a few things to discuss, Persephone."

I could think of a number of things she might have decided to approach me about, none of which were good. Trying to weasel out of the conversation now wasn't going to earn me any points. She motioned toward Nightwood Tower, and I walked over with her, bracing myself.

My mother didn't say anything else as she pushed into the hall and led the way not up toward the classrooms but down to the basement room where the Desensitization sessions were held. I guessed that space had more guarantee of privacy. Still, the cooler air washing over my skin and the faint buzz of the artificial lights set my nerves even more on edge. I'd gotten better control over my reactions to the illusions the chamber showed me, but I'd had a lot of unpleasant experiences down here.

No sessions were running this late in the day, but Professor Razeden was sitting on one of the benches outside the chamber, flipping through a notebook. His head jerked up at our arrival. He sprang to his feet, undisguised wariness crossing his gaunt face at the sight of my mother.

"Baron," he said with a dip of his head. "What can I—"

"My daughter and I will be making use of this space for some time," my mother said, flicking her hand toward the Desensitization chamber. She strode over and opened the door without waiting for his response.

Razeden's throat bobbed. His eyes caught mine searchingly, but I didn't know what to tell him.

"Any activities conducted in there, it's best if I oversee them," he said quickly. "If you're simply looking for an out-of-the-way place to talk, I can vacate the hall here and see that you're not disturbed."

A definite chill crept into my mother's voice. "That

won't be necessary. I remember the procedures well enough."

I followed her into the domed chamber, resisting the growing urge to hug myself. The baron shut the door firmly behind us. I knew from past sessions that no sound penetrated the thick stone walls, painted as black as the floor behind our feet. The light at the peak of the dome shone over us with an eerie glow.

I hung back by the door. It was in the center of the space that the illusions took hold. They wouldn't start up unless activated, but I had no desire to remind myself of those times in any way.

My mother spun to face me. "I thought we had thoroughly covered your concerns about the new school policy the last time we spoke. Lying to avoid a difficult discussion with me should be beneath you, Persephone."

A finger of ice slid down my spine. This was about the Naries, then, one way or another. It didn't seem wise to give her more information that she might already have.

"I'm not sure what you mean," I said carefully.

Her gaze bored into me. There were no drafts in the tightly sealed chamber, but enough magic raced through her body that the energy alone stirred her hair where it grazed her shoulders. My pulse skittered, probably helping fuel that energy.

This woman was my mother, but she was also the most powerful of the elite fearmancers that ruled over us. And clearly her imprisonment hadn't diminished her ability to wield that power.

"We need to get a few things straight," she said. "I

realize I haven't been a part of your life for most of it, and that you found your footing in this world without having to take my perspective into account. But I am here now. I'm both your mother and your baron, and you will respect those roles. If you have questions or concerns, you come to me, and we'll talk them through until you're satisfied. You do *not* spread ideas or take actions that go against our family's goals behind my back."

I couldn't hold back a shiver at the furor rising in her voice. "Of course not," I said. "If you could tell me where I went wrong—"

Anger flashed in her eyes, and my mouth snapped shut. Her shoulders had gone rigid.

"Do you expect me to believe you don't know? You spoke out against using the feebs in front of an entire class —vehemently, from what I understand. I have reason to believe you also directly interfered with a session involving them this morning. I know you're not so stupid as to believe I'd approve of either of those instances. Don't treat me as if *I'm* stupid enough not to see that."

I fumbled for my tongue. My voice came out barely above a whisper. "I know you're not stupid. I—I was only giving my opinion in class." I wasn't going to address this morning. It didn't sound like she had definite proof it'd been me. She was either guessing based on my first transgression, or Professor Crowford had gotten a glimpse of me that hadn't been clear enough for certainty.

"Your opinion that we should stay weak and let the Naries lord over us and this world." My mother jabbed her finger at me. It shook for an instant before steadying.

"That's not how a Bloodstone thinks. That's not how you should have been raised. Those damned joymancers taught you nothing but how to be afraid—of your power, of your people, of using the people who weren't worthy of being granted the same talents we have."

"That's not—"

"You'll learn to cope with those fears and rise above them to take your proper place," she said, cutting me off. The gleam in her eyes had gone wild. "However many times it takes until you understand. This is what you *need*. Take your spot, now." She pointed to the middle of the room.

My legs balked, every inch of my skin crawling with the longing to get away from her while she was in this state. "No," I said, reaching for the door. "I won't—"

"*Walk to the center of the chamber, no more arguing,*" my mother snapped out. A sear of persuasive magic sliced through my mental shields as if they'd been made of tissue paper. It felt as if the spell stabbed right into my brain with a cold shock of pain rattling my thoughts. Before I could even process that, my feet were moving, carrying me to the spot she'd indicated.

"Mom." The word broke from my throat like a plea. It was the first time I'd ever called her that, shocked out of me by the terror racing up inside me, as if the woman I was calling out to wasn't the same person causing that terror.

Something stuttered in my mother's expression, but so briefly I couldn't have said whether it was sympathy or disgust or something else altogether. "Begin!" she hollered at the room, her hand already on the doorknob. The light blinked out. Through the darkness came the sound of the door thudding.

She'd left me alone. Alone in this place with whatever would rise up to—

Forms were already emerging from the darkness, lit up with an unnatural glow that didn't diminish my horror. My mother stood over Shelby, sprawled slack on a table. She lifted a glinting knife over my friend's body.

"No!" I cried, throwing myself at them. My mother jerked her fingers, and the air closed around me like a vise. She plunged the knife into Shelby's chest.

Blood spurted up and splashed across Shelby's clothes, the floor, my face. The sticky substance burned my skin as my nose clogged with the metallic smell. My stomach lurched.

My mother dug the knife deeper. A gristly sound filled my ears. My muscles strained against the magical hold, and something clicked in my head beneath the panic.

This was just one more Desensitization illusion. None of it was real. I knew how to deal with this scenario now. My mother's declaration had put me so off-balance that I'd reacted out of emotion rather than any mental preparation. I could get back the calm I needed and push away the horrors.

I closed my eyes and stopped resisting the invisible vise around me. The bloody smell filled my lungs with each slow breath, but I kept up their even pace anyway. "You can't really hurt her like that," I said in the steadiest voice I could manage. "I won't let you. I'll protect her. Nothing that happens in here has anything to do with the world out there."

The stink started to fade. The sounds fell away. After a few more breaths, I let myself open my eyes.

The illusion hadn't disappeared. My mother was still standing there, motionless now, over Shelby's gutted body. I opened my mouth to repeat the mantra I'd just said, this time to her face, and two more figures plunged out of the darkness that surrounded us.

One of them was the woman I'd always thought of as Mom. The other was the man who'd tried to blast me and ended up disintegrating Deborah when I'd fled the joymancer headquarters last month. They lunged at my mother from both sides, conjured blades shimmering in their hands. A sound of protest broke from my throat an instant before they stabbed those weapons into my mother's back.

She crumpled, but the violence didn't stop there. The man hurtled onward and slashed his blade through Mom's chest the way the fearmancers had all those months ago. Both of my mothers, the one in practice and the one by birth, collapsed on the floor in a gush of blood.

My heart wrenched. I spun around, trying to focus my breaths again. "It's not real," I reminded myself. "None of this is happening. None of this matters. It can't touch me or anyone I care about."

A gurgled breath rose up behind me. I winced and trained my mind harder on the memory of the empty room, the black stillness of it. A gasp of pain rang out, just as clear as before.

Nothing was working. Had my mother intensified the spells on the chamber somehow, added power to them to make them even harder to subdue? Was I stuck in here until she decided to come back and release me?

How long would *that* take? I had to get out—I was supposed to be helping Connar—the guys couldn't pull off our plan without me there.

With a quiver of inspiration, my hand rose up to touch the dragon charm on my necklace. The magic in the chamber was a combination of insight and illusion spells. The insight part couldn't hurt me if it didn't generate the illusions. If I activated the spell on my charm, it'd show the falseness of the illusions, prevent them from working on my mind anymore.

But Professor Burnbuck had warned me when he'd placed the spell that it wouldn't work indefinitely. I'd get a limited number of uses before I drained its power. Challenging the entire Desensitization chamber would probably take a lot.

Connar didn't just need me. He needed this necklace too. I couldn't take the chance that I'd use up the rest of that magic on myself.

Probably drawn from my immediate thoughts, yet another form stepped forward. Connar glared at me, his chiseled jaw so tightly clenched the sinews stood out in his neck. I straightened my posture, committing to enduring what the chamber threw at me for as long as I could.

It wasn't enough just to brace myself. The Stormhurst scion charged at me with a snarl, shoving me so hard that I stumbled backward with the force of the impact even though it was all in my head. My heels jarred against something on the floor—one of my mother's bodies?—and skidded on tacky blood. I tripped and only just managed to fling myself to the side so I landed on bare floor rather than right on top of a corpse.

"Traitor!" Connar shouted at me. "You useless fucking bitch!" He swung a kick at my side, and pain slammed through my ribs. I scrambled away—and found myself crouched next to yet another body, this one cold and tinted black and blue where the flesh was starting to rot.

Imogen. A putrid stench filled my nose. I gagged and backpedaled, and she sat up with a jerk, her eyes snapping open, pale and filmy. She stared at me. Bile spilled from her lips when she opened her mouth.

"You killed me. Murderer. Some fucking friend. Making stupid promises you never intend to keep. You care too much about keeping *yourself* safe. Who cares about worthless Imogen?"

"No," I couldn't help gasping out. "I didn't—I never thought that way. If I'd known they were going to come after you—"

Connar hadn't vanished with Imogen's arrival. My fears were multiplying on themselves rather than the chamber focusing on just one. "That's right," he hollered at me. "Stay down on your hands and knees where you belong. You don't deserve to stand with us after what you've done."

The hurled insults and the awful mingling smells were making me dizzy. I shoved myself away to a clear spot of floor and hunched there with my face pressed to my knees and my arms wrapped around my legs. Not a graceful pose by any means, but the most impenetrable ball I could form.

All I had to do was wait it out. All I had to do was listen to the rasp of my breath and tune out the sneers and the smell and, oh god, the viscous liquid seeping under me and soaking through my dress—

It didn't matter. It wasn't real. It wasn't true. Not at all. Not at all.

Someone yanked at my hair, smacked the side of my head. The smell thickened. I hugged myself tighter, repeating those words over and over to myself. The rest of my thoughts were fragmenting with panic and despair.

It was too much. Somewhere in there, my mind blanked out.

I came back to myself with a spill of light over me and a waft of fresher air. A hand rested tentatively on my shoulder. I realized I was rocking in place, my cheeks damp and eyes aching from tears I hadn't noticed falling. My neck ached when I raised my head.

Professor Razeden was kneeling next to me, his mouth bent at an anguished angle. "It's all right," he said in his dry voice, not quite as even as it usually was. "It's over now. I—I'm sorry. Your mother put a spell on the door to stop anyone from opening it. I didn't have the skill to unravel it. It took even Isla quite a while to break through."

He glanced up, and I followed his gaze to the other teacher in the room. Professor Viceport was standing over us, her stance rigid, her face even more sallow than usual. I tensed automatically at the sight of my mentor. If it'd been a physicality spell sealing the door, it made sense that Razeden would have gone to her, but I couldn't imagine this incident was improving her opinion of me.

I swiped hastily at my eyes and moved to stand. My legs wobbled, cramped from having stayed in that awkward position. Razeden grasped my arm gently to help me up.

"Thank you," I said to both of them, fighting the urge to cringe at the thought of the state they'd found me in. "I tried to think my way through it the way we're supposed to—it just didn't work."

"The chamber's magic isn't meant to be amplified," Razeden muttered, confirming my suspicions.

My gaze darted toward the open doorway. "Is she still here?" My voice quavered despite myself.

Razeden's grip firmed with a reassuring squeeze. "As far as I know, she left campus as soon as she'd finished with you here."

"Okay." No relief came with that knowledge. What did it matter whether my mother was here right now? She'd outright told me that she'd do this all over again until I was acting the way she expected of her heir.

My arms crossed over my chest again. The words spilled out on the back of a wave of fear. "I don't know what to do. I can't be the person she wants me to be. I—"

I forced my mouth to close before I could babble any more of the desperate thoughts racing through my mind. *I'm not strong enough. I can't stand up to her.*

But I had to. I'd find a way. I was still a fucking

Bloodstone. Even if right now I felt like a stone that'd been shattered into too many pieces to fit myself back together.

Viceport's gaze darted to the floor and then back to me. Something passed through her expression. Was that a… flinch? Her jaw worked.

"I'm sorry," she said abruptly. "I haven't been the support you've needed—I haven't done my job as your mentor or your professor anywhere near as well as I should have. That was unfair of me. We should set another meeting, soon, so we can get properly on track. And if there's anything I can offer you right now…"

Right now. Those words cut through my surprise at her admission and the shakiness that still gripped me. There was somewhere I was supposed to be.

"What time is it?" I blurted out.

Both of the professors blinked at me. Razeden murmured a casting word. "Eight o'clock," he said.

Urgency rattled my nerves. I'd been shut up in the chamber for nearly an hour. "I've got to go," I said. "I—I'll set up that meeting as soon as I have time." Then I was dashing for the stairs, hoping I wasn't too late.

CHAPTER TWENTY-THREE

Rory

There was no sign of any of the scions when I burst into Ashgrave Hall. I walked as swiftly as I could to the door to the lounge stairs, not wanting to draw too many stares from the other students I passed, and then raced down those steps as fast as my feet would carry me.

When I barreled through the doorway, just Jude and Declan were standing there by the threshold waiting. "There you are!" Jude said triumphantly as Declan let out a sigh of relief.

"I'm sorry," I said, reaching to unclasp the silver chain from around my neck. "I—I got held up." There wasn't time to get into the punishment my mother had subjected me to.

Declan was already tapping a message into his phone. "Malcolm was able to dawdle for a few minutes since you hadn't arrived," he said. "As soon as I give him the signal, he'll get Connar over here."

"Connar's still listening to him?" I asked.

"Well, Malcolm hasn't announced an epic failure yet, so at the very least he hasn't given up," Jude said in a chipper tone that had a manic edge. He bobbed on his feet as he stepped closer to his post right next to the door. As the illusions expert among us, he was going to be the key player in unraveling this spell once we'd subdued Connar… if we even managed to do that much.

None of the guys had spelled it out when we were discussing the plan, but I could tell they were all nervous about trying to restrain a guy who was both physically stronger than any of them and a master of Physicality. Who knew how the rage built into his parents' spell would fire him up on top of that? We'd all have preferred to find some way to get through to him without launching what he'd take as a full-out attack, but there didn't seem to be any options left.

If this worked, the temporary distress we'd put him and ourselves through would be worth it.

Declan braced himself by the other side of the door, and I stepped off to the side beyond the entertainment system, so Connar wouldn't be able to see me until he was already inside. My fingers closed around either end of the necklace. My part in this first stage of the plan was going to be plenty challenging too.

A minute slipped by, and then another. A prickle ran down my back. I was just starting to worry that maybe Malcolm's nonmagical persuasive techniques hadn't managed to win his best friend over enough to get Connar all the way to us when footsteps sounded on the stairs. Both Jude and Declan tensed. I readied myself, the metal links digging into my fingertips.

"I don't really see why you're so convinced—" Connar was saying as he pushed open the door.

Declan and Jude rattled off casting words simultaneously. Malcolm's voice carried from behind Connar. The Stormhurst scion winced and froze in place with an awkward stiffness as if he'd been wrapped in invisible bindings—which technically, he had.

"What the fuck—" he started to demand as Malcolm stepped in and shut the door. I hurried toward him, and Connar's gaze caught on me. So much fury lit in his eyes that it might as well have scalded me.

He spat out a casting word of his own, his muscles flexing all across his brawny body. The other guys called out to reinforce their spell, but not quickly enough. Connar's limbs wrenched away from their hold.

He lunged at me with a snarl and rage contorting his face. He looked… he looked like he had when the illusion of him had battered me in the Desensitization chamber less than an hour ago.

My heart stopped. The impulse shot through me to turn tail and run, to get as far away from the guy rampaging toward me as I could. In that instant, I could believe he'd happily tear me to pieces—and that he was capable of doing that in a matter of seconds.

This must have been what his brother had faced when their parents' torment had pushed Connar over the edge.

He didn't want this. He wasn't in control. He'd have *hated* the way they were using him.

That thought helped me hold my ground. I jerked my hands up, putting all my trust in the other scions' support.

Malcolm threw himself at Connar with a rough word that seemed to tangle the Stormhurst scion's feet. As Connar lurched, he shoved Malcolm so hard the other guy smacked into the sofa with a pained grunt. Jude and Declan were hollering too. Connar spun around, lashing out with his fists, one of them connecting with Jude's jaw before he could dodge all the way clear. Jude's head snapped around, his shoulder slamming into the wall.

Declan threw out another hoarse word, and Connar's arms momentarily stilled. His lips parted to form another casting. My pulse stuttered. "Shut!" I shouted with a jab of guilt through my gut as Malcolm barked a casting word that I suspected had the same effect.

Between the two of our efforts, a magical force clamped on Connar's mouth. His eyes blazed. His muscles bulged beneath his shirt as he fought the bindings the only way he could, and even in that second I saw him regain a little movement.

In whatever time I had to see this through, I leapt forward and slung the chain around his neck. Connar swung his head at me in an attempt to crack my skull with his. I whipped myself as far to the side as I could, but his forehead glanced off my temple. Pain radiated through my face. My fingers fumbled with the chain.

My head spinning, I gripped the necklace with all my might and jammed my thumb down on the clasp. The click of the pieces joining was the most welcome sound I'd ever heard. I yanked my hands back, pausing for just long enough to press the two trigger points on the charm before letting it fall against Connar's chest.

As I darted backward, out of range if his arms wrenched free again, he strained against the magic for a moment longer. Then the fury in his expression started to dim. He blinked, his stance going slack, his forehead furrowing.

I spoke a quick word to let him speak again.

"What?" he mumbled. "I—There was—"

Jude had recovered, rubbing his jaw where a red blotch had already formed from the punch. "We're going to make things a whole lot clearer for you, big guy. Just hold steady."

"I don't… What's going on?"

His bewilderment made my chest ache. We gathered closer around him now that he wasn't fighting us. Malcolm moved in front of him to meet his eyes. His voice came out with the lilt of a gentle persuasion spell. "*Focus on me.* This could take some time, but we're doing everything we can to help you. It'll be okay. *Relax as well as you can.*"

Connar let out a shuddering breath. Jude, Declan, and I started to murmur together, focusing our attention on the quiver of magic we could all sense housed at the base of Connar's spine. I was the strongest at physicality magic after Connar, so we'd decided that I would work on breaking apart the bodily construct while Jude tackled the illusion elements of the spell and Declan pitched in where he seemed most needed.

We were all on guard for some sort of secondary effect once we disabled the main spell. I had no idea what Connar's parents might have decided was appropriate for that purpose, but the barons had included a little surprise in Professor Banefield's spell, so it was hard to believe they'd pass up the opportunity to cause even more damage if they could.

"Damn, that's a messed up one," Jude muttered. He spoke a few more casting words, his brow knitting with concentration.

"Conducting," I said to myself under my breath, drawing even more of my thoughts toward the spot where Connar's parents had lodged the spell. I could trace the shape of it with the magic I'd extended: a small raised mark like Banefield's mole, hollowed in just the right way to contain and amplify the spell they'd placed in it, just like the traditional conducting pieces made out of stone or metal.

When I'd destroyed the spell on my former mentor, I'd only managed it by summoning up all the determination and frustrated emotion I had in me. My anger at Connar's parents and my concern for him were already stewing inside me.

I thought back to the way he'd reacted the first time he'd seen me after I'd gotten back from California, to his violent reaction after discovering me in the lounge the other day, to his hostile disdain in Professor Crowford's classroom. With each memory, I grasped onto the anguish that surged up, until my hands had clenched and my breath was coming short.

I sent my mind back to the little tour of the Fortress of the Pentacle that my mother had given me—to the cold satisfaction on Baron Stormhurst's face, knowing the pain she was putting us all through. To my mother herself, abandoning me in the Desensitization chamber to face that pain and others expanded in horrifying brutality.

We would stop them. We *had* to stop them, here and in every other way they were tearing apart the things I actually supported in the fearmancer world.

Connar stirred. His arm twitched where the binding spell still held it by his side. "I don't like it," he said, an edge coming back into his voice. "Stop it—let me go."

His parents' magic hadn't been only illusionary. My necklace wouldn't stop the other factors from acting on him—and even the illusions would burn out the charm's power if they kept rising up often enough. We might not have much time.

I willed all the fervor in me through the thrum of magic collected behind my collarbone and out with my voice. "Get out!" I commanded.

The words came out ragged. The spot of energy jittered but didn't budge. I gathered myself even more and poured every ounce of my energy into the casting. "Get *out*! Break and deflate! Begone and get the fuck away from him!"

A crackle raced through that last demand. Through the blast of my magic, I felt the construct snap. Jude let out a victorious cry and intoned another hasty word. Malcolm was trying to talk Connar down, and Declan was murmuring his own spells, and the toxic magic that had possessed Connar spilled out of him like the breaking of a boil.

I had just enough time to enjoy one jolt of victory before Connar roared and magic blazed over us like a thunderclap.

He whipped around, faster than any guy that bulky had the right to move, socking Malcolm in the face and Declan in the gut before any of us even blinked. The aftershock of the spell's destruction had split apart our own spells on him and, from the looks of things, enraged him twice as much as before.

All of us shouted out words to renew his bindings, stumbling out of his reach at the same time. He shoved the sofa so hard it toppled over onto its back and sent a kick into the shelf of video games that smashed one shelf. Then he hurtled toward Jude.

Panic lanced through me. "Stop!" I snapped out. "Block him." Whatever I'd managed to conjure alongside the other guys, it made Connar's stride lurch. He fell to his knees and then shoved forward again.

"Calm," I said, pouring more of my magic into his body as well as I could. "Cool." This fury couldn't last without the conducting construct maintaining it—it had to burn out. But not necessarily all that soon if we couldn't find a way to simmer it down.

The others must have been taking a similar tactic. Connar faltered in mid-stride, the ferocious light fading from his eyes. He wavered on his feet.

Slowly, he turned to look around at us. His shoulders came down, his hands drifting back to his sides. The others said a few more words, and the Stormhurst scion stopped moving completely, just staring at us.

As his expression softened and his gaze cleared, I saw the guy I knew fully there for the first time in over a week. My heart skipped a beat.

"Connar?" I said cautiously.

His attention shifted to me. In that moment, he looked so lost that tears crept up behind my eyes at the sight.

"Rory?" he croaked. "I don't know what's going on. What are we doing here? What *happened* to me?"

He pressed the heel of his hand to his forehead as if to push back a headache.

Malcolm grasped his shoulder. "It's good to have you back, Conn," he said, sounding a tad choked up himself. "Your parents cast a hell of a spell on you. You'll need to take some time to rest and recover now."

Connar glanced at the sofa, at the broken shelf, at the bruise forming on Jude's jaw. "I was fighting you." His voice came out hollow with shock.

"Thankfully, the four of us were just barely a match for one of you," Jude said lightly. He motioned to Declan, and they righted the sofa together. At Malcolm's nudge, Connar sank down on it. He touched his temple again.

"It's all so muddled."

His gaze sought me out. He opened his mouth and then hesitated as if afraid of how I might react to whatever he was going to say. I swallowed thickly and eased onto the sofa next to him, tipping my head against his shoulder and wrapping my arm around his torso. In the first instant as I touched him, my body braced, still expecting him to recoil. When he didn't, I leaned into him, soaking in his warmth and offering my own in return.

His arm slid around my back, and then he was hugging me to him as if his life depended on doing so. I closed my eyes, drank in his smoky scent, and fought back a sob for what might have happened if we'd failed. For the state the spell had left him in even though we'd succeeded.

CHAPTER TWENTY-FOUR

Connar

Nothing had ever felt quite as right as having Rory in my arms. Her body was soft but solid against mine, each rise and fall of her breath coming with a faint rasp that showed the exertion she'd put herself through, her familiar caramel-sweet smell washing over me.

Everything about her presence was so perfectly real compared to the chaos flitting this way and that in my head. I might as well have been seeing my own memories through an insight spell rather than directly, a mishmash of impressions I couldn't make sense of.

Rory was in some of them. I'd been *angry* with her, for reasons I couldn't decipher now. From the glimpses that came to me of her face, I suspected I'd thrown that anger at her in awful ways.

At my friends too. They'd all come together, they'd snapped me out of the hazy nightmare of my recent existence, even though I couldn't remember being anything but antagonistic or suspicious around them in… in however long it'd been.

"I'm sorry," I said, my voice partly muffled where I'd bowed my head by Rory's. My lips grazed her hair. I might not know exactly what I was apologizing for, but I was sure there were plenty of offenses. I'd sworn to myself I'd never hurt this woman again, and I—and I— My throat closed up as I tried to fit the fragments of memory together.

Rory hugged me tighter. "It wasn't your fault. It wasn't *you*. I knew that the whole time, even if it was hard. I'm just glad we managed to break the spell."

They had. Of course it'd been magic. My mother—

I winced at the pain that stabbed through my skull when I tried to remember that specific detail. "Thank you," I said to Rory, and then raised my head enough to take in the guys. "Thank you."

Malcolm tipped his head, the corner of his mouth curled with a relieved smile. "You'd have done the same for any of us."

Jude shifted on his feet, his hands tucked awkwardly in his pockets. Declan glanced at the other two and made some gesture I couldn't quite catch but that made the others pull straighter. He turned back to me and Rory. "It's you two who were pushed apart the most. We should give you some time to talk. If you need anything, just give us a shout."

They headed out, leaving me alone with Rory. I pressed my face to her hair and just held her for a while longer, not able to bring myself to do much else. She seemed happy enough to stay right there too. Her fingers curled into the fabric of my shirt as if to make it harder for me to detach her, if I'd even wanted to.

What had I done to the woman who owned my heart?

As much as I tried to escape into our embrace, that question kept niggling at me. Finally, I pulled back enough to look into her eyes.

"Will you tell me what happened? All of it, even the bad parts? I can— There are bits and pieces in my head, but they don't really connect, and it's all kind of a blur."

"That's not surprising. You had a lot of magic coloring your thoughts and memories. Mostly illusion, but probably some persuasion in there too." She touched her glass dragon charm, which I abruptly realized was hanging against *my* chest rather than hers. "I can't feel the spell Professor Burnbuck imbued it with anymore. Tackling all the illusions you were being hit with must have drained it."

She'd used up her summer project prize on me. A fresh wave of agony rushed through me. "I'm—"

Rory touched her finger to my mouth. "Don't say you're sorry. *I'm* not sorry. I'm *glad* I had a tool like that to help us save you. I can't think of any better use I could have put that prize to. So don't you dare tell me I should regret it."

I swallowed the rest of my apology. Instead, I reached back to open the chain and tucked it around her neck where it belonged. The broken base of the dragon's body reminded me of other times I'd failed to save her from pain I should have prevented.

"Declan says your mother came by campus the night after I left," Rory said, nestling her head against me again. "He mentioned her presence to you, and then he didn't see you again until you turned up a couple days later. Do you remember anything about that?"

I reached farther back in my mind to where my recollections were steadier. "I remember that conversation with him. I found her at her car, and she said I should get in so we could talk. She brought up my relationship with you." My jaw clenched at the memory. "She wanted me to break up with you in whatever way would be the most painful, and I couldn't convince her otherwise, so I... I told her I *wanted* to be with you and she didn't get to have any say in it."

Rory let out a sputtering sound. "I'm sure she was just thrilled to hear that."

I couldn't stop the upward twitch of my lips at her dry sarcasm. "She didn't congratulate us, that's for sure. She—I tried to get out of the car, and she cast a spell to stop me —I couldn't move—" I frowned. "That's where it gets hazy. We drove somewhere, and my dad came, and they were working magic, but I think she must have put me in some kind of stupor. And then everything's really distorted after that."

"They embedded a spell on you so that it would sustain its power after you came back to campus," Rory said. "That was a little more than a week ago. It... It made you believe that I'd been trying to sabotage all the scions, that I'd lied to and manipulated you and was still doing that to the others. You couldn't stand to be around me. We tried to tackle the spell more peacefully, but as soon as our magic touched theirs, you had an awful reaction. The only way we could help you was by force."

"I yelled at you a lot. Said horrible things." I closed my eyes, my stomach knotting. "You didn't deserve that."

"I know. But like I said before, I also know it wasn't you. That spell ran deep. Your mother was using you like a puppet to mess with the bond we've all formed. But it didn't work." Rory paused. "There's also—there've been some developments at school to do with the Nary students."

"Developments?" I said, and she gave a quick explanation of the plan the barons had approved, the way a select group of fearmancer students was using the Naries to boost their power—and how I'd inadvertently supported that effort. Her horror at the new policy rang through her voice, her body tensing as she described the effects.

"And I've given them more justification," I said, bile rising in the back of my mouth.

"Just the once, and only a little. I'm sure we can still turn it around. It's just a matter of figuring out the best approach. And not being too overt about it. I—"

She cut herself off with a pained press of her lips.

"Rory?" I said.

"I don't want to talk about that part right now. I just want to enjoy the fact that you're back with us the way you should be."

I wasn't going to push her if there were things she wasn't ready to say. Instead I held her close, pressing a kiss to the top of her head. "I won't let it happen again. I promise you that. I wasn't cautious enough with my mother—she's not going to get the jump on me that way again."

"Good," Rory said. "And even if she does, we know we're stronger than her."

They'd been stronger, not me. The queasy sensation stayed with me as my gaze passed over the broken video game shelf, the altercation we'd just had here in the lounge coming back to me in disorienting flashes. The room felt abruptly too small, too constricting, too harsh with the beaming of its artificial lights.

"Do you want to get out of here?" I said. "We could go for a walk. I think I could use some fresh air."

"Of course." Rory leapt up, so quick to do whatever she could to help me that it brought out a renewed ache in my chest.

I had to make this past week up to her one way or another. She might not blame me, but I'd still been a part of it. It would still be my face and my voice in *her* memories.

The lights in the hall upstairs were dim, the space quiet. The library never officially closed, but anyone who wanted to keep studying into the night generally took the books back to their room. We slipped past it and out into the night.

A couple of students were just ducking into Killbrook Hall, their animated voices carrying briefly across the green, and then we were alone out there too. I turned instinctively toward the eastern woods, the stretch of forest that held both the Shifting Grounds and my cliffside haven.

The grass whispered under our feet as we crossed the field. I clasped my hand around Rory's, and she eased closer to me as we stepped into the thicker darkness between the trees.

We hadn't gone very far when I realized a walk on an autumn night might not have been the wisest idea ever. A chilly breeze washed over us, and a shiver ran through Rory's body. Her dress fell to mid-calf, but her legs below it were bare, and the jacket she had on over it was thin. She hadn't anticipated this excursion.

Before I could say anything about that, she nodded to the forest around us, keeping her voice low. "Did you want to go out to the Shifting Grounds?"

The possibility would have been more tempting if my parents hadn't used that spot once to badger me about my involvement with Rory. That memory soured all the good ones I had there.

"No," I said. "I feel more like rambling around. It's more peaceful out here than it is most of the time on campus."

"Especially lately," Rory agreed with a short laugh. She squeezed my hand tighter and then shivered a second time.

I stopped and tugged her around to face me. "You're cold. We can go back."

She shook her head. "It's all right. I don't really *want*

to go back just yet." She hesitated, and a coy smile crossed her face even as a tremor of anxiety rippled off her. "I'm sure you could figure out a few ways to warm me up."

Hell yes, I could. But her nervousness dredged up a flickering of images: my hand on her breast, the taste of her skin on my lips, her gasp, and… Malcolm's cajoling voice?

We'd done something while my mind hadn't been my own. Something that might have left her even more uncertain of my reactions than the cruel comments and the shunning had. If it would write over that moment, I'd show her every bit of affection and desire I had for her.

I touched her cheek and bent down to kiss her. She looped her arms behind my neck, her body swaying toward mine, and *I* already felt twice as warm as I had a second ago. She kissed me back like she'd been waiting years for me to come to her. This past week might have seemed like that long.

With a few careful steps, I walked her backward until her shoulders came to rest against a nearby tree. I left one hand at her waist, tracing a curving pattern on her belly with my thumb, and slid the other up beneath her jacket to caress her breast through her dress. Rory hummed encouragingly against my mouth.

I eased back just far enough to murmur a quick spell to heat the air. A giggle escaped Rory as the warm current wrapped around us. "Exactly what I needed," she said, and drew me in for another kiss.

She felt even more right with her arms twined around me, her hips arching toward me to brush my groin. I was already hard, drunk on her scent and the sweetness of her mouth. I wanted to tumble into her, to reach that place where there was no telling where one of us ended and the other began, but I reined in my longing. Tonight had to be for her first. I owed her that much.

In the warmed air, I eased down the zipper of her dress so I could tug the neckline lower. As I slipped my fingers under her bra, I dipped my other hand to tease over her inner thighs. Rory let out a little growl and kissed me hard enough that her teeth nicked my lip. The spark of pain amid the pleasure only inflamed me more.

She tugged up my shirt and reached under it to trace my bare chest, every sweep of her fingertips making me hungrier for her. When she tweaked one of my nipples, I let out a growl of my own. Unable to resist, I cupped her right between the thighs. She arched into my touch with a sigh.

I gripped the soft fabric of her dress to pull it higher, but the rasp of her jacket against the tree's rough bark made me pause. I didn't want to see that delicate skin scraped.

We didn't need the tree at all. I could take care of her in every possible way with my own power.

The moment the idea came to me, my patience fled me. I yanked the skirt of her dress up to her waist and trailed my fingers over her panties. Thankfully, Rory was just as eager. Her hips bucked to meet me, her breath stuttering. The dampness between her legs sent a bolt of desire straight through my groin. My cock strained against my slacks.

As I tugged her panties down, Rory snapped open the top of my fly. If I'd had any doubts about how much she wanted this too, the firm stroke of her hand over my cock would have chased them away. I groaned with the sear of pleasure and claimed her mouth again, catching her cry as my thumb flicked over her clit.

With a heft of my arms and a murmur of magic, I lifted her flush against me. Rory clutched my shoulder and my side, her thighs squeezing against me, but she relaxed when she realized how fully I was supporting her. Her head bowed next to mine as I settled her into just the right position, my hands on the small of her back and her hip, the spell I'd cast steadying her upper body. As I plunged into her, a hot gasp of her breath spilled over my neck.

God, the slick heat of her knocked every other thought from my head. I kissed her jaw, the crook of her shoulder, as we rocked against each other. Every thrust, every giddy sound she made in response, sent pleasure pulsing through my veins. I kept just enough wherewithal to work a few words from my throat.

"I've got you. And you'll always have me."

Rory turned to seek out my mouth with her lips. I adjusted her angle against me just slightly, and the kiss broke with a moan. My favorite sound. Her fingers curled against the back of my neck, and I thrust into her faster, pulling her tighter against me. It only took a few seconds more before her head tipped back with the shudder of her orgasm.

The clench of her channel around my cock pulled me over the edge with her. I spilled myself inside her with a release that left me groaning and sated. Rory wrapped her legs around me, hugging me to her as if she never intended to let me go either.

As we clung there together in that blissful embrace, a chill that had nothing to do with the weather seeped through my chest.

I'd promised her I'd never let myself be torn from her again. I'd rather die than let that happen. But I couldn't completely avoid my parents for the next dozen or so years while my mother was still baron and I was only her heir.

As long as she ruled over me and the rest of fearmancer society, how the hell could I be sure of keeping any promise at all?

CHAPTER TWENTY-FIVE

Rory

Having Connar back should have taken a huge weight off me. But even with the memory of his embrace fresh in my mind, when I woke up the next morning, my stomach knotted.

Too many other things had happened yesterday. I'd tried to push back against the barons' plans for the Naries and maybe shown too much of my hand. My mother had shown more of *her* hand than ever before: a willingness to brutally punish me for perceived slights less than two weeks into restoring our relationship.

What would I face if I defied her expectations again? *Could* I even behave in a way that would make her happy?

While I showered and dressed, my mind crept back to that extended, amplified session in the Desensitization chamber—to the horrific images it had shown me, to my helplessness when I'd tried to resist them, and to the professors who'd come to my rescue.

Professor Viceport had seemed genuinely remorseful about our past interactions and eager to make up for them. If she was around this morning, maybe I should take her up on her offer to talk further. At the very least, she was one of the only people on campus who already knew how my mother had treated me, so I wouldn't have to worry about how to broach that subject.

I wolfed down a quick breakfast and headed over to Killbrook Hall. The green was already bustling with students heading to the first classes of the day. The sight of the gold pins on several of their collars made my gut twist all over again.

There had to be something the other scions and I could do for them. It just might take time to work around the barons, and I wished we could have protected all of the Naries right now.

When I reached Viceport's office, another student was just leaving, the professor stepping out behind him. My mentor saw me and paused, her hand still on the door. A shadow of emotion crossed her face. She pushed the door wider.

I hesitated. "If you have something else to get to, it's okay. I know I'm showing up unannounced."

"No, it's not a problem. My other plans can wait." She motioned me in. "You've been waiting much longer for me to really fulfill my role as mentor."

Once I was inside the office, though, an awkward silence settled between us. I sat in my usual seat, and

Viceport paced behind her desk a couple times before sinking into her own chair across from me. She ran her hand through her wispy hair.

"I'm assuming that anything we talk about today won't be passed on to Baron Bloodstone," she said, catching my eyes.

I offered a wry but pained smile. "I can't even tell her about most of the things *I'm* doing or thinking about. I don't think keeping one more conversation under wraps should be an issue."

"All right." She fell silent again and then dragged in a breath. "I should apologize again. I've been unfair to you from the start. I can't really justify it. There are certain assumptions you learn to make within this community… but you weren't really from this community. I let my prejudices get ahead of really seeing who you are."

"Prejudices?" I repeated.

"I…" She trailed off before seeming to gird herself to the conversation. "Your mother and I don't have the most pleasant history—let's put it that way. We attended Blood U as students around the same time. I heard things, saw things… I don't like or trust her, and it makes me nervous having her in place as one of our rulers."

Her gaze came back to me, and her voice dropped. "You look so much like she did back then. You're a Bloodstone. You arrived, and everyone was awed, and you appeared to be stirring up all sorts of conflicts. I let that color my opinion of you before I'd even given you a chance."

"The more I'm getting to know my mother, the more

it's clear to me that there's very little we agree about," I had to say.

"Yes. That's becoming clear to me too." Viceport rubbed her mouth. "I should have seen it sooner. I kept waiting to catch on to the larger plan behind your activities here, but there really hasn't been one, has there? You've honestly believed in the things you've said and done."

A trace of disbelief still lingered in her tone. I guessed being honestly kind and upfront wasn't a quality one witnessed very often among fearmancers, let alone the families of the barony.

"I don't know who I'd be if I'd grown up here like I was supposed to," I said. "But I was raised by joymancers —good ones, even if some of them have questionable motives too. I spent most of my life seeing magic as something meant to be tied to joy, to be used to help people... Those ideas didn't just disappear the moment I stepped on campus. I've had to adjust some of my views with the things I've learned, but I still don't like seeing anyone purposefully hurt."

"And because of that, your mother tried to hurt you in the worst way she could." Viceport shook her head. "I don't know if I could have done anything to prevent what happened yesterday, but I wish I'd at least offered some real support before it did. You should have felt you could turn to me."

I ran my fingers over the curved wood at the end of the chair arms and debated my next question. "Would you tell me what happened between you and my mother before? No one I've been able to talk openly with even knew her before she was taken prisoner… I haven't had much frame of reference."

"That's fair. I suppose I owe you that much." Viceport leaned back in her chair, her pale eyes going distant. Her mouth slanted tightly downward before she spoke again.

"It wasn't really *me* that anything happened with. I'm a few years younger than your mother, so we weren't often in the same circles. But my older sister was the same age as her, and they… did not get along. There were occasional spats in public. Then, in their last year, my sister did something that made your mother furious. I don't even know what, only that everyone was buzzing about the Bloodstone scion taking offense."

"Your sister didn't tell you what it was?" I asked.

"No. We were close, and frankly I was a little annoyed at the time that she wouldn't explain, but afterward… I realized she might have simply been doing what she could to prevent me from becoming a secondary target." Viceport's jaw worked. "Not long after that, there was an incident out at the Casting Grounds. They were arguing again, and it turned into a fight. One of the spells your mother cast crushed my sister's heart."

My skin chilled. It took me a moment to find the words. "I'm so sorry."

Viceport raised her shoulders in a weak shrug. "The few witnesses who'd been present said my sister provoked her, attacked first, that your mother was only defending herself. She had a couple of magical wounds to lend proof to that idea. But the witnesses were all people eager to keep her favor, and my sister wasn't the type to resort to violence. I'd seen how firmly and viciously your mother enforced her position when she felt anyone had even mildly challenged it."

I could believe it. I'd experienced that cool callousness in the way Baron Bloodstone had sentenced me to that Desensitization session yesterday. I'd seen how the other older barons reacted to anyone who went against their authority.

"I guess it makes sense that you'd still be carrying some resentment against the Bloodstones, then," I said.

"I'm not asking you to absolve me," Viceport said. "I'm a teacher. I should be able to treat my students based on who *they* are, not their family name. But you asked, and maybe that will at least explain why I struggled."

"It does." I found, after everything I'd been through at the hands of the barons and, for a time, their scions, that it made her reaction to me much easier to swallow. "We can put that behind us now, I hope? I won't hold it against you as long as you don't hold my family against me anymore?"

For the first time since I'd come in, Viceport managed a small smile. "That sounds more than fair."

Which meant that maybe we could get started on the helpful side of mentoring right now. I had other questions about my mother that I hadn't been able to ask anyone before.

"I'm not sure if you would have noticed," I said tentatively, "but back then, when my mother was here at the school, or afterward, even when she became baron...

did she ever seem outright paranoid to you? Not just reacting to things people said or did that she didn't like, but constantly worried that even her friends might be undermining her or trying to hurt her behind her back, checking for spells and that sort of thing?"

The professor's brow knit. "Not that I can think of. If anything, she gave me the impression of being overconfident in her ability to handle anything that came at her. She'd have been more inclined to go about her business as if nothing could shake her, waiting until anyone attacked her in a way overt enough to be obvious. Then she'd have that much more excuse to crush them as thoroughly as possible."

The anxieties I'd seen were probably new, then. How could my mother *not* be shaken by being imprisoned and drained of her power for nearly two decades? I'd bet she didn't even fully trust her fellow barons. The trauma had left her permanently suspicious and on edge.

"Thank you," I said. "That's useful to know."

Viceport studied me. "Is there anything else I can do for you right now, in terms of information or guidance or otherwise? I'm sure you understand I'm not in a position to challenge a baron, not without ceasing to be both your mentor and a professor here rather quickly, but I'll do the best I can behind the scenes."

The earnestness of the offer eased the last of my nerves. I took a moment to consider the challenges that had come up over the last several months. Tackling most of them *would* require challenging the barons in turn. But...

"I've been wanting to adapt to using casting words

rather than literal ones for my spells," I said. "I think I'm ready, but it doesn't really come up in class since all the other senior students picked that up in their junior studies. It'd be especially handy if I ever happen to need to cast a spell I'd rather not be totally obvious to those around me."

Viceport's smile came back, a little wider this time. "I can certainly help you with that. To begin, I think it's ideal to have quite a bit of space and no audience, as things can go somewhat wrong when you're switching over from having the literal meaning to help shape the spell. I believe the Casting Grounds will be free for most of this afternoon. I could meet you there at two?"

I found myself smiling back. "That sounds perfect. Thank you."

Nothing had really been resolved, but the weight I'd been carrying felt easier to bear as I walked back onto the green. I had more allies than I knew; I had a better idea what I was dealing with when it came to my mother.

I was heading back to the dorms, wondering if I could manage to get all of the guys together for a proper scion meeting now that all five of us were really present, when a broken sound split the air from somewhere above.

I whirled around with a hitch of my pulse. My gaze jerked to the upper reaches of Nightwood Tower.

A figure was leaning out of a window on one of the upper floors—no, not just leaning, climbing onto the ledge. Her legs wobbled and her hair drifted limp around her face. She let out the sound again: a rough sob.

I took in all that in the space of a few seconds. Before I

could even process what she was doing, she flung herself from the window.

"No!" The cry lurched out of me automatically. I fumbled for some kind of spell to catch her, to cushion her fall—but she plummeted so fast. I'd only forced out one syllable when her body hit the ground back-first with a sickening crack of bones.

Blood gushed through her pale hair and into the grass. Everyone on the green around me had stopped to stare. My stomach turned, on the verge of expelling the meager breakfast I'd forced down. I clamped down on my nausea and forced myself to step forward, to try to see if I knew her. Had one of the other students compelled her out the window? What the hell—

My thoughts stilled in my head and my feet froze under me when a golden glint reached my eyes. She was wearing a leaf pin—she was one of the Nary students.

Had a spell from one of those terror sessions stuck with her unexpectedly? Had the buried distress overwhelmed her? There was no way to tell, but I had no doubt at all that her death had been caused by the new policy my mother was championing.

Less than two weeks, and it'd already caused one death. How many more were coming?

I turned, wrapping my arms around my belly, and locked gazes with Shelby, who must have just been coming out of Ashgrave Hall when the girl had jumped. Her eyes had gone wide and watery. I opened my mouth, wanting to say something to her—but what could I say?

It was my people who'd done this. My mother who'd

encouraged them. And for all I knew, Shelby could be next. Wasn't she lucky to have me as a friend?

She swayed on her feet and hurried back into the hall as the first professors emerged from the buildings to deal with the growing crowd. My heart wrenched.

I followed her, but only as far as the foyer. There, I stopped and leaned against the wall, resolve searing up through my chest alongside my guilt.

I might not be able to save all the Naries right now, but I *would* save the one who'd shown me the first kindness I'd received here, the one who wouldn't still be here at all if it wasn't for me. I didn't deserve to be a scion if I couldn't manage that. I just had to find the right angle...

Inspiration flashed through my mind. I snatched up my phone and tapped a quick text to Malcolm.

When do you have a chunk of free time for a little field trip? I think I need a persuasion expert.

CHAPTER TWENTY-SIX

Rory

"You know," Malcolm said, looking around the ornate lobby of the concert hall, "if all you want is a little persuasion on a Nary, you could have handled that yourself. It doesn't really take an expert."

"Then it shouldn't be any trouble at all for you," I said, elbowing him. "I'd like this spell to stick as long as possible to make sure everything's set up by the time he comes out of it. Unless helping me with this is too big a hassle?"

The Nightwood scion held up his hands, giving me his characteristic smirk. I didn't mind it now that it came with a gleam of affection in his dark eyes. "Not at all. I was just making a statement of fact." He stepped a little closer— close enough that he could brush a kiss to my temple and say under his breath, "I enjoy knowing that you need me, Glinda."

I rolled my eyes, but his smooth tone sent a quiver of heat through me all the same. We hadn't had a chance to repeat the other day's orgasmic encounter yet, and when he talked like that, it was hard not to wonder how soon we could make it happen again.

Right now, though, I had a life to potentially save—or at least to set on a much better course.

We eased apart as footsteps rapped toward us. The director of one of the most renowned orchestras in the state strode from one of the side halls across the deep red carpeting to meet us. His trim black suit looked somber in the light from the crystal fixtures overhead.

He glanced us over, his expression turning puzzled, maybe because of our age. "I don't fully understand what this is about," he started, already shifting his weight back as if to turn away.

Malcolm slipped into his persuasive tone without missing a beat. "*There's a promising new musician you want to hear about. Better than any of the auditions you've seen for the new celloist.*"

The director blinked, and hope washed over his face. "We do need to fill that position soon," he said. "Is the applicant here?"

"She couldn't make it today, but if you call her in for an audition, she'll get down here as quickly as she can," I assured him. I hadn't wanted to say anything to Shelby until I'd pulled this off, but this was exactly the kind of job she'd been hoping her time at Blood U would qualify her for. I couldn't imagine her turning down an offer just because it'd come earlier than expected.

I pulled out my phone and brought up the video I'd recorded of Shelby playing last night. I'd asked her to show me one of her favorite pieces. Even through the tiny speakers, you could hear the passion she was pouring into the song, each sway of the melody tugging at my emotions.

The university staff only took the most promising talents into their programs in the first place, so that they could maintain the reputation of their scholarship programs. Even without any persuasive influence, the director could tell Shelby had impressive skills. His eyes widened as he listened.

"Her name is Shelby Hughes," Malcolm said, and shifted back into casting. "*You'll want to call her as soon as possible, before someone else snatches her up. You're sure she'll be a perfect fit. It's just a matter of seeing through the formalities, and then you'll make her an official offer of employment.*"

Even if Shelby should be a shoo-in, I wasn't so naïve as to think she'd be the only talented musician auditioning for this role, or that internal politics might not sway the hiring decision away from her if we left it completely to chance. The persuasion was just to grease the wheels to move everything along faster and more smoothly. Once she'd gotten her spot here and proven herself on this level of professionalism, she'd never need to consider coming back to Blood U.

It didn't feel like nearly enough considering everything that was happening to the Nary students, but it was the most important thing I could accomplish right now.

"Yes, of course," the director said, nodding emphatically. "We have to get her in here. You can give me her contact information?"

"Here's her phone number," I said, handing him the paper I'd prepared. "She's currently finishing up an advanced program at Bloodstone University, just a couple hours from here, but I'm sure she'll jump at the chance to be a part of your fantastic organization."

The director was already pulling out his phone. Malcolm's spell had sunk in deep. The Nightwood scion flashed a smile at me as the director walked off with the phone at his ear, so intent on landing Shelby for the position that he didn't even bother saying good-bye to us.

"Mission accomplished," Malcolm said, wiping his hands together with a satisfied air. His smile faded as we headed out to his car. "I get why you wanted to do this, but it's going to be tough for you, isn't it? You and her were pretty close."

And with Deborah and Imogen dead, I didn't have anyone else I could call any kind of friend beyond the scions. My chest tightened at the thought, but I'd already pushed aside that sense of loss. "This is what a real friend would do. She won't be *that* far away. I'll still be able to visit her. I just don't want her coming anywhere near campus after I can get her away from here."

"Well, we can take comfort in the fact that the barons shouldn't have any idea we were involved in removing one Nary from their grasp. It's not totally unusual for employers to poach the students before they're finished with the programs."

"Thank God," I said, trying not to think of how my mother would react if she did find out. Which became significantly more difficult with the chime of my phone.

"While we're out here, we could take our time, grab some lunch," Malcolm was starting to say.

I held up my hand with a lurch of my heart, staring at my phone's screen. "My mother and Lillian are coming by the university this afternoon to look into the 'incident.' Soon. If she gets there and I'm *not* around…"

Malcolm gunned the engine. "All right. No taking our time. Let's see how many speed records I can break without letting a single cop notice."

I'd have liked to enjoy the trip, knowing I had set one small thing right, but it was hard to dwell on anything except the thought of seeing my mother again. Before now, she hadn't reached out to me at all since that night in the Desensitization. How was she going to expect me to act around her? Would she get upset if I didn't throw myself at her feet full of apologies?

No. I was pretty sure that she wouldn't want her heir prostrating for anyone, even her. She wanted me to be strong, just… strong while I supported the same ideals. That was one minor mercy.

I still wasn't looking forward to navigating the latest consequences of her plan. At this point, I didn't have much hope she'd see it as a clear indication that the new policy had been a mistake.

By some miracle—and a whole lot of Malcolm's magic —we made it back to the university in just over an hour without hearing sirens wail behind us even once. Malcolm caught my hand before we got out of the car. "Do you want me with you when you go meet her?" he asked. "I don't know how much help I'll be, but she does like my father, at least."

My emotions tore down the middle, half of me longing to have some kind of supportive presence at my side and the other half recoiling from the idea of any of my lovers seeing how my mother might treat me. Malcolm had warned me she might be harsh if I pushed back against her plans. It wasn't as if he'd be surprised. But still…

She was *my* mother. I wouldn't always have backup when I was dealing with her. I had to find a way to work with her and around her on my own.

"Thanks," I said, "but I've got this. I wouldn't want her realizing I brought you along to side with me, anyway. We still want your father to think you're his loyal heir, don't we?"

"We'll see how long it makes sense to keep that ruse up," Malcolm muttered, but he didn't argue. He leaned across the seat to steal a kiss that left my heart thumping for totally different reasons. "Text us as soon as you know how they've decided to handle the situation."

"I will."

I lingered by my car for a few minutes as he left so no one would notice us emerging from the garage together. It shouldn't matter, but I wasn't sure what my mother would make of our trip when she was so busy watching everyone around her for signs of treachery, especially if she connected it to one of the Nary students who happened to be from my dorm making an abrupt departure.

As I came out, a gold Lexus was cruising into view up the road from town, a blacksuit sedan right behind it. We'd made it back just in time.

I ambled over to the open parking lot in front of Killbrook Hall to meet the arrivals. My mother and Lillian got out at the same time and immediately converged, my mother checking something on her phone while they talked together. Maggie slipped out of the car and trailed behind them. I paused to let them cross the rest of the distance to me, my skin prickling at the sight of the blacksuit.

I had another friend I owed a debt to. Another enemy to deal with—and one my mother was in so tight with. Maybe Baron Bloodstone didn't care about Imogen's murder. Maybe she'd see the slaughter of an innocent student by the people who were supposed to protect us fearmancers as no worse than what she'd done to Professor Viceport's sister. But was she also totally fine with all the lies Lillian had told me, with the way she'd helped the other barons nearly hobble my magic?

Did she even know? She'd never said anything to me to confirm it one way or the other.

My mother looked up as they reached me and gave me her usual careful smile. "I was about to let you know we'd gotten here. You didn't need to wait for us."

"I happened to be passing this way anyway," I said in the most lighthearted tone I could summon.

Apparently my mother wasn't even going to

acknowledge any uneasy emotions I might be feeling after what she'd put me through, just as she'd never made any mention of my birthday. She walked on, expecting me to fall in stride along with her as she headed onto the green. "This death is an unfortunate event," she said, not sounding remotely concerned. "I'm sure it's stirred the students up. Have you heard any questionable sentiments among your classmates?"

"People are speculating about why the girl did it, but that's all. Nothing outrageous." Although maybe her real question was whether *I* was having a questionable reaction to the girl's suicide, considering the sentiments I'd expressed before. There hadn't really been any need for a baron to come out to campus over this, had there?

She might not be talking about her suspicions of me, but she was checking up on me all the same.

"Well, some of them are even more feeble-minded than others. It's unsurprising that now and then one cracks under the pressures of the school." She glanced at Lillian. "There may be some additional talk when it comes to the next phase, but I think we can quell that fairly quickly."

"I don't expect there'll be much of a hitch in your plans," Lillian confirmed. "I've gone over every aspect on my end thoroughly."

"Next phase?" I asked, my stomach sinking. Did I *want* to know what more the barons might be planning? Not really, but I needed to.

My mother brushed the question off with a twitch of her hand. "It'll all come together soon enough. For now, the blacksuits simply need to make certain no foul play was involved in the death."

"Standard procedure," Lillian said with a crooked smile of her own.

After everything she'd done to me, she was now running around helping my mother with her schemes in every way she could. How many more people were going to die before the two of them were finished?

The comment slipped out before I'd totally thought it through. "And hopefully I won't get accused of murder all over again."

Lillian's expression twitched, but my mother wasn't looking at her. She brushed her fingers over my hair, ruffling it, and said, "Let's not dwell on the unfortunate happenstances of the past. I can't see an awful set of circumstances coming together like that again."

She spoke casually rather than pointedly, as if she really did think it'd all been a matter of coincidence.

"I'm sure I wouldn't make a mistake like that," Lillian said with a short chuckle that only solidified my impression. She hadn't told my mother her part in that story after all.

She set off toward Nightwood Tower with Maggie at her heels. The assistant shot a quick look over her shoulder at me, but then she turned her attention back to her boss. And I was left with my mother.

"I hope you didn't have any personal connection to the poor girl," the baron said.

I shook my head automatically. "No. I didn't know her at all." Which didn't mean I thought she deserved what'd happened to her. But my thoughts were whirling now with a shiver of agitated excitement.

My mother was wary even of Lillian, from what I'd seen. What if I *could* give Imogen something like the justice she deserved? What if I could strip my mother of her possibly greatest ally with the same stroke?

It might get me nowhere. Hell, for all I knew my mother would see any mention of the subject as whining. But on the other hand, there had to be a reason Lillian hadn't filled her in.

I kept my own voice quiet but as casual as possible, even though I chose every word with care.

"It's kind of ironic, Lillian investigating this death when she's the one responsible for that other one."

My mother's gaze had been roaming over the green. At my remark, it snapped to my face. "What was that?" she said, her voice tightly even.

"You know." I glanced around as if making sure no one was close enough to overhear. "She killed my dormmate to arrange my arrest. I realize she must have had her reasons…"

I trailed off, not entirely by design, at the tensing of my mother's face. Her eyes had gone even darker than usual. "Where did you hear that?" she demanded. "Is that what people are saying? Absolutely ridiculous."

I frowned. "It isn't, though. I saw the proof—just not anything solid enough that I could use it in the trial." I couldn't bring Deborah into this, let her rest in peace. Hugging myself, I rubbed my arms. A little show of vulnerability might help me in this one moment. "I assumed she'd have told you. I—I'm sorry. Seeing how close you two are was part of the reason I was nervous opening up to you very much about, well, everything."

The admission had the ring of truth because in a lot of ways it was true. My mother's gaze shot back to Lillian, who was standing at the base of Nightwood Tower now. "She wouldn't," she started, but then didn't seem sure how to go on.

"Maybe I got mixed up somehow," I said in a doubtful tone. "I guess all it'd take is an insight spell to clear that up, anyway."

My mother squared her shoulders. "Stay here," she said, her voice turning firm and even cooler. "I'll see that this is sorted out."

She set off across the green with a fierce air that I wouldn't have wanted to be on the receiving end of. Another shiver passed through me as I watched her, this one all nerves. What if this gambit backfired on me?

The impression rose up that I'd just moved a key piece on the board of a dangerous game, with stakes I wasn't totally prepared to face.

My mother drew Lillian a short distance to the side. Her hand jerked through the air as she spoke, her voice too low for me to make out.

Lillian's whole body went rigid. In the space of a second, the lioness she'd always come across as vanished in the place of a gazelle inches from a predator's jaws. Her mouth moved quickly, and I caught a couple of snippets of her hasty explanation: "...best option at the..." "... interference with our..."

However she was trying to justify herself, my mother's stance didn't relax. She leaned closer, so much fury twisting her expression as she gave her response that it chilled me to the bone. Then, with a flit of her fingers, Lillian's mouth jammed shut and her wrists smacked together in front of her as if bound by invisible handcuffs.

The baron was arresting her.

I couldn't help staring after them as my mother marched the blacksuit back toward their cars. My gaze slid away as they passed behind Killbrook Hall—and collided with Maggie's.

Lillian's assistant was still standing by the tower, watching me watching them. Her hands had balled at her sides. Her mouth flattened as just for a second she outright glared at me, and then she was hurrying off after her employer without a backward glance.

I dragged in a breath. I'd done it—I'd revealed Lillian's crimes, and to someone who was actually going to see her face retribution for them, even if my mother saw the offense as more against her than against Imogen.

Whatever this precarious game was, I'd thrown myself into it now, and I couldn't see any way of turning back.

CHAPTER TWENTY-SEVEN

Jude

About five minutes after I'd come down to the lounge, I started to think this was all a terrible idea. I could be blowing up the little bit of stability I still had in my life. I hadn't even let Rory come along for moral support, as much as I missed her presence now.

This was between me and the guys I'd known since we were kids. She shouldn't have to step in. If I deserved their respect, I'd damn well better show it.

I lingered over the liquor cabinet, the tangy scents that drifted from the bottles tempting me, but after a moment's wavering, I just grabbed a Coke from the mini-fridge. Something to occupy my hands and my mouth but that wouldn't potentially loosen my tongue more than was beneficial. I had too much experience with hangovers and regrets.

Malcolm sauntered in first with his usual princely

aura. *He* poured himself a whiskey sour, which I couldn't help eyeing with a little pang of longing. I clutched my can tighter and took a fizzy sweet gulp.

Declan showed up next, with Connar right behind him. The Ashgrave scion went to fix himself an espresso, which maybe I'd have gone for if I'd seen any use in making myself more wired. No, thank you, I already felt about ready to leap right out of my skin.

Connar stopped by the sofa and glanced at each of us before his gaze came to rest on me. The bruise on my jaw where he'd clocked me tingled. A little of the haunted look that'd come over him after we'd snapped him out of Baron Stormhurst's spell returned. His mouth twisted.

"If this has anything to do with anything *I* did while the spell was acting on me—"

I held up my hands. "Nothing to worry about. I'm all interventioned out for the next few years at least. This is— this is just a me thing."

Once I'd said that, there really wasn't any shifting back to regular small talk to ease into the subject. Connar sat down, and the other two guys came over to join him. I stayed standing next to the armchair they'd left empty, holding onto my pop can as if for dear life.

I was not off to a great start here.

Malcolm raised his eyebrows at me. "Didn't you invite Rory? I'd have thought you'd want her included in any scion business from now on?" His tone was only mildly provocative.

I looked at the floor and then back at them. "Rory already knows what I'm going to tell you. I thought, considering our history— It's been just the four of us for a long time—"

I shut up, because I had no idea where I was going with that. The guys all watched me, Declan's forehead furrowing with concern.

Fuck, I was nervous because of *them*, so they had to all be able to feel it, little tremors of anxiety feeding their magic for reasons they couldn't even have suspected. I strode farther into the center of the room and then, feeling too exposed, back to the chair, but I couldn't quite bring myself to sit down either.

This spot wasn't far from where I'd been standing when I'd severed the illusions that'd been gripping Connar the other day. I let myself sink into that memory for a moment, because it'd been that night that'd convinced me I should do this. We'd all worked together, every one of us vital to the plan, me no less than anyone else. We'd worked together as *friends*, without a word about our future responsibilities.

What Rory had said was true—I couldn't expect to rely on just her for the rest of my life. If I'd earned the right to more than disdain from anyone in the community, it was these guys here in front of me. Maybe I couldn't claim the barony, maybe I'd never deserved to be called scion, but they couldn't say I hadn't stepped up when they'd needed me as people, not as their roles.

At least, they'd better see it that way. Because otherwise I was epically screwed.

"Jude," Declan started, still looking so fucking concerned.

I waved him off. "It's all right. I'm just figuring out where to begin." More accurately, I was working up to beginning at all, but I didn't need to say that.

I took another swig from my Coke and managed to turn that jolt of sugar into some kind of courage. As I lowered my hand, I drew my posture straighter.

"What I'm about to tell you, you can't mention to anyone else except Rory," I said in the most serious tone I had in me. "Word getting out to the wrong person would be a death sentence. So I hope you'll understand why it's taken me this long to tell even you."

"Tell us *what?*" Malcolm burst out. "Let's hear it already, Killbrook."

"Malcolm," Declan said chidingly, and Malcolm mock-grimaced at him. The Nightwood scion shifted in his chair, his gaze coming back to me, and it occurred to me as maybe it wouldn't have even a week ago that he wasn't impatient because he wanted to be done with me. He was impatient because he was waiting to hear how *he* could step up and defend me from whatever horror I was about to tell them.

Which would be great for me if he still felt the same way once he knew. At least his comment had given me a perfect opening.

"That's the thing right there," I said. My voice went hoarse despite my best efforts. "I'm not—I'm not a Killbrook. I'm not a scion. It's all been a fucking sham."

The second the words spilled out, I'd have given anything to take them back. The other guys stared at me in deathly silence. Connar's jaw had gone slack. Then

Declan, with that furrowed forehead and of course his academic precision, said, "When you say you're not, you literally mean—"

"Yes," I said before he had to form the whole question. "I have no genetic relationship to Baron Killbrook or anyone else who was born a Killbrook. I... It's a long story."

My body had tensed as if I might need to bolt for the door. Connar managed to shut his mouth. Malcolm kept staring at me, but he didn't look angry, so that was a small win.

"I think you'd better lay it all out, then," he said.

My legs abruptly decided they weren't inclined to hold me up any longer. I sank onto the padded arm of the chair, my head bowing forward. "You all know how uptight the barons can get about ensuring succession and solidifying their family line," I said. "My... well, the man who calls himself my father is the oldest of the current barons; he was the first to take his spot at the pentacle. He'd been trying for an heir for years, but all the other barons were popping out kids and he couldn't and—I guess he panicked."

I told them the rest of the story as well as I knew it from the argument I'd overheard between my mother and the baron and the pieces I'd fit together in the seven years afterward: the way he'd convinced her to let him compel another mage to impregnate her, the way he'd treated me after he'd gotten what he thought he wanted, the way my impending sibling had left my position ten times as precarious.

The scions let me talk without interruption, taking it all in with varying expressions of shock. By the time I wrapped up the story, an ache had filled my throat. I couldn't quite look any of them in the eye. I pushed myself to my feet again, my gaze fixed on my pop can.

"I didn't *enjoy* lying to you for so long. For most of that time, I didn't want to even let myself accept it. I'm sure I've taken out far too many of my frustrations on all of you, and I wish I could have figured out a better way to handle the whole mess. I just—"

Declan stood up and moved to grasp my shoulder. "It's *okay*, Jude," he said, his own voice a little raw. "He put you in an impossible position and left you to fend for yourself —we're not going to be upset because you weren't perfectly graceful in dealing with his shittiness."

The Ashgrave scion didn't often lower himself to coarse language. That and the impassioned tenor to his words gave me the will to meet his eyes. He was pissed off, yes— on my behalf, not with me. He gazed back at me steadily, his mouth slanted at a sympathetic angle.

I'd always scoffed when Malcolm or occasionally the others would refer to the pentacle as a "family." Mostly, I supposed, because I'd assumed I didn't belong to it either way. It struck me right then that Declan was exactly the older brother I'd have wanted if I'd allowed myself to want anywhere near that much, and something in me cracked.

"I'm sorry," I said, not even sure what I was apologizing for now.

Declan let out a sputter of a laugh. I wasn't sure who moved first, but we collided in a brief but firm hug, his arm squeezing tight across my shoulders as if he thought he could press the reassurance he intended into me. I stepped back, embarrassingly choked up.

Malcolm and Connar had gotten up too, but thankfully neither of them attempted quite the same demonstration of acceptance. Malcolm did clap me on the back with a rough guffaw.

"And you had me worried *you'd* created some kind of catastrophe."

"It is a catastrophe no matter how you look at it," I muttered. "And I shouldn't really even be in this room."

Connar let out a disgruntled sound. "Fuck that," he said. "You're one of us in every way that counts. Your father's shitty decisions don't change that. I don't know how we're going to sort this out, but there's got to be a way."

For a second, their show of solidarity overwhelmed me. I swiped my hand across my mouth.

"I just want to stay alive," I said. "Whether I'd want the barony or not has no bearing on the situation. I *couldn't* take it even if someone handed it to me on a silver platter. And Baron Killbrook knows that if I'm ever put in the position to try to claim it, or if anyone finds out I'm not really his son in some other way, he'll be hung for treason. I'm not sure how long I have before he decides to get ahead of that problem by hanging *me*, by whatever method he deems most effective."

"He's got no reason to think there's any urgency about it, does he?" Malcolm said. "You kept it quiet that you knew."

"Well…" I winced. "I was more upfront with him than maybe was smart a few weeks ago, thinking if I showed I knew and wasn't going to make problems for him, it'd get him off my back. It didn't appear from his reaction that I achieved the intended effect. I thought I was reasonably safe until after my sister arrives and they're sure she's healthy, but… after that, it's become less clear. As long as he doesn't think I've been spreading the information around, at least—"

Declan's expression fell. "He might already think that. Damn it. If I'd had any idea, Jude… I was trying to negotiate with him the other day, and I said something about uncertainty with his heirs, and he reacted as if I'd accused him of something terrible. I had no idea what that was about. I told him I only meant that it seemed he was removing you as scion, but—I'm not sure he believed me."

My heart dropped. "Fucking hell."

"It doesn't matter," Malcolm announced. "He's not touching a hair on your head. He didn't want you? Well, you're ours now. Honorary scion. No take-backs." His body was tensed, but he shot me a wry smirk.

He could say that all he wanted—I was still in even deeper shit than I'd been before. Or perhaps not. Because I also had three allies standing around me that I hadn't been sure I could trust before.

Baron Killbrook would come for me, somehow or other, but I wouldn't be facing him alone. Not by a longshot.

CHAPTER TWENTY-EIGHT

Rory

"It seems crazy that it happened so fast," Shelby said as she stuffed another sweater into her suitcase, which was yawning open next to me on the bed. "They said they saw a video someone had of me performing—I guess from one of the recent public recitals—and got my info… I still can't believe they really want me to be part of the orchestra." She paused and hugged herself with a giddy smile.

I grinned back with a pang in my chest. I loved seeing her so happy, but the good-bye was still hard. Once she was gone, I'd be stuck with Victory's trio and the dormmates who'd always simply kept their distance. With every new ally I discovered, the barons' machinations were peeling away the ones I'd already had.

"You're amazing on that cello," I said. "Anyone can tell. And I'm sure you aced that audition."

"I was *so* nervous." She giggled. "But I can't wait to get started. I'm sure I'm going to learn so much from the other musicians. It feels a little weird dropping out of school, but I'll probably get an even better education learning things hands on, surrounded by that many pros."

"For sure. I'm looking forward to coming to your first official performance." I'd promised her I'd make it out there for that.

I glanced around the room as she fit a couple more pieces of clothing into the suitcase, leaving her closet empty. "Is there anything you need help packing or getting to the car?" One of the university's on-call chauffeurs had agreed to drive her out to her new accommodations.

"I think that's everything." Shelby swiped her hands against her sides and took in the room that was now stripped of her personal touches. Her mouth slanted at a bittersweet angle. "It's funny—this place stressed me out so often, but I'm going to miss parts of it too."

"I'm going to miss *you*," I told her, getting up. "Call me or text me with all the news, okay? I want to hear everything about the glamorous orchestra life."

She laughed again, her cheeks flushing, and gave me a quick hug. "I'd have been a lot more stressed the last few terms if it wasn't for you. You let me know any exciting developments on your end too."

I didn't think any pending developments were likely to be exciting in a way I could share or that it'd be fun to talk about, so I just smiled. "Of course."

I walked her down to the parking lot and helped heft her luggage into the trunk. The pang in my chest sharpened as I watched the car whisk her off down the road. Then I turned to head across campus. I had one more painful conversation to get through, but at least it might alleviate a little pain for someone else.

My mother had called me this morning to let me know Lillian's fate. The blacksuits were keeping her exact crimes quiet, deciding with the barons' agreement that it would unnerve the general community too much to know what one of their high ranking members had done. No doubt my mother also didn't want it getting out how easily her heir had been framed. But Lillian had been stripped of her position and at least temporarily of her magic via those blacksuit cuffs, and she'd remain in their detention center for the next year until they could re-evaluate.

Baron Bloodstone had relayed all this information in a chilly tone. She didn't need to tell me how furious she still was with the woman who'd once been her closest friend. Her voice had made me shiver, but this was the best outcome I could have hoped for. She'd lost one of her key allies too.

It didn't sound as if Lillian had revealed the other barons' role in my arrest, or perhaps she had and my mother had dismissed the idea. They'd been good at covering their tracks. Lillian might have been afraid she'd lose even more than she already had if she'd tried to implicate them.

That was fine. *I* knew. And if the right moment arrived, I wouldn't hesitate to make use of that information.

Inside the maintenance building, the door to the main office stood slightly ajar. I knocked on it anyway.

Mr. Wakeburn's voice reached me with the same hint of strain it'd had when he'd called me for a meeting a couple weeks ago. "Come in."

When I stepped inside, a strange combination of emotions crossed his face. Somehow he both brightened and deflated, as if seeing me simultaneously gave him hope and sapped it away.

"Miss Bloodstone," he said, managing a smile. "To what do I owe this visit?"

It seemed blunt to jump straight to the point, but the idea of making some kind of small talk leading up to it made my stomach clench. I clasped my hands in front of me.

"I just wanted to let you know that I've done what you asked for Imogen. The details aren't being made public, which wasn't my choice, but—her killer is facing justice. She won't be in a position to hurt anyone else like that again." At least, I certainly hoped not.

I was about to add that I wished I could tell him more, but Mr. Wakeburn was already getting up behind his desk, nothing but relief in his expression now. "Thank you," he said. "I understand—the politics and all can be so complicated—it's enough just to know something's been done. I wasn't sure it was even possible."

My smile came out tight. "Neither was I. I'm glad I got the chance to set things a little right, for Imogen's sake. It was the least she deserved."

I left the office with my spirits lighter, one small

weight lifted off them. Unfortunately, the largest one remained—and would for a long time, I suspected.

Gold leaf pins flashed amid the students crossing the green. There were so many more Naries here that so many of my fellow students were eager to terrorize. And I still didn't know how the barons were hoping to escalate those plans. My mother had made it clear this was only the first stage in some larger scheme.

I couldn't get them all out of here like I had Shelby—and if I did, the staff would simply bring in more eager applicants to fill their places. So, I'd just have to find some other strategy. I wasn't standing down.

There'd been a moment, before Lillian had brought the news that my mother was still alive, when I'd been able to see how different the fearmancer world could be with Declan and me joining the pentacle of barons, and later the other scions taking their spots too. I had to believe we could still have that world I'd pictured. That we could stop the current barons from ruining our chances of getting there before we even had the opportunity.

Even if the methods I might have to use along the way made me queasy.

As I headed to the garage, I texted the guys. *Going to meet with my mother now. Should be back in a few hours.*

The replies popped up one after the other, Jude's first: *Go get her, secret agent girl. We'll be ready to send a rescue party!*

I didn't think he was completely joking about that.

Then Declan, with practical advice I automatically heard in his measured voice: *Keep those mental shields solid.*

You've got one more strength than her, and she's out of practice —just don't give her any openings.

Connar, short but sweet: *You've got this, Princess Bloodstone.*

And finally Malcolm, echoing the words he'd said after the five of us had discussed—and argued about—my decision last night: *She's got no idea what she's up against. Just make sure it stays that way. We'll have your back, no matter what.*

The messages soothed my nerves for a little while, but by the time I parked outside the mirrored office building where I'd talked with my mother before, my heart was thudding out a staccato rhythm. I took a few deep breaths in the car before getting out and striding inside.

When I reached the space the Bloodstone family owned, my mother was sitting at the same desk as before, glancing between the papers on her desk and a tablet. She looked up at my entrance and gave me a smile that held a hint of warmth.

"Persephone. You made good time."

"Traffic wasn't too bad. And I'm looking forward to really getting started with our work." I pulled over another chair to sit down across from her.

My mother leaned over her papers, her hair falling forward to shadow her face, as dark as mine except for the silvered strands. There was strength and power in that slim body, along with enough cool ferocity to terrify me, but her imprisonment had left her with cracks of fragility too.

Today I began the most fearmancer-like task I'd ever taken on. I was going to show this woman what she wanted to see and say what she wanted to hear until I understood both what she planned to do and how to shatter those plans, and then I was going to betray her. I was never going to be the heir she so obviously wanted. I just hoped I could pretend long and well enough to be the heir *I* intended to be.

I might not have been prepared for this deadly game, but I was in it now, and there was a hell of a lot more than just my happiness on the line. So I was going to play it with everything I had in me.

I shot a smile back at her—the smile of a daughter relieved that she could rely on her mother now that an enemy no longer lurked nearby. "What's on our plate today, Mom?"

ABOUT THE AUTHOR

Eva Chase lives in Canada with her family. She loves stories both swoony and supernatural, and strong women and the men who appreciate them. Along with the Royals of Villain Academy series, she is the author of the Moriarty's Men series, the Looking-Glass Curse trilogy, the Their Dark Valkyrie series, the Witch's Consorts series, the Dragon Shifter's Mates series, the Demons of Fame Romance series, the Legends Reborn trilogy, and the Alpha Project Psychic Romance series.

Connect with Eva online:
www.evachase.com
eva@evachase.com

Made in the USA
Las Vegas, NV
16 March 2024